Probably
Ruby

A NOVEL

...

Lisa Bird-Wilson

HOGARTH

LONDON / NEW YORK

Copyright © 2020 by Lisa Bird-Wilson

All rights reserved.

Published in the United States by Hogarth,
an imprint of Random House, a division of
Penguin Random House LLC, New York.

HOGARTH is a trademark of the Random House Group Limited,
and the H colophon is a trademark of Penguin Random House LLC.

Originally published in Canada by Coteau Books, Regina, Saskatchewan, in 2020.

LIBRARY OF CONGRESS CATALOGING-IN-PUBLICATION DATA
NAMES: Bird-Wilson, Lisa, author.
TITLE: Probably Ruby : a novel / Lisa Bird-Wilson.
DESCRIPTION: London ; New York : Hogarth, 2022.
IDENTIFIERS: LCCN 2021015917 (print) | LCCN 2021015918 (ebook) |
ISBN 9780593448670 (hardcover) | ISBN 9780593448687 (ebook)
SUBJECTS: LCSH: Métis women—Fiction. | Adoptees—Fiction. |
Identity (Psychology)—Fiction.
CLASSIFICATION: LCC PR9199.4.B524 P76 2022 (print) |
LCC PR9199.4.B524 (ebook) | DDC 813/.6—dc23
LC record available at https://lccn.loc.gov/2021015917
LC ebook record available at https://lccn.loc.gov/2021015918

Printed in Canada on acid-free paper

randomhousebooks.com

9 8 7 6 5 4 3 2 1

First U.S. Edition

Relationship web by Tanner K. Wilson

Book design by Barbara M. Bachman

FOR MY FAMILY

kisâkihitin

We are what we imagine. Our very existence consists in our imagination of ourselves. Our best destiny is to imagine, at least, completely, who and what, and *that* we are. The greatest tragedy that can befall us is to go unimagined.

—N. SCOTT MOMADAY

My dear young woman, appearances are the only true reality.

—EMILY CROY BARKER,
*THE THINKING WOMAN'S
GUIDE TO REAL MAGIC*

RUBY'S
RELATIONSHIP
WEB

———

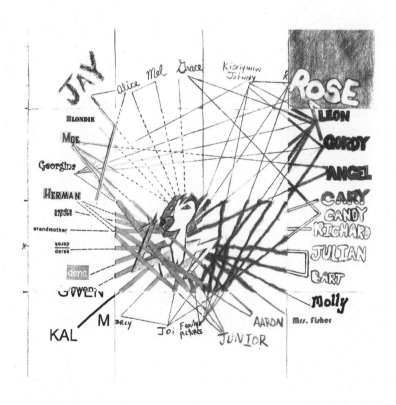

PROBABLY

RUBY

Kal

2 0 1 3

...

"**I** LIKE TO BE IN CHARGE," SAID RUBY. "I PRETEND I LIKE watching him jerk off, just so I won't have to touch him. My commitment level's kind of low on this one."

Kal's face showed no emotion. Instead he looked at the sunglasses resting on top of Ruby's head. Kal's office was in the interior of a downtown building and had no windows. Outside, it had been raining for days. He asked, "Is it sunny out there now, Ruby?"

His question made her laugh. She had a royal, attention-getting laugh, big enough to be heard out in Kal's waiting room. Which was good. Ruby wanted anyone out there to know Kal and she were having a *great* time. *Try and top that, sucker.* That's what she hoped her laugh said to any waiting client she'd subconsciously pegged as a rival for Kal's affections. And by "anyone" she mostly meant the shiny, obvious "Lori," seen on one occasion leaving his office and stopping to make an appointment on her way out; and, another time, waiting for

Kal as Ruby left. In an effort to make him even more uniquely hers, she tried out a variety of nicknames on Kal. "Hey, Mister K," she'd said when she arrived today, to which he just shook his head and smiled, motioning for her to come in. She was pleased to make him smile like that.

Ruby carried on with the chitchat about her new boyfriend. "I say the dirtiest things to him, Kal. To get it over with quicker."

He nodded.

"Why are guys always so turned on by the *idea* of coming on your face?" she asked, pausing so he could think about that one. Ruby knew Kal was divorced and had recently started dating. He often told her personal things about himself as a way to relate to what she was going through. Because of this, he was her favorite kind of counselor. She listened carefully to his disclosures.

SOMETIMES SHE HIT IT off with a new counselor and sometimes she didn't. She usually gave it two appointments to decide, but honestly, a lot of them only deserved one chance, and even then she'd been known to cut the first hour short.

Take the counselor before Kal: Larry, with the huge wooden cross around his neck. So effing big, as if he was compensating for something. Or dragging it around doing penance. He had a serious Jesus complex, that one. She decided quickly: Jesus-counselor was not going to get the benefit of her attention—he said one thing about the "sanctity of the marriage bed" and she threw up a little bit in her mouth before she fled. After that she made sure to tell the assigning agent at the insurance company that she didn't want "Christian" counseling, thank you very much.

IN HER EXPERIENCE, THE people who stressed things the most or the loudest were the first ones to break their own rules. That's why she always liked to hear one of her counselors say they would "never" date a client. When they said that she couldn't help but think, *Great*. Now *we're getting somewhere*.

Ruby always fell for her counselors. That was the point, really. I mean here was this person and they only had eyes and ears for you. How could you not be crazy about that? You got to be in a room alone with someone who listened hard and cared about what you were saying. Ruby was also counselor-monogamous, as far as that went. That was, if monogamy meant one at a time, one after another.

"You're really aware of your anxiety," Kal said during their first or second session. "You just don't quite know how to manage it." He was right. She hated to be alone. She sometimes felt she'd had kids to save her from being alone. But she could still be lonely.

"I'm not all parent," she told Kal once. "I'm a person, too. I'm often selfish and greedy." In some ways, the boys were the only thing, and in other ways she needed so much more to save her from her sadness.

Today Kal and she were four sessions in and she was trying to decide if she would renew with him. That was, if her insurance would allow it. Six was the upper limit on the first assignment, and she got six because "her stepdad died." Which was not really true but, as far as she could tell, insurance companies had no truth-auditing process. She didn't have a stepdad. But if she *did* he might have died, because he'd have been old, right? Ruby's parents were old, because she was adopted. They were the same age as her real grandparents, and by "real" she meant "birth" grandparents. So if her mom had remarried someone who was even older than her—which he likely would be, because that's how patriarchy works—well, then he would be so old that he might have died. In that case, it was entirely believable that Ruby could have had a stepdad who died. Really, Alice had broken up with all the losers she dated after the divorce, thank god, but still, Ruby was starting to feel a bit sad about the whole dead-stepdad thing, once she'd thought it through like that.

Her options with Kal at this point were to try to renew her insurance so she could stay connected to him, or to be brave and make a move on him soon. She just didn't know if he was ready. And then, just as she was weighing all the options, during appointment number four, Kal said this: "Do you want to book your next appointment at my home office? I find it quieter, and it might be a nice change of scenery for our discussion."

Aha. Up to now, they'd always met at his downtown office, where there was a chaperone. Okay, secretary. At his home office Ruby imagined there would be no one but the two of them. In his *house.* This was looking promising.

SHE ARRIVED EXACTLY FIFTEEN minutes early—if there was some Lori before her, she wanted to see her leaving. But there was no one. She was relieved to see Kal's house wasn't smelly or desperate. Or, worse yet, too clean. It looked mostly ordinary. As he led her inside she pointed to a yellow sombrero hanging on the wall between the kitchen and living room.

"Nice," she commented.

He laughed. "Mexico. Last winter. I should probably take it down."

"Don't you dare," she said. "It's the best."

Hoodies on the coat pegs and sneakers near the back door provided evidence of his kids, who were older teenagers. He shared custody with his so-called ex.

Once, during appointment number three, when Ruby talked about her irrational devotion to Dana, Kal told her, "I understand how you feel. I'm still in love with my ex."

"Are you? Would you go back with her?" she asked. This turn of events had never occurred to her before. She'd taken at face value his previous pronouncements of "ex," whom she had started to think of by that name. *Ex*, in her mind, had been a final, strongly held identity. Now Ruby was all wound up like a jewelry-box ballerina. Who knew which direction she might end up facing? One minute, he said "ex" as if he meant it; the next he was pining to get her back. Ruby realized she didn't even know Ex's real name.

They stopped in the kitchen while he finished making two cups of tea.

"We drank a lot of tea as kids," he said. "With loads of milk." She identified drinking milky tea as a kid as a Métis thing. She loved that Kal was part Métis, like her. Only *she* didn't grow up with her "real" family, and she never drank tea as a kid, her mother Alice being partial to instant coffee, which had a completely different vibe altogether. She watched Kal pour the hot water into the teapot and longed to know more, to connect to that part of herself she'd never had.

"I bet you were a cute kid," she said, and filled the room with her big laugh. Kal just smiled and poured the tea.

THEY SETTLED INTO HIS OFFICE, which was more like an overstuffed den, with couches and a big chair. She sat on the couch with its back against the wall. She noticed right away the Métis sashes draped over the end tables and along a shelf. Blown-glass ornaments lined up on the sash on the shelf; more glass works scattered on the side and coffee tables. Bowls, paperweights, ornaments—colorful blues, oranges, greens, and purples, swirls of molten glass hardened shiny and cold. On the table beside the couch sat a perfectly round glass marble, slightly smaller than a golf ball: clear glass, with a purple-and-green flower trapped inside. Ruby knew Ex was an artisan, a glassblower. These must be hers.

After some general small talk, Kal asked her an unexpected question.

"Tell me what kind of kid *you* were."

"*That's* a great question," she said, a big believer in warranted compliments.

He smiled a bit despite himself. "So? What were you like?"

"I was a serious tomboy," she confessed. "I had short hair and I dressed like a boy and ran wild. All my friends were boys, and all I wanted to do was play sports and smoke cigarettes and break shit."

"What do you think that was about?" he asked.

"Kal. You're too obvious," she said. "It's like I can read your mind."

He blushed! She loved him even more.

She'd had this kind of question before. About the tomboy thing. She said, "You think I've got some repressed butch/masculine-female something or another going on, don't you?"

Kal just looked at her the way a "good" counselor was supposed to, to encourage her to answer her own questions.

"That's not it," she told him. "I've thought about that and I really don't think that's it," she said, not wanting to discount his insightful suggestion. She did, after all, sometimes present as if she was the boss of the world. "What I really think is that I saw boys getting all the good stuff and I wanted to get it too."

"*Good stuff* like what?"

"Like cap guns and Hot Wheels and radio sets. Walkie-talkies. Jean jackets. All the cool stuff."

"Penises?" he asked. Kal was full of surprises.

"Okay," she nodded slowly. "Even penises, I guess. Only because I had no idea what *my* parts were all about." A thought popped into her head. A memory. She laughed breathlessly, sitting forward on the couch. "I asked my mom—" She laughed again and started over. "*When I was little,* I asked my mom when it would happen that I'd grow *my* penis so I could pee standing up."

He smiled too. "What did she say?"

"Sent me to my room and poured herself a drink."

———

IF KAL HAD NOTICED she was always the first one to call time on their sessions, he hadn't let on. She spent her life being told she was chosen but constantly needing people to prove it. With Kal, she didn't want to be confronted with the fact that this was a business relationship. She didn't want him pointing out that time was up and she had to leave. She'd rather leave of her own accord. It was like breaking up. She was always the first to call it over.

As they were wrapping up, Kal asked her to fill in a questionnaire about how useful the session was and how close she felt to resolving her issue, on a scale of one to ten. She didn't want to make Kal feel bad by giving him a low score, so she gave it an eight, but on instant reflection knew that was too optimistic. She definitely thought they'd made some progress, though—he invited her to his house, after all.

When he turned to his filing drawer to return her file, she did something she had no idea she would do. She palmed the glass marble. As he was turning back to face her she grabbed her bag as if she was looking for something, dropping the marble into her bag at the same time. She pulled out her bus pass and gave Kal an award-winning smile.

When she left he gave her a hug at the front door. A bit paternal, but still. Physical contact. She squeezed good and tight but not *sexy* tight or *needy* tight. Just *I appreciate you* tight.

She decided to walk. Kal lived in the east end of the city and she was in the west. She walked down one of the city's busiest arteries, full of bars, restaurants, tire shops, love shops, you name it. The day had warmed up and she felt light on her feet. She considered whether she should text Kal to say thanks for today's session. She thought she probably would. She was feeling so good she decided to stop at a familiar pub. It was only 4 P.M. and the place was nearly deserted. She took a seat at the bar.

She ordered a pint of beer and enjoyed the first cold swallow, anticipating the spread of warmth that would let her shoulders relax and eventually fill her with curiosity and cuteness. She fished out her phone to text Kal now, before she had too many drinks. Two things she'd learned to be careful about. One, she always lied to her counselors about drinking—some of them had their own hang-ups about alcohol and drugs, and she didn't want any of them confusing their issues with hers. The second thing she'd learned was don't drunk-text, drunk-email, drunk-Facebook, and so on. Best to get any follow-up texts to Kal out of her system now, pre-drink. But before she had a chance to do that, she sensed someone occupying the barstool next to hers.

"Next one's on me," said a familiar voice.

She closed her eyes for just a second. "Dana. Oh my god," she said, as if she was not at all surprised. "I was literally *just* talking about you."

He looked confused.

"To my counselor," she said.

"All good things, I'm sure," he laughed, as if they were a couple of corny business buddies out for happy hour. As if he wasn't really bad news. As if she wasn't still in love with him.

"Actually, I was saying how when I first met you I wondered if your beard would give me razor burn when you went down on me. But then, after you did, I realized I shouldn't have worried." She laughed her spectacular laugh, so he could remember what he'd been missing.

He looked around the bar like he was anxious to see someone, anyone else. "How you been keeping?" he finally asked.

That's it? she wondered. *After everything?*

She reached out and petted his face like a Chia. "Beard's no worse for wear, so to speak. Still soft."

"Yep," he said, riding his barstool like it was a horse, leaning forward and really digging his elbows into the bar, as if he hoped to hurt himself. The flash of his teeth and his full bottom lip caught her eye. She thought of the groveling she'd done. Pictured herself lying down on the dirty floor so he could walk over her on his way out. Envisioned his hands gripping her wrists above her head, holding her down because she told him to. She thought about calling him dirty names the whole time he was on top of her splayed body.

When the bartender came by, Dana ordered another round. The bartender plunked a new pint in front of Ruby. Dana said, "Big head on that one."

"I don't mind a bit of head," she said, taking up her line like there had never been a break between them.

"You wanna get out of this place?" he asked.

She diffused her laugh all over the bar. "It's gonna take a lot more than two beers to get *me* out of here."

RUBY WAS DEEP INTO her fourth pint when Dana wandered off to the toilet. She knew other women watched him as he made his way through the bar. Part of her wished he wouldn't come back.

She pulled her phone out of her bag to distract herself and remembered she was going to message Kal. She texted: "I felt better after talking to you today . . . thanks, man in the yellow hat." She had to close one eye to get the words to work out straight.

He texted back almost right away: "No problem, I am happy to help."

Not quite the stellar conversation she'd hoped to start. She ordered another beer.

"I know we only have one session left but maybe I can see you outside of that?" *Send.*

DANA CAME BACK TO his seat and occupied it in a way similar to the moon blocking the sun. His presence was heavy and full of their bodily knowledge of each other.

"I thought Crees couldn't grow beards?" she teased Dana, examining his nearly black pelt, his low hairline and dark hair, still thick.

"What is it with you and my beard?" he asked. "Do you want it that bad? You want to feel it here." He made a drunken grab for her crotch, more or less missed.

"There," she said, pointing her finger, letting it graze his chest. "There it is. That's more like the Dana I know." She hated that she was slurring her words now. "Your beard is a Métis beard, isn't it?" She turned back to the bar, sipped her beer. "That explains it," she said to the bartender standing nearby, her eyes big. "The Métis needed beards to stay warm." She shrugged her shoulders. "I forgot." Her tone implied she was stating the obvious.

KAL HADN'T RESPONDED TO her text. She imagined him thinking his way through her question. She realized only one of them had had the benefit of alcohol to facilitate this conversation. Finally, he texted: "We can try to get more sessions approved, if that's what you mean."

"Not exactly," she sent back.

"I'm not sure what you're asking," he texted, ever the professional.

"I never really wanted a penis." *Send*. "I was just unaware of the options." *Send*. And finally: "You know too much about me." *Send*.

From him, silence. Then he said: "That's the problem."

She wrote, "I think I'm falling for you." *Send*. "That's the problem." *Send*.

SHE ORDERED A ROUND of shots for her and Dana. The shot glasses were full of a red, sweet concoction, so they had two rounds. Then three.

"RUBY. LET'S GO FOR a walk," Dana said, sliding off his barstool.

"Okay. Let's walk." She puddled off her seat. "You ruined

me," she muttered. "But it's not enough yet." And then she said, "I can't walk. You'll have to carry me."

THE NEXT DAY SHE woke up at Dana's, in his bed, naked from the waist down, her eyes gummed shut and her shriveled tongue stuck to the roof of her mouth. Her collapsed brain cells cried for water. Slowly she remembered the stumbling walk from the bar, the taxi, getting sick outside his apartment building. More drinks inside, his bed, her straddling his face in muscle-memory mode, rubbing herself all over his beard so she would smell herself later when they kissed. Him on top of her, coming, telling her to slap him, "Harder. Harder!" Her palm striking his bearded cheek. Slapping him, taking him deeply.

She couldn't remember using a condom so got up to look for evidence of one—the thing itself, a wrapper, the ripped edge of a wrapper, even. She looked all around the bed, under the pillows, in the bathroom garbage, and in the kitchen. No sign. There were burnt bits of hash all over the stove, bits of tinfoil, and two blackened knives wedged in the cold burner rings. She drank from the kitchen tap, looked around for pain meds, found a bottle, took four.

She went back to the bed. Dana was asleep, curled on his side. She lay down beside him, didn't touch him, just watched. He was snoring lightly so she knew he wasn't pretending. Her impulse was to caress him, wake him, take more, get more, demand something, extract all she could. She resisted the urge. Sick and willing and almost overwhelming, she resisted the longing to press herself against him, to get as close as possible as if she could absorb him, fill up on the parts she longed for. She knew indulging this physical desire wouldn't produce satisfying results. Instead she thought *fill, fill, fill* as her eyes traced his tragic cheekbones, swollen brown lips, vain penis withdrawn now into its dark pubic patch. Finally, she got up and left. Last one in, first one out.

She stopped to throw up in the hedges beside the sidewalk, looked back one last time before she started running. A dog barked, and soon she slowed down. She walked after that, all the way home, a solid three miles. She listened to music on her headphones. The first song up on the random shuffle: "Sweet Dreams," Eurythmics. She laughed and walked faster.

SHE KEPT HER NEXT appointment with Kal. She didn't tell him about the night with Dana, about later texting Dana with condom questions and getting no response, about going to the clinic to get tested. Instead, she told Kal about the feeling of wanting to fill up on other people. As if she couldn't or wouldn't get enough. As if the people she loved might just disappear or be withdrawn at any moment.

"What do you mean, *fill up*?" Kal asked.

"Watch everything, memorize details, absorb it all." She thought about the stolen marble. It occurred to her that this single transgression might ruin everything. She felt ridiculous for having risked her relationship with Kal. Foolish for thinking it meant anything for her to have that piece of Ex's glass. Or for him *not* to have it anymore.

"As if you're empty," Kal stated.

Captain Obvious, she thought. She searched her bag for a tissue.

"What's the matter, Ruby?"

"I have allergies."

"So you're not crying?"

"No, definitely not. Not crying."

"Are you sad?" he asked.

She looked at Kal straight and hard. "We're all *sad,*" she said, surprised he didn't know this already. "We're all fucking *sad.*" She wiped her eyes and laughed her above-average laugh.

She looked at Ex's ornaments, the blown glass, the cold hardness. She wondered about Kal, if he was just as predictable as the rest in the end. "Don't settle for something," she said. She didn't even know anymore which of them she was talking to. "Just don't settle," she repeated.

Kal looked at her, then to the spot where the marble once was. Ruby closed her eyes and remembered throwing it.

Throwing the clear glass marble with its silly little flower.

Drawing her outfielder's arm back and letting it fly, hard, at Dana's apartment building. At his bedroom window. Then running away, the sound of breaking glass at her back. A dog started barking but she kept on running.

Alice

1981

. . .

THE WEATHER WAS HOT FOR LATE SEPTEMBER. AN "INDIAN summer," her mother called it. But real summer was over; the other kids in the neighborhood returned to school. Ruby's days became longer and took on a new rhythm.

"Ru-by"—her mother voiced a warning.

She froze.

"Ruby," her mother repeated. "Did you *pee* in the *yard*?" Mother's tone suggested she could hardly believe such a vile thing, as if Ruby had done something as horrible as poop in her pants, which Ruby most certainly would never do. Ruby might only have been six but even so, she knew the massive gulf between number one and number two on the scale of what was disgusting.

"No?" Ruby answered.

"Don't lie to me," Mother said, a phrase so familiar that Ruby almost couldn't hear it. Familiar, but dangerous. *Don't lie to me* seemed, at first, to convey the notion that lying was the real offense and the other thing, the peeing, was secondary.

It suggested that if you simply didn't lie about it, then peeing in the yard would somehow be forgiven. But Ruby wouldn't be fooled again—she knew for a fact that peeing in the yard was a very terrible offense on her mother's list of infractions. Her mother referred to peeing in the yard in a wrinkled tone of disgust. Lying was definitely the secondary offense in this case.

"No," Ruby said more firmly, standing up straight under her mother's gaze, looking ahead at her mother's soft hands. Without thinking, Ruby reached out and stroked the velvety skin on the back of her mother's hand.

Mother paused. "Well," she said, more tenderly, "you didn't come in to pee this morning. I don't want you peeing in the yard. You never know who's watching." Mother brushed Ruby's hair with her free hand. "You're not some kind of animal, you know." Mother, who was also called Alice, put her hand over Ruby's small stroking fingers for a moment, trapping them in a pillowy embrace before letting go and moving to the sink to rattle the dishes into submission.

RUBY *HAD* PEED in the yard that morning, squatting in the small fenced-in square between her house and the Wrights'. Safe and perfectly invisible to the soulless kitchen window, the small square patch of grass had a clean view between the pickets to the street in front of the house and David on his bicycle. She imagined her father had fenced this small space just for her, a hideaway, a place of her own to curl into, out of her mother's sight. But she couldn't hide away in the fenced-off square for too long, because that alarmed Alice.

If Ruby spent too long in the square spot, then her mother turned up at the back door with a small panic in her throat, calling Ruby's name. And Ruby would have to come running to assure Mother she was still within the boundary of the fence, where she was allowed to be.

"Where were you?" her mother would ask, and Ruby would point.

"Over there."

The fenced-in square was where Alice one day caught Ruby peeing in the grass, propped against the painted cedar of the house, white cotton panties stretched ankle to ankle. She didn't hear Mother coming because Ruby was lock-eyed with David, who was across the street in his usual position on his bicycle. David, who she imagined lived somewhere down the crescent that started across the road, watched her crouching in the short grass, the fence between them like a force field. David never took his eyes off hers and yet he still shouted out as each car approached, sensing it coming with perfect timing. Something in the changed quality of his shouts suggested to Ruby that he heralded the approaching cars as a way to warn her or make her aware of their presence. Ruby was impressed by his talent, how in tune he was with his main objective of yelling at the cars. He couldn't be thrown off by something as insignificant as Ruby peeing in the grass.

Of course, Mother was mortified. At least she didn't realize Ruby knew David was watching her. In fact, Mother didn't see David until after she grabbed Ruby's arm and startled her, making her pee on her socks and shoes. Mother yanked Ruby's panties up and made outraged, fierce whispering sounds and that's when Mother saw David, across the street, watching with his naked gaze. Mother's lips clamped shut and her hand tightened dangerously around Ruby's small arm. Mother's eyes narrowed and went hard as she stared at David, who continued to stare at Ruby. Then Mother turned her attention to Ruby and said, "See?" shaking Ruby by her arm.

"Ow," Ruby whined.

"See?" Mother repeated. But that was all.

Mother dragged Ruby back into the center of the yard, where she picked up Ruby's dropped hat. "Keep that on, for heaven's sake," she said, tugging the hat onto Ruby's head firmly, "or you'll be darker than Christmas." She left Ruby standing on the grass. Mother went inside.

Later, Mother called Ruby and gave her a ham sandwich on white bread spread with smooth, cool butter. And a half a glass of milk. Her mother said nothing and Ruby soon forgot to think about it.

David's eyes, locked on hers, were more reassuring than alarming. Also comforting was the way David showed up every day at the same time, like she could count on him. A scheduled actor in her daily drama.

David had short, dark hair and dressed in a white button-up shirt, brown pants, and hard lace-up shoes—like a uniform. He looked like a boy dressed like a man going to work. His bike had a front basket. David had an older brother, John, who dressed the same way and also rode his bike to the corner. They took turns—only one of them ever showed up at a time. Ruby decided she liked David better because he was closer to her age.

Ruby guessed David and John were allowed to ride their bikes only to the spot on the corner. When they arrived at the mailbox, each stopped like he'd hit an invisible fence, a boundary as real as Ruby's fenced-in yard. David always stayed on the wide brown seat of his bike and held the mailbox for support. Keeping his feet on the pedals, he watched the traffic. At the approach of every car he shouted out something incoherent, something like a code to be cracked. It was a busy street and so there was a lot of shouting. John did the same when it was his turn.

"Poor thing," Mother said one day, watching David out the front window. This caught Ruby's attention. Sympathetic expressions from her mother were rare.

"Why does he do that?" Ruby asked.

"He's not right. *Retarded*," her mother said, talking slowly as if Ruby was in danger of misunderstanding or not hearing correctly. Her mother rarely took the trouble to enunciate so clearly.

"What's that?" Ruby asked after a minute.

"There's something wrong with him," her mother said, shaking her head sadly.

David had a healthy, deep voice. He seemed quite robust to Ruby. But she resolved to keep a closer eye on him.

A THREE-FOOT FENCE ENCLOSED Ruby's yard with wide white pickets, spaced evenly apart, three inches between each picket like clockwork. What Alice didn't know was that Ruby's yard included a front world and a back world. Mother couldn't see the secret front world from the back window, the window that seemed the embodiment of Alice. Almost the entire back world—where Ruby played in the gravel next to the fence, making little piles and then neatly transferring the pebbles from one to the other; skipping hopscotch endlessly up and down the slab walk that led like a cement breadcrumb trail from the door to the gate and back again—was visible from Alice's window. Even if Ruby couldn't specifically see her mother in the dark window, she felt her like a prickly heat at the back of her neck, keeping score of something that would later need to be accounted for.

Mother could also watch Ruby standing patiently on the bottom fence-rail. Ruby's father built the fence before he disappeared. Ruby was convinced that he had made the lower rail, which made a perfect ledge for her to stand on, just so she could look over the fence. She linked the fence to her absent father as if they were the same. From time to time she thought of her father. His hands were bigger than any hands she knew. They were strong and capable, but also a bit scary. Unpredictable. Sometimes impatient. Those big hands could build a fence, but Ruby knew they could tear it down, too, if they wanted.

RUBY STOOD ON THE LEDGE and waited for the Fisher kids to come home from school for lunch. The Fisher kids lived at the other-next-door. The Wrights on one side, the Fishers on the other. The Fishers were forced to pass Ruby's yard, right past Ruby's fence, each day. They always walked down the alley-

way and, most thrillingly, the Fisher children were strictly off-
limits to Ruby, according to Mother. The Fishers were many in
number, some so old they attended high school; the high school
ones didn't traipse down the lane, though, only the ones who
went to the elementary school.

Ruby waited for the Fisher children each and every school
day at noon when they came home for lunch, and after school
when they tore down the alley—some of them in their dirty
bare feet—to squeal and holler and bang their back door, in
and out, in and out, while Ruby watched them through the
fence. The Fisher children were so self-contained, so satisfied
with one another's company, that they paid exactly zero attention to Ruby. The boy, Dusty, was nearest her age, one year
older than her. Dusty went to school.

Every day, Ruby asked her mother, "When can *I* go to
school?"

And her mother said "Not until next fall" again and again,
an answer that held little meaning for Ruby, who'd taught herself to tell time so she could gauge when to expect the Fisher
children to come down the alley, but had not yet mastered the
calendar or the seasons well enough to comprehend what "next
fall" meant.

"Is that tomorrow?" she asked.

WHILE RUBY WAITED FOR the Fisher kids to come home for
lunch, she took off her shoes and socks and walked as fearlessly
as possible over the rough gravel patch. Once there had been a

trailer for camping in the summertime, parked on that patch. But the trailer, the camping trips, and her daddy had disappeared all about the same time. Ruby practiced on the gravel until she could walk one end to the other in her bare feet almost without flinching, limping, or wincing.

She dreamed of being able to run down the back alley in her bare feet all the way to the elementary school, which she guessed was red and located, curiously, at the end of the alley. She'd never seen the school but she believed in it the same way she believed in Santa Claus, the Easter Bunny, and the tooth fairy, which is to say fervently and reverently and with mystical love, adoration, and fascination. She imagined the song she had sung at preschool, "Baa baa black sheep, have you any wool," was connected to the red school and the back lane somehow. She pictured the sheep situated outside the red school building, waiting for her, on the day she was finally allowed to go there. She imagined herself stripping off her shoes and socks as the Fishers did and running down the lane to join them at school. She would pet the sheep affectionately and meet the principal with his bag of wool.

THE FISHER KIDS HAD a rusted coffee can that formed the basis of many of their activities. They used it for games, including a version of hide-and-seek that involved ultimately running to kick the upside-down can, placed in the center of the yard, high up in the air, its hollow metal echo and the glorious cries of the winner resounding off the many decrepit cars and sheds that occupied the Fisher yard. Once the runner kicked the can in victory, all the still-hiding children emerged from their concealed places in the yard. Heather might roll from under the decaying red truck, Cindy might jump out from behind the corner shed, Billy might toss aside a sheet of flimsy metal leaning against the fence that he had crawled beneath. They all emerged and congregated noisily at the spot, one of them retrieving the can and placing it back in its place upside down on the grass, which immediately restarted the counting melody from the one who was It. "One. TWO."

The can also served as a digging implement. The Fishers had a large muddy hole in their yard near the back fence that they alternately concentrated on making larger or ignoring altogether.

"What are you doing over there?" she asked Dusty one day.

"Digging."

"Yeah, but what are you making?"

"This is the hole."

"But why?"

"Because it's a good idea. We can catch robbers."

The hole was a booby trap. It would be camouflaged so thoroughly that some unsuspecting person would walk right on top of it and SURPRISE! Fall in. *WHAM-O!* Ruby was thrilled and troubled by the prospect.

She imagined Mr. Fisher falling in the hole. Mr. Fisher, who appeared now and then at the back door with his riotous black hair and his incredible, outrageously bare brown stomach. Mr. Fisher always appeared unsteady on his feet, which were also consistently bare. He wore only a pair of blue jeans. He'd pause at the back door as if thinking, tottering like a top-heavy toy before rolling over the doorstep and into the yard.

"SOME PEOPLE SHOULDN'T BE allowed to have children," Ruby heard her mother proclaim to the elderly Mrs. Wright. Ruby imagined the police or a stern teacher shaking their finger "No" at Mr. Fisher and preventing all the Fisher children from existing. The scandal was partly because there were two Mrs. Fishers. All those people lived in the same house together all the time.

How can you live right next door to someone, know them, and yet not know them at all? That was how it was with the Fishers. Ruby felt wholly connected to their world, to their daily in-and-out struggles. When she saw Billy punch Dusty in the chest hard enough to knock Dusty down and make him cry, she nearly cried too. Dusty was carefree and indifferent. He was tough enough to walk the alley in his bare blackened feet, over jagged stones and the sharp bits of broken pop bottles—green and clear jewels glinting in the sun.

Ruby wanted to help Dusty, loved Dusty, in fact, but only in the way you might love your perfect self, the self you wished to be someday.

Ruby's mother grew raspberries in the back garden next to the fence. Though Mother had been gathering them since the summer, there were still so many unpicked berries. Ruby braved the thicket of canes, half filled a margarine container, and waited with it by the side fence, unsure what she would say but wanting terribly to say something. When she saw Dusty come out, she knew she had picked the raspberries for him. She poked her toes onto the bottom fence-rail and hiked herself up, hooking her elbows over the pickets.

"Want some?" she offered, holding the container out, the start of a raspberry thorn rash on the back of her hand.

Dusty ignored her.

She screwed up her nerve a notch higher and repeated, "I've got raspberries."

"So?"

"Want some?" she asked again.

"What is it?" he asked, coming closer, relenting a bit. He took a handful, recklessly dropping several. He put them all in his mouth at once and swallowed. Ruby didn't believe he even chewed a single time.

She shook the margarine container. "You can have them," she said. "I don't even like them."

"You're crazy," he said, grabbing the container out of her hand and leaving her standing at the fence. The back door banged shut behind him.

RIGHT AFTER LUNCH, RUBY saw her grandmother's big car approach the front of the house and come to a halt. David shouted at the car and Grandmother unfolded herself from behind the steering wheel. Ruby decided to stay behind the fence, sitting cross-legged in the cool grass, her back propped against the cement foundation of the house. She kept an eye out for daddy longlegs, who liked to climb now and then onto her bare arms and sometimes into her hair. She wasn't afraid of them—

they were so light and innocent. Grandmother approached the sidewalk in front of the house, the handle of her blue purse over the crook of her arm in an I-mean-business kind of way.

Just then, David yelled, making Grandmother pause and look across the road. Ruby couldn't see Grandmother's expression but imagined her frowning mouth and her skeptical eyes, sizing up David on his bicycle. For a moment Ruby wanted to save David from her grandmother—he didn't deserve her sharp look. It was the same look Ruby saw Grandmother give her father, who didn't warrant it either, but in a different way than how David didn't deserve it.

"He keeps the neighborhood on its toes," Mrs. Wright called out to Grandmother from her front yard.

"I'll say," Grandmother replied, making a *tsk*-ing sound with her tongue and teeth. Ruby tried it, tapping her tongue against-and-away from her closed front teeth to quietly replicate the noise.

"It's one thing to have that accident once." Mrs. Wright paused and lowered her voice. "But imagine—*twice*."

Both women *tsk*-ed and examined David across the street as if he were a specimen.

"Well, I guess you never know how these things come to be," said Mrs. Wright philosophically.

Grandmother eyed the house as if it were an embodiment of Ruby's mother. "I advised Alice against adopting. I told her, *You never know what you're going to get*."

"Ah. Yes," said Mrs. Wright. "The little girl."

"Well," said Grandmother.

"Native?"

"Partly," Grandmother said. "But different."

"Oh, yes," said Mrs. Wright.

Grandmother looked as though she'd swallowed a pickle.

Ruby remembered overhearing her mother telling Mrs. Wright that Ruby was prone to nightmares. But Mother didn't know the content of the nightmares, about the recurring rooster that frequented her dreams. The rooster of her bad dreams was lately combined with the bottomless pit in the Fishers' yard, in which she was falling and falling, yelling into eternity. And within the bottomless pit, hollering loudly while holding her gaze, David with his bicycle, hanging on tightly, maintaining his seated position on the bike, yelling overtop her screams, louder and louder, holding her eye. Billy slapped Ruby in the dream, a stinging shock, and all Ruby wanted to do was tell on Billy, to tell and get him in trouble. And then she woke up and it was her mother who had slapped her in the face and was holding her tightly on her lap, Ruby's head pressed against her mother's legs. Ruby was left with the feeling that her mother, whose actions sometimes surprised her like sharp little razors, like raspberry-cane spikes, couldn't be trusted.

Ruby plucked a leggy spider from her forearm and tossed him gently into the grass, then watched as he righted himself and crawled toward her again as if she were a beacon. When Grandmother went indoors, Ruby stayed hidden in the shadow of the house, hearing the coffee cups clinking. David stopped shouting and rode away on his bicycle. A few minutes later John pedaled up to take his place.

Ruby wandered to the back door. She considered going inside to see if Mother had put out the plate of cookies.

"Now what?" she heard Grandmother ask.

"I don't know, Mother. I'll find a way."

"Well, what do you want from me?" Grandmother asked coldly.

"*Nothing*, Mother." Ruby's mother's voice was hard. "Nothing," she repeated, and Ruby imagined her mother's tight jaw and straight, square shoulders.

"There comes a time to pay the piper, Alice. This is yours."

The sound of a coffee cup clattering into the sink startled Ruby. Seconds passed and then spoons and a plate hit the enamel too, the noise of the dishes surprising but still familiar, the music of her everyday life. A chair scraped, followed by footsteps, and then the front door banged. The engine of Grandmother's big car rumbled as she drove away. John shouted triumphantly.

THE FRIDGE WAS BROKEN. Mother called a repairman and told Ruby to stay outside. This seemed strange to Ruby because Mother never told her to stay outside—she usually had to tell her to come *inside*. The repairman arrived. Ruby saw him park his white van and take his time getting his things and make his way up the walk. Ruby couldn't take her eyes off the full tool belt strapped around his hips. His belly hanging over it.

Ruby's mother told her to stay outside but for once she wanted to go inside, wanted to see the repairman, watch him while he fixed the fridge, see him pluck things from his tool belt without looking, like her daddy used to do. Or maybe watch his fingers wander lightly over the tools until he felt the right one and then withdrew it. Her daddy would sometimes swear in his funny accent while fixing things, and her mother would scold him if she dared.

Ruby went to the back door and heard her mother talking with the repairman. Mother's voice was funny, softer. It reminded Ruby of individual crystals of sugar. Careful and sparkly, but fragile too. Ruby went in to ask for a drink of water.

"Well, it's so nice to have a man in the house," Ruby's mother said as Ruby slunk into the kitchen and headed for the sink. Mother and the repairman stood in front of the refrigerator. The repairman looked from the fridge to Mother, as if he wasn't sure which to pay attention to first. Mother was wearing a red dress that wrapped around and showed off her narrow waist. And she had on high-heeled sandals and a necklace, as if she planned to go out. Ruby looked closer and noticed Mother's teased hair and lipstick. Perfume hung in the air. As she stood there with one hip jutted out, Mother's delicate fingers played with the necklace, twirling it while she admired the repairman as if he were a shiny new car.

"Where are you going?" Ruby asked.

"Oh. Ruby." Her mother dropped the necklace and stood up straight. "I thought you were outside playing!" Her voice was supposed to sound sweet but there was a hard look in her eye as she approached Ruby and filled a cup of water without even letting it run to get cold. She gave Ruby the cup and steered her outside. "That's okay, honey," she said, "take it with you."

As Ruby exited the back door she heard her mother sprinkle

laughter in the repairman's direction and say, "Kids. They can
be such a handful." Mother giggled again. Ruby let the screen
door slam and sat on the back step with her water. She listened
for a while as her mother and the repairman talked, Mother
laughing crazily.

RUBY SET HER CUP on the step and went to the fence. She
stood on the fence, her elbows hooked over the top of the pickets, and surveyed the Fishers' backyard. The empty margarine
container, she noticed with pleasure, had been added as a tool
for the digging of the bottomless pit. The kids were at school
but one of the Mrs. Fishers was in the yard, pulling weeds from
a bushy patch of shrubs. Ruby watched the backs of Mrs. Fisher's bare legs as she bent to rip the weeds. It seemed a funny
thing to do when the rest of the yard was such a mess—for
Mrs. Fisher to tend to one corner of the yard where something
was growing on purpose, when the whole rest of the yard was
so haphazard.

Suddenly Mrs. Fisher straightened and saw Ruby at the
fence.

"Hello," she called and waved her hand, full of weeds. *Come
over,* she motioned.

At that moment Ruby had a choice. She knew she might say
no, as Mother would expect. Except Mother was in the house
being stupid with the repairman.

"Astum. Come," Mrs. Fisher said. She had a generous smile.
Ruby needed no further encouragement.

Ruby jumped from the bottom rail, hung over the posts on her stomach, stretched a leg onto the top rail, and climbed over the fence. It was the first time she'd done such a thing.

Mrs. Fisher brought out treats, and she and Ruby sat on the back step side by side, licking their dripping Popsicles. Afterward, Mrs. Fisher rinsed the sticky red drips from their hands with the garden hose and let Ruby take a drink from the hose. She went back to pulling weeds.

There was a pond in the Fishers' yard, among the junk, that Ruby had never seen from her side of the fence. The pond was fed with a pump to circulate the water. Long grass grew all around it. Upon close inspection Ruby noticed it was alive with movement. Orange fish with long flowing tail fins curved and swirled beneath the surface of the water, from one end of the pool to the other. To Ruby they appeared nervous. She felt bad for them as they bumped against the rocks again and again, endlessly curling in on themselves and flipping the other way to try anew. Over and over they did the same dance; over and over they got the same result.

"What's the matter with them?" she asked Mrs. Fisher.

"Maybe they're trying to escape?" Mrs. Fisher replied, as if she was seriously considering Ruby's question.

"Are they blind?" Ruby asked.

"It's just their job," Mrs. Fisher said, shaking her head. "It's the thing they were meant to do. Swim like that."

"Maybe they're retarded," Ruby said, trying out her mother's word, even though she couldn't quite remember what it meant.

"Oh, child," Mrs. Fisher murmured, putting her hand on

Ruby's head. It felt warm and soft, resting there. Several seconds passed before Mrs. Fisher removed her hand.

"Come look at my flowers," she offered. They went to the tended patch and she snipped a delicate pink flower from a thorny bush. "Here," Mrs. Fisher said. "You can press this in a book and it will keep forever."

When Ruby looked unsure, Mrs. Fisher explained further, "Take a heavy book, the heaviest one you've got. And lay the flower between two pages. Then close the book and maybe put more books on top of it. Let it sit for a very long time."

"How long?" Ruby asked.

"Well . . ." Mrs. Fisher thought for a moment. "When's your birthday?"

"August twenty-fourth." Ruby beamed.

"Okay, you press this today and take it out on your birthday and it'll be dry." Ruby held the flower carefully in her fingertips.

"Don't worry too much," Mrs. Fisher said. "It looks delicate but it's kind of tough, too." Mrs. Fisher laughed out loud. "A bit like you, I suspect," she said, chuckling again. "You're a good kid." Then Mrs. Fisher said it was time for her to go back inside and she left Ruby alone in the yard.

Ruby began to climb the fence back to her own yard, but it was harder from the Fishers' side because the horizontal bottom and top rails were only on Ruby's side of the fence. As she was hoisting herself up, trying to hold the flower carefully and also hurry in case Mother came to the window or the door, Ruby fell hard, with one leg on either side of the fence. She landed with all her weight on the inverted V of her crotch and felt the wooden fence-picket bruise her bony groin. Tears sprang to her eyes and she transferred her weight onto her hands. She swung her body forward and brought her second leg over the fence. Once back on her own side, Ruby pressed her right hand into her groin until the sting subsided. She still held the flower in her left hand like a prize.

AFTER A TIME, RUBY went to the step and picked up her empty cup. Through the screen door, the house was quiet. Ruby no longer heard her mother giggling or talking to the repairman. It was too silent. Had Mother left? She entered quietly and ventured up the three short steps. There was no one in the kitchen. Cup still in one hand, flower in the other, Ruby peered down the hallway. Her parents' bedroom door was closed. Was the repairman already gone? Was Mother taking a nap? She turned back to the kitchen to put the cup in the sink and saw the tool belt on the kitchen chair. Ruby heard muffled noises now from the bedroom but she was disoriented. Her mother, who was always so predictably *there,* in the kitchen, in the dark and quiet house, watching and seemingly waiting, was suddenly not where she'd always been. Ruby put the cup by the sink and absently laid the flower on a little-used corner of the counter, near the junk drawer. She went out the back door and into the warm sunshine.

She went to the little patch of grass by the front fence and saw that the repair truck was still parked out front. Across the street, David yelled at the cars and balanced on his bicycle, one hand on the mailbox.

———

LATER, AFTER THE REPAIRMAN was gone and Ruby had scrutinized Mother's flushed cheeks until she tired of it, Ruby went to the bathroom and discovered blood on her panties. She recalled the sharp pain of the fence when she fell. All the same, she called Mother.

"Did somebody touch you?" Mother asked, examining the stained underwear. And Ruby thought about Mrs. Fisher and her warm hand on Ruby's head like the sun.

"No?" she said.

"Oh my god, did somebody touch you!" Mother shrieked.

Mother put Ruby to bed and called the doctor.

Ruby was left alone to fear she had mortally wounded herself instead of incurring the smallest of childhood scrapes and bruises. Eventually, the doctor came. He talked with Mother before entering Ruby's room.

The doctor insisted that Ruby take her clothes off and lie on top of the blankets on her bed. Ruby didn't want to but Mother was so stern, the doctor so full of angry authority. Ruby didn't know what she had done that was bad enough to make this happen, but thought about the delicate flower and her forbidden visit with Mrs. Fisher. She understood that a lie was better than the truth.

The doctor sent her mother for a flashlight. While Mother was gone the doctor looked at Ruby with a cold eye.

"I don't want to hear any nonsense from you. Right?" he said.

Mother returned with the flashlight in one hand and the delicate pink flower in the other. There was something unreadable in Mother's eye.

"Where did you get this?" she demanded.

"I don't know?" Ruby answered, fumbling with the hem of her pants, undressing as slowly as possible.

"You left the yard," Mother declared. To the doctor she said, "She left the yard and somebody touched her." Mother's voice was rising. "I knew this would happen. I always knew this would happen," Mother cried.

Mother yanked at Ruby's panties and removed Ruby's clothing because Ruby wasn't doing it fast enough. Ruby was made to lie on the bed.

"Put your knees up," the doctor instructed. "Feet flat. Ankles together," he commanded. He forced her rigid knees apart. Mother exhaled hard as she shone the flashlight. Ruby trembled and the doctor prodded her soft flesh with his callous fingers. Ruby pleaded with them not to do what was already done. The doctor told her to be a good girl and be quiet. All the while Mother breathed indignantly from behind the flashlight.

Ruby watched the familiar flaking paint on the ceiling, counting in her head the swirling orange fish from the pond. Her body was no longer hers. She no longer heard their words. Her chin set. She became resolved against them, the adults who betrayed her. No matter what they did to her, she wouldn't tell. She would keep inside how she'd climbed the fence that day and visited Mrs. Fisher to eat Popsicles and drink from the hose. How Mrs. Fisher was nice to her. And most of all, the way Mrs. Fisher laid her hand on her head like a warm ray of sunshine. Ruby held on. She held on and on.

Leon

1993

...

L EON TOOK A LONG DRAW OF WHISKEY, LEANED OVER, and slung the bottle into the glove box. He jammed his bare foot onto the clutch, turned the rusty ignition, and ground the gears as he yanked on the three-in-a-tree shifter. The night moon behind the clouds conspired with the dense bush to obscure him in a deep well of darkness. He flicked on the headlights to illuminate the narrow dirt road in front of him. The truck jolted forward and Leon heard the ax slide across the bare metal floor of the old truck amid a clatter of empty beer bottles.

There was ringing in Leon's ears along with the memory-sensation of punching the bedroom door, creating a fist-sized hole, moving to the living room, leaning over, one knee on the pullout couch, and punching the pillows and blankets where he visualized Cynthia, if she were there with him. He still felt, on the knuckles of his right fist, how he punched down the pulpy pillows like yeast, thinking of her soft belly, the fleshiness of her face, her large breasts. The couch springs cried out softly, which he found oddly satisfying, as if it protested his assault. *Someone should,* he thought. *Someone should protest.* Leon's right fist planted itself over and over against the thin mattress of the pullout.

He had followed up the punching by putting on his headlamp and making his way in the dark to the woodpile where he picked up the heavy splitter, the same one now sliding around in his truck. He'd lined up the cut logs one at a time on the chopping stump and then raised the ax all the way up over his head, spread his legs wide in case he missed, not wanting to come down on his bare toes. He's still dressed as he was then, in nothing but a grimy pair of blue jeans. And then, each time he held the ax high over his head, he closed one eye to aim, really aim, finding through the alcohol a certain concentration, and then came down with the ax to shatter the wood clean, one piece after the other cleaved and cleaved and cleaved from itself.

And he thought about Cynthia the whole time he killed that wood. The hot energy in his shoulders and back, biceps and forearms, combined with the white rage behind his eyes. Enough to almost blind him and at the same time frighten him nearly sober. Yet he couldn't stop until there was nothing left of his shredded muscles. He didn't worry about anyone hearing the crack of the ax again and again like dull gunshots in the middle of the night; the cabin was so isolated in the bush, the nearest neighbor was at least three kilometers away.

Immediately after the chopping, the sting of sweat in his eyes, Leon decided he would drive back to the city. He couldn't recall, in the flush of his anger and exhaustion, exactly why he had thought it so important to leave his own damn house in the first place. Alcohol clouded his memory and he found he couldn't quite pull into focus his reasons just then. He tossed the ax into the back seat of his truck cab where it bounced on the floor among the beer bottles, then went back to the cabin for what remained of his second case of beer. He laid the case crosswise on the front bench seat, like a divider.

"I'll show *you*," he muttered to no one, puffing his chest.

MEANWHILE, SOMEWHERE NEAR RURAL highway 945, Joi and Marcy emerged from the bush. Marcy dragged her suitcase and Joi picked leaves from her long dark hair.

"I can't believe my luggage got lost," Joi complained.

"That's not the only thing lost," Marcy said, hauling the suitcase with two hands up the embankment to the dark road, the muscles in her sinewy forearms dancing. No cars were in sight. Cloud cover filtered the moonlight.

Joi followed and stood on the road. She stuck out her hitch-hiker's thumb, left hand on hip, cocking her body into a faux-sexy pose.

Marcy laughed. "Maybe a chicken hawk will pick us up. That's about our only hope." She looked left and right, up and down the road. "Which way?"

"Let's flip a coin," said Joi. "That's as good as anything." Joi took a lipstick from her purse and applied it expertly in the dark. It was black, the same color as her hair, making Joi's face look pale.

"Golly, I'm thirsty," Marcy said to no one in particular. "I'd kill for a drink right now!"

"Is it possible," Joi mused, turning serious, "that we've come to the wrong place?"

"No," said Marcy. "This is it. I'm nearly certain." She extended her hand to Joi. Her fingers, with their black fingernails, motioned for the lipstick.

"*Nearly* certain?" asked Joi, handing over the tube.

"Yes. I think we should wait. Someone will be along soon." Marcy applied the lipstick. "They'll come," she said confidently.

Joi narrowed her eyes, rimmed in black eyeliner.

LEON GUIDED THE TRUCK to the main road, a narrow secondary highway that he knew was straight and uncomplicated, but with a steep ditch. It was as easy as keeping an eye on the center line. No harder than that.

"Just. Keep. Your eye. On. The dotted. Line," he told himself, and then burst out uncontrollably, "Cunt!" He fixated on the center line, his eyes flicking back and forth to the speedometer as he tried to keep a steady speed. He leaned forward as if he could will the truck to move faster.

"No, no, no, no, no," he said, hitting the steering wheel with each denial. His mind whirled at what he might find when he reached the house. Betrayal sat behind his eyes like dull warm pudding. He groaned when he thought about the last couple of months. How he sensed Cynthia changing but couldn't put his finger on what was happening. About how he pressed her, in his own way, to talk to him. She always had excuses not to. How she had changed bit by bit over the past weeks, and who knew how long it was going on before he noticed. He boiled thinking about her indifference to him, the way she pulled further and further away. The way he practically begged her to do things with him, things like talk about baseball, go with him to the bar, or even just sit with him on the couch—each instance rebuffed for the reason he knew now. Dennis. *Dennis,* for Christ's sake.

"Center line," he said. "Center line, center line, center line"—a chant, a rule to be followed at all costs. The road was narrow and there was no shoulder, the edge broken pavement that hadn't been patched in years.

And then it happened. Almost in slow motion.

He was following the center line diligently, with a single-minded focus. His concentration was so acute he didn't register the one, then two dark figures on the road until they split apart and one moved into the path of his truck. Gradually he picked his eyes off the center line and steered gently left in an effort to avoid whatever it was that had moved into the path of his vehicle, thinking slowly, thinking he would avoid the creature. But it kept moving left with him, the other dark figure staying on the right-hand side of the road.

Leon's sluggish response time meant he was forced, at the last minute, to stomp the clutch and brake to avoid hitting the person on the road. He heard the ax slide, fast and heavy, head-first along the floor amid a jangle of bottles; it slid deeper under his seat. He stopped the truck completely, surprised it had really come to this, and the vehicle sat still and quiet in the middle of the wrong side of the dark road. The figures, dressed in black, were two girls.

The first girl, the one who'd walked out on the road and forced him to stop, approached his open driver's-side window; the other opened the passenger door—she dragged a large black suitcase on wheels behind her. He couldn't keep up with the two of them at once. Both girls were out of breath.

"Can you give us a ride?" The girl at the window gave him the once-over. Leon fathomed she smelled the alcohol, took in the bleeding knuckles of his right hand on the wheel, his bare chest; he sensed a flicker of apprehension on her part, maybe even fear, despite her goth, tough-girl lineup of impressive ear piercings. She wore black lipstick and her dark hair was long and straight.

The other girl, already in the act of pushing the split-bench seatback forward and wrestling her heavy suitcase into the tiny back seat, left the front seat for her friend. They didn't look any older than late teens at best. The first girl, taking note of her friend, ran in front of the truck to the passenger side while the other one cleared a path through the beer bottles and crumpled papers in the back with her high-top sneakers as she got comfortable. He thought about offering her the middle bitch-seat in front, but his beer was there and that's where he liked it.

Reluctantly he cut away from his daydream about Cynthia and willed himself to relax his grip on the steering wheel. Reluctant because, truth be told, he'd been experiencing mild pleasure, right alongside the anger—the righteousness of his position. Cynthia's betrayal! His moral superiority. The situation suited him. He geared down on the shifter, paid attention to this new turn of events. He started driving again. There were now two underage girls in his truck at 3 A.M.

"What're you girls doing out here?" he asked, trying hard not to slur his words.

"Oh my god, like, thank god you came by. We've been walking for *hours*," the one in the front said. "I'm Joi," she added. "Joi with an *i*," she giggled.

Leon's mind tried to make a word picture out of Joy with an *i*. He came up with *Jiy*. He shook his head as if to clear it. "Where you coming from, Joy with an *i*?" He searched his mind for local landmarks where they might have been, but came up empty. "This is the middle of nowhere," he said and he wasn't exaggerating, not a structure within at least five kilometers, likely more, any way you turned.

"Marcy's *boyfriend* took us out to a cabin to go drinking," Joi with an *i* said, stabbing her thumb in the direction of Marcy in the back seat. "*I* didn't want to go. It turned out bad. We had to leave."

"Do you have any water?" Marcy asked. "I'm so dry."

Leon tried to appear sober.

"I think we got lost," Joi added.

"So you're going into the city?" he asked, still trying to get his bearings.

Instead of answering his question, Joi with an *i* perked up in the front seat, as if she'd suddenly remembered something. She asked, "What are *you* doing out here?"

Leon could feel her gaze on his face. Her suspicion radiated up and down his right cheek. In the air a new, slight glaze of fear mingled with—he wasn't sure what. Excitement?

"Yeah," echoed Marcy from the back seat. "How come you're out so late?"

"Joy ride," he said, then laughed. He wanted to add "Joy with an *i*," but couldn't spit it out because he'd already said it in his head and was laughing too hard to articulate anything just at that moment. He convulsed silently, his shoulders shaking, unable to speak. *These girls are going to think I'm crazy.*

"Joy ride?" Joi in the front asked. "You didn't look all that happy to stop for us." She laughed along with him but didn't seem to catch on to what was funny.

To stop himself laughing he put his chin down and grabbed a beer from the case. He took his hands off the wheel to pop the cap with his lighter. He downed a third of the bottle in one gulp, wiped his mouth with his forearm to rub the smile off his lips. He grunt-choked in answer to her question.

Not good enough.

"But *really,*" she persisted, "what are you doing out *here?*" She spread her hands in front of her to indicate the vast darkness.

"Nothing."

"You must have been going somewhere," she pressed.

"Nowhere." He didn't want to say and then did anyway. "I was at my cabin. Got a place out here."

"Then what are you doing out driving at this time of the night?"

"Thinking," he said. "Driving and thinking."

"About what?"

He didn't know about what exactly. He searched his mind and couldn't quite recall what was so important out here.

I got something to do, he thought. *Cynthia. Fucking Cynthia.* He noticed his hands were gripping too tightly again. He breathed heavily and let up on the wheel.

"You ask a lot of questions, don't you?" He drank again.

"Can I have one?" the girl in the back asked, shifting forward so she was hanging over the center of the front seat and pointing down toward his case with her black-painted fingernails. "I'm so dry, really," she said. He grunted in a way she interpreted as "yes" and she reached for a beer. "You want one too, Joi?" she asked and handed it over without waiting for an answer.

Leon heard her search her purse for a lighter, pop the cap, and guzzle, which made him tip his bottle to his lips and finish off his beer. He cranked down the window and flung his bottle into the deep ditch. Left the window open.

Leon's attention drifted. Cynthia. Dennis. He snorted and hawked up a chunk of something, spit the glob expertly into the sucking wind. He rolled his window up again.

He tried not to think about his own betrayals, the way he'd stepped sideways out of his relationship with Cynthia. He'd had a girlfriend once, only one time, he told himself. And calling her a girlfriend had been a stretch too. But one evening, at her insistence, they had gone dancing, even though Leon's simple stubborn response to Cynthia had always been "I don't dance," as if it were all the explanation required. *No.* His answer to Cynthia had always been no before the question was even asked. And yet when Leon and his girlfriend—one time!—had decided to go dancing it had arisen from a discussion about music. The plan to go out dancing had emerged organically and, in that moment, he'd happily taken her. If he felt guilty at all, it was on that score. But then there was Dennis, he reminded himself. Dennis with his fancy shoes and shoe polish. His hair gel.

"Swine," he cried, upset again. "Pig!"

"Who?" Joi with an *i* exclaimed defensively.

"No," his head spun. "Not you." He tried to change his thoughts. Think about these two tough-tender girls. The one in the front seat. Joy.

"Joy, Joy, tough Joy," he sang, vaguely remembering, incorrectly, the words of a song. "You girls oughta be careful," he said. "You shouldn't be out hitchhiking. Especially in the middle of the night." He wanted to sound as if he meant to impart some fatherly wisdom, but he hiccuped in the middle of "hitchhiking." The two words lurched out of his mouth with exaggerated *h*'s. *H*itch *H*iking. He was aware he sounded both careful and angry at the same time. "You know how women go missing? Bad things can happen."

Both girls fell still.

"You don't know who you're going to meet," he carried on. "You don't know what kind of cock *hic* sucker might pick you up."

The paternal feeling, just then, sparked a foggy memory— a long-ago daughter hovered in the margins of Leon's brain. A baby he never met. An unfulfilled promise. He felt strangely protective all of a sudden.

"*No one* would give us a ride. We were walking *forever*," Joi whined.

"Boy, I needed something to drink," Marcy said as she guzzled her beer. "That helps." She held the empty bottle loosely in her black-lacquered fingertips, tapping its neck, leaning forward on her skinny forearms. She looked around at the back seat. Leon remembered again about the ax, thought maybe if she saw it she might misinterpret its presence, as if he meant to do some harm with it. For a moment he envisioned her taking preemptive action against a vague threat he might pose, saw her planting the ax in the back of his skull to get him first. Or maybe these two girls were car thieves and would attack him regardless. But he doubted it. Marcy leaned in, put the empty in the case, and took another beer, her nails tapping.

He stayed quiet about the beer. Instead he repeated, "You never know who you're going to meet. I want you both to be more careful, all right?"

"But we met *you*," said Joi smiling.

He said nothing, but let his mind wander over the tinkle in her voice, the slight hint of tease. He thought about Cynthia coming out of the bedroom in her lingerie, talking dirty to him. Leon could smell his own peppery sweat and from there he conjured the moist scent of Cynthia's folds.

"I'm Leon Black," he said, talking to himself now, shaking his head. "That name *means* something." He saw his rough work-hands on Cynthia's waist, on her hips, maneuvering her to turn onto all fours so he could take her from behind, guiding her onto him. The two of them fucking all over the big bed and other parts of the house, too—the kitchen, the laundry room, even outside. Cynthia liked the idea of being risky, of maybe getting caught, or being seen. A lot of the dirty talk had to do with who might be watching them. Now it had all taken on a different hue. Dennis had lived with them for the last three months, slept on the couch, the old friend with nowhere else to go, the one they made fun of behind his back. The guy they both felt sorry for.

He should have been driving the center line but he'd lost his concentration.

———

THE FRONT PASSENGER TIRE left the asphalt and bit into the gravel where the shoulder had crumbled away. The truck shook and the wheel jittered in his hands.

"Hey!" Joi in the front seat yelled, grabbing the door handle with her right hand and the dash with her left. The tire bit deeper into the rough gravel and jolted sharply to the right, causing the truck to lurch and tip dangerously forward.

Leon's torso slammed into the steering wheel. His hands lost their grip, braced instead against the dash, while his body shook. The steering wheel spun as the truck bucked into the ditch. He thought they would flip and he put his arms up to protect himself. But the truck remained on all four tires, the wheels straightened, and the vehicle careened nose-first into the steep ditch. He caught at the steering wheel and at the same time jabbed his foot toward the brake.

He was aware of the long dark hair of Joi flying around beside him, the girl's small body jumping like a bean then pressing into the corner of the dash, her head contacting the windshield as her limbs darted out to stop herself, in search of something to fasten onto. The beer case bounced high on the seat between them, bottles clinking madly.

The nose of the vehicle pointed down as it descended the ditch. When the truck hit a deep depression and then the rise beyond it, Leon was thrown up, then forward, and Joi disappeared altogether, a slither of black feathers, skinny arms and legs through the windshield.

A number of things happened all at once, but each with individual clarity. The top of Leon's head smashed on the roof of the truck while the steering wheel caught his thighs midway between hip and knee. His right leg cleared, but his left leg caught. He slid, leg under wheel, up the narrow steering wheel edge until there was no more space for his leg to give. The truck hit the rise on the other side of the ditch vee, hit it hard. His left leg bent above the knee where no natural bend occurred, and his mind blanked on the crack of bone deep inside tissue. Something heavy from the back seat landed on his lower back like a boulder while his neck and spine crunched and compressed on the impact of his head to the truck ceiling. The vehicle shuddered as the engine stalled. The boulder on his back receded, who knew where to. The seats creaked, the truck stopped still, and the shocks groaned. The headlights were on, the ditch grasses swayed in the wind; deep silence followed the settling of the truck into its final, hard resting place.

TIME PASSED. HOW MUCH Leon didn't know, but he was sure it had. The first thing Leon gradually became aware of was the ax, under his right foot. There was no mistaking it. The head was wedged under the brake pedal and the handle under his bare foot. Next, he felt burning in his left thigh, deep in the bone. He reached for the door handle and pulled. It opened. He thrust himself out the door. The grass in the ditch was tall and rough and the truck had wedged itself on a high spot. He fell from the cab into the deep ditch, more than the average step down. He was unprepared for the feeling of the earth falling away from where he'd expected it to be, combined with the giving way of his femur, which failed to hold his weight. The pain shot all the way up through his thigh into his hip and settled like a sick, wet dog in his gut. On the ground, he lifted himself onto his hands, forearms trembling. He allowed himself to fall forward and lie on his chest. *Only for a minute,* he thought.

How long he rested he didn't know. Eventually, by putting his weight on his elbows, he crawled to the truck cab. He reached up to the floor with his hands, pushed his good leg under him, avoiding any pressure on the bad one, and pulled himself up. He reached inside the truck and unwedged the ax before falling back into the long, dry grass, exhausted. He looked up at the dark, cloud-covered sky, wished for stars.

Sometime later he became aware of a murky raven moving in front of the truck lights. She came closer; he recognized her. Her dark hair shiny like wet black feathers. Her lips moved but he wasn't aware of any sound coming out. He remembered she was funny. *Something funny about her,* he thought. He longed to take her to his chest, smooth her dark feathers, and hold her there if she would let him. Hold her there beside his heart, which wasn't really that bad, was it? "There should be more comfort," he said, or thought he said. He didn't move, though. There was no other noise than the wind.

JOI BECAME AWARE OF the rough grass under her cheek first, and then the quiet breeze. The light. It was behind her. The light was radiant and she knew to move toward it. Standing to take a few baby steps as she might have done when she first walked as an infant, her head spun. Her hair was, what? Wet? She ran her hand through her long, dark hair and it came away dripping. She marched forward.

"Marcy," she called. She would find Marcy. Get their shit. Get this over with.

Joi approached the light, the quiet truck lights.

She staggered to the front of the truck and put her hand on the warm hood, leaving a dark handprint. Something in the grass. She looked, got closer, both saw and didn't see the figure in the tall grass, the residual lights still shining in her eyes.

She turned back to the truck, wondered again about Marcy. Back seat, she remembered now. She walked through the lights in front of the truck and approached the passenger side. Why was everything so quiet? Joi wondered. "Marcy?" she whispered and reached for the door.

LEON WAS THIRSTY AND remembered the case of beer like a barricade between the front seats. If he had a girlfriend she would ride on the bench seat where the case was, right beside him so he could sling his arm over her shoulders and she could rub her hand on his leg, up and down on his jeans. He smiled at the thought. All he wanted now was one of those beers from the truck. He tried to tell the girl but she couldn't hear him and moved off somewhere behind him. He was trembling, shirtless, in the night air. He shook uncontrollably and his core muscles ached with the effort.

Leon remembered then. It was unmerciful. It shouldn't have been this way. But he did remember and there was no remedy for it. Once the remembering began it unraveled like a ball of fat yarn. Cynthia. Dennis. The wood splitting. The seat punching. The white light behind his eyes.

"This is my time," he told himself.

He pulled himself up to his elbows. Where did the girl go? *Girls,* he remembered. Two of them. Plural. Dark ravens. He had to get them in the truck. Try and go. He'd be blamed for this.

"Cynthia," he cried hoarsely.

Elbows, then up on one knee, excruciating pain, no way to hold that leg or let it dangle without agony. No matter which way he tried to rise, which way he tried to hold the leg, the sickening pain persisted. The ax was in the grass. He forced himself again onto the knee of his good leg, used the ax as a short crutch, and heaved himself up to the cab of the truck. His arms pulled his body up and over the lip of his seat. Onto his good foot. There was nowhere to put the useless leg but under him. He saw the case of beer wedged in the space between the front seat and the dashboard. He ripped the back of the box open and took a beer, fumbled for his lighter in his jeans, finally guzzled greedily, liquid running down his chin. He finished one and took another and drank heavily of it, too, before swiping his face with his palm. He put the open beer on the seat, leaned it against the seatback. That's when he saw the hand, fingers with their black fingernail polish, hanging loosely over the bench seat.

"Shit!" he exclaimed. "Shit," he said again. The voice startled him. Was it his voice? "Jesus." He pulled back, afraid to touch the hand. Afraid of what it may or may not do in response.

He thought of her then. The baby. The one given up for adoption. She must have been almost this girl's age now? It was hard to think about details. A daughter. Dark-haired. Or so he'd heard. Out there somewhere he had a daughter he'd never met. What was her name? Did he ever know her name? What if something happened to her? What if something like this were to happen?

An urgent need gripped him: *Start the truck. Drive away.*

The keys were in the ignition.

He lay with his broad chest full on the seat, supporting his entire body. He reached for the whiskey in the glove box, took several drinks. Calmed now by the alcohol, he looked at the hand. It was a young hand. He compared it to his work-worn hands, bleeding knuckles, and knew it must be a good fifteen or twenty years younger than his own. "Just a baby," he said. He raised his head long enough to drink again. The alcohol helped the pain.

"Here's the thing," he told the hand, laying his cheek on the grimy seat. "A person can think of these things. Can imagine the destruction. The tearing up. The destroying. Really shattering that person, you know. The raw emotion of it all." Leon reached for the whiskey again. "All of that's possible without really *believing* in it. That's not what I wanted. I wouldn't actually *do* such a thing. You gotta believe me." Leon was tired now. "I didn't mean it. I didn't mean any of this."

With great effort he raised his head and tipped the whiskey to his lips. And then, just like that, he couldn't bear the sight of the hand, not one second longer. He pushed himself away from the seat, lurching backward, falling toward the long grass. He twisted to avoid his left side, crying out anyway as he hit the ground hard, hot knives tearing through his leg. He rolled to his back, panting, and after a while spread his arms as if making a snow angel, his fingers feeling through the long grass for his crutch—the ax. Soon he would look for it more earnestly. Soon.

Perhaps he slept a bit then, it was hard for him to know, but suddenly the clouds had moved off to reveal silvery moonlight. And the girl, the goth girl with the funny name. Happy name. Joy. Yes. It was Joy—Joy, tough Joy.

Joi stood near the front of the truck. Illuminated in the headlights, she looked like a dark angel. A black silhouette. Her long hair like dark feathers hung past her shoulders but Leon couldn't distinguish her features. He pictured her smiling a little enigmatic smile and narrowing her eyes as if she would say something teasing or funny. He would like to know what she was thinking. Leon started to smile back but then he saw it. He saw the ax as she lifted its weight across her body and gripped it with two hands. He tried to formulate a response, or maybe just a question, a simple question. What was it? he wondered. What did he want to say to this tough but tender girl?

It was time to go. The keys were in the ignition and they could go anytime.

Soon. Pretty soon.

Bart

1992

...

"MAYBE WE'RE TWINS," SHE JOKED, BETWEEN SAM-pling Bart's salty lips and his tobacco tongue. "I'm adopted." She bit his bottom lip. "Could be true."

He paused, pulled away, and looked at her, shuffled his feet on the cold aluminum ridges of the baseball bleachers. They were making out behind his old elementary school. *He couldn't think of anywhere else to take me,* she thought. Over his shoul-der, the hulking school building was distracting. Ruby imag-ined authoritarian eyes watching her from the dark square windows. It made her want to walk up to those opaque win-dows and yell, *What are you lookin' at? Huh?* and raise the left side of her lip in a tough-girl sneer. She hated school. School was slow and full of rules and judgment. She wanted fast. And fuck the rules.

"I read about it. They're called *pheromones,*" she prompted Bart. "Like a secret smell." She sniffed the air and pressed her-self up against him. "Yup. We're probably related," she taunted, leaning in to nibble his fat bottom lip with her teeth, licking it with the tip of her tongue. "Ruby and Bart, sitting in a tree," she sang, teasing, still kissing him.

He broke off just long enough to say, "Kissing cousins." He smiled before continuing trying to feel her up under her shirt.

She liked teasing him about their birthdays—the freaky coincidence that they shared the same birth date, August 24, 1975. Both sixteen. Exactly the same age. To. The. Day.

"Beavers do it with their cousins and stuff," she said. She pushed him away, one hand on his chest, and reached into her inside pocket with the other. The inside pocket of *his* jean jacket, which *she* wore because now *she* was his official girlfriend. Officially. Which was the sort of thing that made other girls call her a slut, mostly because they couldn't think of anything more creative to say. All the girls in her school were sheep. *Baaa,* she imagined them saying. *Sluuut.* Seriously. No originality. No thinking for themselves.

As for Julian, Bart's best friend, he was at least slightly more creative. Julian had lotsa creative shit to say, him. All sortsa shit.

From the inside pocket of the jean jacket, Ruby retrieved half a joint she'd saved from the morning and Bart, ever the gentleman, fished out his Zippo, flipped it open, rolled his thumb over the wheel, and sparked her up. The dry weed snapped.

She took a deep drag and held it in. "Where were you born?" she asked from her throat, toke solid in her lungs, squinting against the smoke. She was thinking United General Hospital or Sisters of Charity. One of the usual suspects for their city.

He reached out his hand to take the joint but she twisted her arm back over her shoulder, away from him, shook her head, and blew her smoke in his face.

She turned her head for another hit. "Tell me." She paused before adding, *"Cousin."* She laughed, and let the smoke puff out of her mouth while she threw her head back to look at the sky, blue and close to perfect, even though the spring air was still cold. She handed him the joint.

He hit it and croaked, "North."

"What kinda fuckin' place is that?" She stared at his dark curly hair, long and shaggy, in perfect harmony with his deep brown eyes and dusky skin. *"North,"* she mimicked. *"I'm from da Nort,"* she mocked.

"That's not funny," he said, getting all serious on her.

"Oh hell." She waved her hand to dismiss him. "You know what's gonna happen? We're gonna find out we're beavers. Maybe I'm really from *da Nort* too. Wouldn't that suck? To think you've been doing it with your twin?" She took a toke and let the idea settle. *"Incest,"* she said. "Eww."

BART AND JULIAN HAD known each other since grade one or something. Best friends. Julian—what a trip, man. And not always in a good way. She tried, okay? She really did. But then Julian was such a bastard, she'd started calling him Judas. Sometimes she sang Aerosmith's "Dude Looks Like a Lady" around him and laughed her ass off and he hated her for it. And for calling him "Julie," too. But most of all she really hated her for being Bart's girlfriend, even though he would never admit it. He was just so jealous.

Julian, aka Judas, had this long, dark hair that hung straight down his back, no braid or anything, almost to his waist. And tall! And skinny! His legs were long and he had a spectacular hip swagger that could take an eye out. Tight jeans and a firm little ass. Seriously, so many dudes thought he was a chick at first glance and gave him the drive-by whistle. And when that happened, Julian turned and looked, the guys saw he wasn't a chick and they peeled away, and Julian just went "Like, what the hell, man," put his hands up in a baffled gesture, and kept on doing his sashay-thing down the street. Here was the thing: Julian had this e-*normous* beak on him—you know, like a real noble Indian nose. So when he turned around and the guys with the whistles and pickup lines saw him, they really shut the hell up. Or sometimes they swore at Julian, called him a faggot. Guys are all so macho, they probably responded to their mistake by trading a round of punches in their car and then going somewhere to smoke a joint and try to pretend they all didn't just totally catcall a dude.

One time, though, a guy actually got really pissed off. The guy pulled up behind Julian. Ruby and Bart were about half a block back, holding hands and grabbing each other's asses and generally making Julian sick, so he had walked ahead.

"You working?" the guy said to Julian, when he got close enough.

Julian turned, gave the guy a real good full-schnozzle profile and the finger at the same time. The guy started swearing at Julian. He pulled his car to the curb. He was yelling at Julian and then he got out and just *attacked* him. Serious psycho, you know? He punched Julian right down to the sidewalk, like, *one, two, three,* and Julian just collapsed with each blow: down, down,

down to the cement. Then the guy kicked him in the spine before he jumped back into his car and drove off. The whole thing took, like, seconds. Julian didn't even get to fight back. It happened so fast there was no time to respond. Ruby couldn't stand Julian, in a general sort of way, but no one deserved that, right?

Even so, even given that, Julian was still a first-class prick, as far as Ruby was concerned. As for his creative names for her, he called her Red instead of Ruby, and sometimes added "nipples" or "lips." He always said it in a lewd but grossed-out way. Like he was trying to indirectly convince Bart she was disgusting for being female. Ruby's typical response was to tell him to shut the fuck up, but still he insisted. And it got worse. Her last name was Valentine—her so-called dad was English. As in, from England. Accent and all. Who the hell ever heard of a British Indian? Who ever heard of an Indian called *Ruby Valentine*? What the hell were her parents thinking?

IT WAS LATE, AFTER ELEVEN, and Ruby had Bart in her bedroom. She'd snuck him in through the window. Through the same window where she could hear the trains change cars every night. They crashed and echoed against each other while they hooked up and then endlessly pushed on somewhere else. Huddled on Ruby's narrow bed, Ruby was trying to get Bart to be quiet. He always forgot to whisper. In her tiny house, Ruby's mom was totally going to hear them.

"I have four beers in my closet," she whispered. "You want one?"

Bart smiled. "Where'd you get those?"

"Stole them from Judas, last time we were over there. I know he's your official boyfriend and all, but don't tell him, okay?"

"Oh yeah?" Bart said playfully and pushed her off the bed.

She landed on the floor with a thump. "Jesus," she hissed. "You're going to get us caught."

Her mom's footsteps instantly arrived in the hallway.

Ruby froze, still on the floor. Alice was outside the door. Ruby could hear her breathing.

"Ruby? What're you doing in there?"

Bart stifled a laugh.

"Shut up," she whispered, waving her hands at him.

Alice rattled the doorknob. "Why've you got the door locked?" Her voice was shrill.

"I'm changing! Jeez!" Ruby shouted in her best annoyed voice. "Can't I even *change* in private?"

"You need to let that dog out. I don't want her peeing in your room."

"She doesn't *pee* in my *room*," Ruby yelled, trying to sound offended.

Her mother scoffed and walked away down the hall. The TV blared again. More news about the shooting. Her mom was obsessed with it. She kept talking about it, as if it was supposed to be important to Ruby because she was Native. Or something like that.

Now there was an inquiry into what happened, which was more or less: A white supremacist pulled a gun in a store. A pawnshop. Up north. An Indian man. A Cree man, to be more precise. A trapper. Shot. Shot in the back. Shot in the back as he tried to leave.

This wasn't exactly news, in terms of racism in this town. All the same, Ruby struggled to process the cruelty. Even though she'd grown up seeing it, in different ways, every day. Hard to explain, exactly. Maybe it was this: hearing the story again and again made her throat ache, like she was going to cry. Only she didn't cry, as a rule, so that wasn't quite it. She tried to block out the noise coming from the news. Tried to think of it as just "white noise," ha ha ha.

She petted Hound. Alice hated Hound because Bart gave her to Ruby—a "Valentine's present." He thought her mom wouldn't say no to keeping her if she was a present. She called her Hound after *The Hound of the Baskervilles,* which was her dad's favorite book, even though her Hound wasn't a hound at all. And Ruby had no idea what her dad's favorite book actually was *now,* since it was more than a year since he abandoned them, this time for good, to take his crappy accent back to London. As in England.

Ruby looked at Hound, a Doberman-lookalike mutt, curled in the corner, listening to them talk disrespectfully about her bladder. Ruby made dog-whining sounds and Hound's ears shot up.

"We should run away," she whisper-said to Bart and Hound at the same time. "They're all assholes here."

She rolled to her feet and retrieved two of the beers from the back of her closet, returned to the bed, and sat cross-legged beside Bart. "No opener," she said, handing him a bottle. "Use your teeth."

Bart tipped his head sideways and put the edge of the cap on his bottom back teeth and clamped down. With an upward twist of his wrist he pried the cap off, spit it among the blankets, and handed her the opened bottle. He took the other one, opened it the same way, spit the cap out, and held the bottle up as if to say cheers.

"Let's chug two each," he said, "and then I'll go down on you." He smiled his perfectly charming smile and tipped his head back to drink. She guzzled her beer as well, then stashed the empties in the closet and grabbed the other two. On the way back to the bed she unzipped her jeans and kicked them off.

LATER, BART ASKED HER, "Did you mean what you said? About running away?"

"Hell, yeah." She ran a finger along his jawline. "But where would we go?"

"I have a place," he said, all mysterious. He wanted her to ask where.

"I'm not running away with you to Julian's tree house," she joked.

"You're real funny," he said. "No. My family has a cabin up north. My auntie owns it. But I know where the key's hidden."

"I don't know. What about Hound? Who's going to look after her?"

"We'll take her with us."

"How would we get there?"

"We'll hitch."

"Where is it, exactly?"

"Porcupine Lake. Probably about a two-hour drive from here."

THE NEXT MORNING, RUBY left her mom a note—to convince her not to get all excited about things and call the cops like the other times she'd run away. After all, she reasoned in the note, sixteen was legally old enough to leave home, so technically she wasn't doing anything wrong. She promised to return, to call, and to be safe. She said, truthfully, that she felt more stable and happier than she had in a long time, especially now that it was just the two of them, since Alice had kicked out Jay. Ruby said it was nothing personal, but she needed to get some space to deal with her dad leaving the country, which was the bullshit part, designed to get Alice to leave her in peace and also to let her come back when she was finished "running away," which she knew she was really too old to be doing anyway.

Ruby should have known better; Alice never believed a word Ruby said.

They scored four hits of acid and a quarter-ounce of weed, packed a couple of cans of corn and ravioli, and took off. Standing on the side of the highway taking small sips from a bottle Bart got off his brother, they reconsidered their image after a lot of cars went by. Two dark-haired Native stoners in jean jackets and Adidas, with a Doberman-lookalike pup? With a tiny bladder? Yeah, sure. As if anyone was going to pick them up.

Bart and Hound needed to be out of the picture until Ruby

got someone to stop. The two of them retreated to the scrubby brush near a farmer's barbed-wire fence line. With Ruby alone on the highway, it didn't take long before a guy in a silver Trans Am pulled up. His car was full of crap, the back seat crammed with what looked like fishing gear. She opened the passenger door so he couldn't just drive off.

"Hey man," she said, leaning down and looking the guy over. "Can you give us a ride?"

"Sure. Hop in," he said, throwing his arm over the back of the passenger seat and turning to give her his best macho grin. His green-and-white lumberjack shirt fell open to expose his pale chest with its brown, pube-like tufts around his nipples, trailing a line down his stomach, the same color as his long brown hair and three-day beard. He was wearing jeans and an earring and white sport socks, driving with no shoes on his feet for some reason. He didn't look like much of a fisherman to Ruby. She couldn't begin to guess where his shoes might be.

"Just a sec," she said, looking over her shoulder. "My friend's just taking a piss."

Bart ran to the car, Hound loping all puppy-like and cute behind him.

The guy's demeanor soured but Ruby had the car door open and she could tell he wouldn't pull a complete asswipe and drive off, although the thought of it flickered across his face as plain as the disappointment in his eyes. Ruby pulled the seat forward for Bart and Hound to get in the back. She took the front seat.

The driver turned and faced the road. "Watch out for the

shit in the back," he said, his voice flat. Once they got up to highway speed he asked, "Where you guys going?"

"Porcupine Lake," Bart answered from the back seat. Poor Hound was trying to get comfortable with all the crap in the back. Ruby took a good look around the car. A couple of rods, tackle boxes, rain gear or tarps, hard to tell; rope, maybe camping gear, none of it neatly packed. It looked as if he'd just tossed anything he thought he might need into his car in under five minutes and took off with no shoes. Why was he in such a hurry? she wondered.

Across the center console, near the shifter, was a large hunting knife in a leather case. Ruby thought then about the guy who attacked Julian.

After a while the driver flipped on the radio. The news again.

". . . after a couple of shots into the floor," the newsreader said. *Who shoots a gun into a floor?* That was when Leo LaChance was shot in the back: after the couple of shots into the floor. What were those shots about? Warning? Intimidation? LaChance was leaving the store when he was shot in the back with the third shot from an assault rifle. He was as good as gone. They didn't need to make him go. He was practically out the door. An assault rifle. Like shooting him was sport.

"They should give the guy a medal," the driver said.

At first, she thought he meant Leo LaChance. Then she saw what he meant. He looked at her sideways, his eyes darting from the road to her face, back and forth. As if challenging her to say different. Bart drew in his breath.

Ruby leaned over and pointed to his socks. "What's the deal?" she asked. "Where's your shoes?" She leaned way over, trying to get a good look at his sock feet.

He laughed. "Long story," he said. "Lost them at a party." Then he added, "Or something like that," and smirked.

"Something like a party?" Ruby asked. She tucked the hunting knife under her armpit. Sat back up straight.

"Huh? No." He shook his head. "It *was* a party. My shoes were—oh fuckin' never mind." He reached into his pocket and took out a pack of smokes. Ruby took out Bart's bottle and had a slug. Handed it back to Bart. She felt the driver's sharp eyes follow her. He lit his smoke and rolled his window down a crack. The air rushed in. In that moment of distraction, Ruby tossed the knife to Bart in the back seat. "Check this out," she said.

The driver turned to see what they found, but it was already too late for him to do anything about it. Bart pulled the knife out of its case. Not menacing, really. Or maybe just the right amount of maybe-dangerous.

The driver's face turned red. "Don't fuck around," he said.

"Exactly," Ruby said. "Don't fuck around. No one should fuck around." Then she added, "Bart here doesn't need any medals today."

At the first turnoff, the guy couldn't get rid of them quickly enough. She gave his car the finger as he fishtailed away. Bart unsheathed the knife and flashed it in the sun, but soon the quiet settled around them and they began the long walk along the access road, hemmed in by trees. Ruby remembered the first family fiction she'd ever made up: a story about how her real mother walked very far when she was pregnant with her. She asked Bart if he wanted to hear it.

"This is about my *real* mother," she emphasized. She had never tried telling the story to anyone before.

Her mother walked and walked, big and pregnant, until she ended up under a tree—a great big, swaying weeping willow—ready to have her baby. She'd hunched on her haunches and gripped that tree, hugged it like it was her own mother, forehead on the rough cool bark, gaining strength and courage from the tree, whose strong deep roots would help sustain her during a difficult childbirth. She was tired from walking and thirsty, but the baby was coming and the tree propped her up, gave her shade and encouragement. Finally, the baby was born and her mother buried the placenta under the tree to help nourish it and to pay the tree back for how it had helped her out.

"Now, every time I walk near a willow tree," she told Bart, "I feel like I'm walking over my mother's heart." Ruby regularly applied herself to creating and owning the many fragments of her existence.

BART FOUND THE KEY under a rock at the side of the cabin, just like he'd said.

The front of the cabin faced the road. The back faced the lake. The main room was one large space with a couch and a kitchen table, a counter with a sink, a hot plate, and a fridge. There was one bedroom off the main living space. Outhouse for a bathroom. Got it, all in a matter of seconds.

"Is that a phone?" she asked.

"It's a party line."

She had no idea what that was but nodded and said, "Oh. I like parties."

Bart laughed. "Not that kind of party. It means other people use it. You can sometimes pick up the phone and there's other people on it. We never use it because it costs a lot to call long distance. Here"—he put his hand on the receiver and looked at her. "Shhh," he said, then carefully picked up the handset and put it to his ear. He smiled and motioned her over with his hand. He held the receiver so she could hear. She leaned in to listen, expecting the thrill of overhearing someone else's private conversation. But it was only dial tone. He laughed at her disappointed face.

"Well, sometimes you get people talking. The ring for here is one long and two short."

There was a dock, with a canoe on shore. The sun was warm.

"Let's go swimming," Ruby said.

"The water's fucking cold."

"Skinny-dipping!"

"Someone will see us," he said, but she heard the give in his voice. He liked the idea of being naked together. Guys always wanted to have sex in weird places.

"There's no one out here," she argued. "It's only the start of May. No one does lake stuff until the long weekend, right? We probably won't see anyone."

"Let's get some wood for the fireplace," he suggested. "Then we can take our clothes off." He smiled. She examined his perfect teeth. Jesus.

Instead of skinny-dipping, they sat on the couch and smoked a joint. A ghetto blaster and a shoebox of tapes were the only items of interest. She dragged the box to the couch and they looked through them. Most of them were marked. Some of the music was not bad, like Blondie, Pink Floyd, Queen, Led Zeppelin, and even some Alice Cooper. But then they found bad stuff like Jefferson Starship, Olivia Newton-John, and Bette Midler. "Kenny Loggins! Air Supply!" Ruby shrieked. "Oh my god, whose music *is* this?"

"My brother and cousin made a lot of the tapes," Bart said, "but some belong to my uncle and auntie. I don't really know, they're just always here."

"Well, I don't mind 'The Rose,'" she said, holding the Bette Midler tape.

Bart pretended to stick his finger down his throat and gag.

"I taught myself how to play it on the recorder in grade seven."

"Oooh, talented." Bart whistled, mock-impressed.

"Shut up," she said. "It wasn't that easy."

They checked out the bed and Ruby decided to get naked under the covers while Bart built a fire. She heard it crackling and smelled the smoke. The cassette clicked and the sound of Queen filled the cabin. Bart came to the bedroom and whipped the covers off her.

"Don't! It's cold," she shrieked, grabbing them back.

"I'll warm you up," Bart said, pulling his clothes off and jumping into the bed, putting his warm flesh next to hers. They kissed and kissed for so long she felt lost. He put her hand down so she could feel his hardness, like he wanted her to know something about him. She grabbed his hand and pressed his fingers between her legs. After they finished fucking they lay under the blankets and Ruby put her head on Bart's shoulder. She played with his one free hand, pushing his arm in the air, looking at their hands together, fingers entwined. He was darker than her, his knuckles brown and smooth. His fingernails squared off, trimmed and even.

"This makes me happy," she said. "I wish we could stay here forever. Right here. In this bed."

"But we're going *swimming*," he laughed.

"Okay, well. How about we take the canoe out instead? There's probably paddles somewhere?"

"I have an idea," Bart said, sitting up and looking at her. "Let's take one hit of acid each. And eat something, I got the munchies."

They mixed together a can of corn and a can of ravioli and heated it on the hot plate. Ruby found a radio station with music and danced around the cabin. They found the end of a bottle of whiskey in the cupboard over the fridge and took turns drinking shots straight from the bottle.

Bart picked up the party phone and called Julian. Told Julian to come. To bring beer and food. "We've got the munchies," he laughed.

"We love you!" Ruby yelled at the phone receiver, the acid hitting hard.

IT WAS NEARLY SUNSET by the time they found the paddles and pushed the dark-green canoe into the shallow water.

"No, Hound," she scolded. "You stay here." Hound whined, prancing her front paws on the sand, watching them. "No," Ruby said more sternly.

Ruby attempted to enter the boat first, trying to save her shoes from getting wet. As soon as she got one foot in, with Bart standing at the edge of the water and holding the canoe to steady it, the canoe wobbled and she nearly fell, grasping for the edges. Her free foot got soaked with cold water. She screamed and lunged forward, throwing herself into the canoe. Her weight scraped the boat bottom on the sand and rocks. She laughed.

"Sit down," Bart yelled.

Hound whined from the shore.

"Fuck off," she said to Bart. She resented being yelled at. Especially when she was in such a good mood.

Bart pushed out further, jumped in, trailing water from his sneakers, and nearly tipped them over.

"Don't boss me around like that," Ruby said, trying to make a point. "Buzzkill," she muttered.

"Well, you can't stand up in a canoe," he snapped. "You'll tip it."

"Right," she said, with much the same tone she would say *fuck you,* and she stood up in the boat, lifting her leg as if to step over the side of the canoe, which then tipped sharply, pitching Ruby face-first into the icy water. She fell to her hands and knees; water splashed up her nose.

Behind her, Bart choked on a laugh; he managed to stay upright in the canoe. Hound splashed into the water. Ruby put her hand on Hound's strong neck and together they waded

through the shallow water to shore. Ruby was so mad she ignored Bart calling to her from the canoe. She walked away, up
the beach, fuming that he hadn't even come to help her. Prick.
She left him behind, still sitting in the boat.

Ruby didn't notice the cold at first. She walked fast and
angry, trying to put space between her and Bart. If she could
have, she'd have walked all the way back to the city. Soon,
though, she slowed down and the sharp awareness of being
high on acid took over again. The moon was beautiful—full,
luminous. Hound ran ahead and back, disappearing into the
darkness and then resurfacing. They walked for what seemed
like a long time before she noticed she was shivering.

There was only one cabin on the shoreline with lights on.
Bart's cabin was somewhere that felt like a long way behind
her. People were at the cabin with the lights. Ruby walked right
up to the porch and looked in the window of the door. A circle
of chairs and several people sitting around the circle. The
lights were low, a fire in the fireplace. Someone opened the
door for her. Warm air, ripe with the scent of sweetgrass and
sage. She stepped in, Hound at her heels. The door closed behind them. She felt shy but no one really looked at her. She had
a small revelation: she wasn't special; she wasn't un-special.
She was just there. No one was surprised, not even her.

"Bart," she said out loud. She didn't know what she was trying to say. Her voice sounded thin and far away.

"Astum," an older, heavyset man said in a slow northern accent. "Sit down, Bart. Sit down here"—he motioned to a chair,
a smile tipping the corners of his mouth.

Ruby laughed and took her place where he said. Did he

think her name was Bart, or was he teasing her? She was aware of the amber light in the room, the brilliant color of the flame from the fireplace, and the smell of burning wood and sage. A woman with shoulder-length dark hair and kind eyes draped a blanket around Ruby's shoulders.

They were talking, those people in the circle, about a lot of things. And then Ruby heard them talk about the shooting. Sort of. In a roundabout way. She only heard some of the conversation because she was too heavy. Somewhere in there she thought she fell asleep.

MAKE HIM DANCE. THERE were three men in the store, drinking alcohol. Drinking and firing a gun. Not just any gun. An assault rifle. Into the floor. They were firing the gun into the floor. They were making Leo LaChance dance. *Dance.* LaChance.

There once was a man named LaChance.

She drifted.

A LOUD KNOCK AT the door. The old man shook her shoulder gently. "Bart," he said, still teasing, but also serious. "I think that's for you. Better get ready."

Cops. And a woman, who told Ruby she was Bart's auntie. The cabin was hers. Ruby and Bart were overheard on the party line, calling Julian. Ruby heard the words *runaway* and *dangerous. Stealing.* She thought about the Trans Am guy and the knife. She searched the face of the old man, who she thought was being nice to her, teasing her like an old moshom. The woman who brought her the blanket. They called the cops on her, she realized, betrayed.

Someone took the wet blanket and gave her a dry one. She sat in the back of the cop car. They wouldn't let Hound in with her and she was immediately defensive. They questioned her again and again. Sternly. Gently. With patience and impatience. They asked about Bart.

"I'm not mad anymore," she said.

She laughed a few times, even though it was wrong to laugh—she couldn't help it. They asked if she was stoned and she only told them about the pot and the whiskey because adults couldn't handle the truth. She told them she'd done it before and no, she did not need to go to the hospital.

"Where's Bart?" she asked.

"We don't know," his auntie told her, maybe for the first time.

Oh.

They were searching for him. The canoe was gone.

After that, they let her out of the car, left her alone on the beach where she could hear them, calling, searching. Ruby and Hound lay down on the sand and she wrapped herself around Hound's warm body. She thought about Bart, maybe out on the lake. Was he cold too? She willed him back to shore. She thought about Leo LaChance on the cold street after being shot. All bad news is cold.

There once was a man named LaChance

She pulled Bart in with her mind. She held his beautiful hand.

They wanted to see him tap-dance

Someone tried to take her to the cabin but she resisted.

"No. I need to stay here," she pleaded. They left her alone again.

Two shots in the floor

Julian arrived. How long had it been?

"Where's Bart?" she asked him. She already knew it had been way too long.

And one out the door

Julian lay down on the sand with her. He folded his arms around her from behind and held her there. She buried her nose into the collar of Bart's jean jacket. It smelled like wet lake and Bart.

He didn't have even a chance

Gwen

. . .

ONCE GWEN HAD PACKED HER CAR, SHE CAME AROUND
to Ruby's house to say goodbye. Ruby rushed from the house
to squeeze Gwen's remaining items like puzzle pieces into
the already overflowing vehicle. These were probably Ruby's
last moments with Gwen and she spent them cramming all
of Gwen's possessions, a surprising number and assortment
of items—*Why a tennis racket?* she wondered—into the car.
Ruby was determined to make sure all physical traces of Gwen
would be gone.

A couple of days after Gwen left, Ruby held a letter just inside the mouth of the mailbox—the letter addressed to Gwen,
with Gwen's new address, in Gwen's new city, scribbled on the
front. Ruby let her fingers linger for a moment on the corner of
the envelope before dropping it, the *never contact me again* letter, irretrievable, into the belly of the red letterbox.

Done, she thought. She forced herself to smile.

"The brain doesn't know everything," she said out loud. A
woman waited nearby to drop in her own letters. "It knows

what the body tells it to know. So smile!" She beamed at the woman, who smiled back involuntarily.

Ruby laughed and skipped away.

She had a history of moving on. Moving on from people, that is. Ruby collected friends like the tooth fairy collected baby teeth. So many little chiclets just clicking around, tapping against each other. Not even serious teeth; they didn't even have roots. Just little washed-out baby milk teeth.

Like Lonnie and Jessie, her supposed best friends in high school, especially close after her boyfriend Bart died. At the end of grade twelve, the three of them applied to be camp counselors, but only Jessie and Lonnie were selected. That meant Ruby would have to stay behind in the city for the summer. The night before they left for summer camp, Jessie and Lonnie came to Ruby's house to say goodbye. She didn't really understand what the big goodbye was all about. They'd see each other in eight weeks, no big deal. Ruby preferred quick endings. She wasn't fond of, or good at, goodbyes.

A little while after Jessie and Lonnie left her house that night, Ruby, still feeling weird about the visit, noticed her new black lipstick missing, the one she'd shoplifted just that week. Then, a pair of silver hoop earrings that were really her mother's. She investigated further and realized her special Quick Tan suntanning lotion was also gone from the dresser. Jessie and Lonnie hadn't come to say goodbye at all. They came to steal things they wanted to have at summer camp. Ruby decided then and there that her summer would be spectacularly different than Jessie and Lonnie's summer. While they were off being children at camp, Ruby would grow the fuck up.

Ruby met Moe as he unloaded a truck at one of the neighbors' houses. He was older, had been out of school for three years already, and none of her friends knew him, which made him perfect. They started hanging out every day. Like Ruby, Moe was also part Native. Unlike Ruby, he was not adopted, but jeez he might as well have been, you'd never know he was Native by how his family acted. Ruby knew being adopted made her awkward in her own skin, as if she'd had after-factory modifications.

Something Ruby didn't tell anyone: She could spot an Indigenous adoptee a mile away. Pick them out of the crowd like it was a serious parlor game. Sixth sense. And it wasn't just a visibility thing, a Native kid with their non-Native parents. Take the so-called parents out of the picture and she could still recognize them—likely, she thought, because of that window, a blank spot like a slipped stitch in a knitted scarf—once it was missed there was no going back to fix it. It just existed. Ruby recognized that spot a mile away.

As a child, two things were likely to happen when she went out in public with her parents. Other kids would look around and, if they could spot a Native woman anywhere in the vicinity, they would ask, *Is that your mom?* Or, if she was obviously with her white parents, they would say, *Are you adopted?* No pretending allowed.

Siblings in other families would play the adopted card to torment one another, saying, *You're really adopted,* because being adopted was supposed to make a kid cry.

She'd assumed Moe was adopted—he gave off the vibe—but later realized he wasn't, after all. She had no explanation for Moe's family's discomfort with themselves. Aside from being able to get a really great tan in the summer and making comments about "showing their roots," they didn't have much to do with the Native world.

"Their politics are so complicated," Moe's mother complained, watching a news clip about political discord in the Assembly of First Nations. "They can't even get along with each other."

"What's all this *they* shit?" Ruby later asked Moe, but he only shrugged his shoulders and told her not to listen to his mom. But it was hard. For the longest time, whenever Moe's mom saw Ruby she would break into the Kenny Rogers song, singing "Roooo-bee, don't take your love to town" in her fake falsetto. A veiled insult, Ruby was sure. Especially when she listened to the lyrics, which talked about the narrator shooting and burying Ruby in the ground. But Ruby set aside her uncomplimentary thoughts about Moe's mom and married Moe before the fall, not long after her eighteenth birthday.

ONCE THE BOYS WERE born, Ruby, who had always missed the family she imagined she should have—aunties, cousins, grandparents, sisters, mother—saw too late that by having her kids she'd created another generation who would miss this unknown family too. She had no idea how to create for them an entire world she'd never known. So she filled their home with Native art, cheap prints from secondhand stores, portraits of children and Elders from villages she didn't know where. And she told her boys these were their cousins, aunties, uncles, moshoms and kohkums, and made up stories about them based on the little she had pieced together in her short lifetime. She created a mythology for them. Fabricated family. To try and save her kids from the longing she'd felt her whole life. From the weird amnesia about something that didn't happen. From the yearning for something that should've happened, for something she felt in her blood.

She saw the "family pictures" as a terrible but necessary lie. It was Ruby's attempt to dream herself back together.

BY THE TIME IT came to Gwen, Ruby had successfully moved on from several friends and lovers. One of the mistakes Ruby kept making was to believe that each person in her life loved her unconditionally. She didn't question that love until she was given a reason to, but by then it was usually too late—she was in deep. After that, Ruby acted swiftly to cut her losses. She got out while the getting was good.

There were certainly things Ruby loved about Gwen: She drank a lot and ate what she liked. She had a little paunch from all the beer and she took up as much space as she wanted. Gwen had 1,064 unread emails and she kept a bottle of red wine in the trunk of her car, "in case of emergencies."

With Gwen, Ruby stopped obsessing about her weight. Her terrible eating habits settled down. The less Gwen gave a shit about diets and weight, the healthier Ruby got.

Ruby had never met anyone like Gwen, who randomly held Ruby's hand or put her arm around her, kissed her on the cheek even, for nothing and any old time. When they were walking somewhere, enjoying the nice weather, faces turned to catch the sun, and Gwen reached for Ruby's hand or linked arms with her, it made an already lovely day perfectly glorious. Her easy smile suggested nothing stuck to her. In Ruby's experience, only beautiful people got away with Gwen's kind of carelessness.

Gwen fussed over Ruby's style and in response Ruby stepped up her game, building a wild but fabulous wardrobe out of thrift shop finds and self-altered garments. Ruby's sewing machine took up semi-permanent residence at one end of the kitchen table and she was forever creating or transforming some article of clothing. "You're like a walking art piece," Gwen told her. Modern art, more like it. Kind of collage-effect. Once in a while another woman would stop her in the Sally Ann and say, "I love your outfit," and look at her with an approving eye. Ruby's cachet bloomed.

On one shopping spree to the thrift store, Gwen picked up a cardboard suitcase. She showed it to Ruby.

"I've never seen anything like that." Ruby's tone was approving.

"I'm getting it. And then, I want to travel somewhere with it." Gwen's voice was dreamy.

"Is it really meant as luggage?"

"I don't know, but I like the idea."

"The idea of what?"

"I don't know." Gwen shrugged as she examined the suitcase. "The idea of trusting something so fragile for something so important."

"Well, that sounds about right." Ruby laughed loud and hard, but Gwen didn't see what was so funny.

———

RUBY WAS SITTING AT the kitchen table cutting a tag out of a new used shirt with a pair of baby nail clippers.

"Can't find the scissors," she said. One tiny snip at a time. "Probably in the boys' room. Under the bed or something." *Snip. Snip.* Gwen was flipping through one of Ruby's fashion magazines.

"What's your favorite color?" she asked, looking at a spread of color-coded clothes and accessories.

"I like the blue," said Ruby, looking up for a second. Then back to her snipping.

"Why are you putting those two patterns together?" Gwen pointed to Ruby's outfit, floral on the top, a very small check on the bottom.

Ruby stared at Gwen. "Because it works."

"I'd never think to do that. You're so clever."

Ruby laughed. "Well, I don't know if I'd go *that* far," she said, pleased.

"Which would you rather have, the white boots or the choker?" Gwen pointed to the magazine.

Ruby loved beautiful things. Made a habit of looking away from as many ugly things as possible. "The world is full of ugly, after all," she would say. "Why not choose beauty?" In the same way, she always preferred a lie to the ugly truth. A mountain of lies to one dirty fact.

Gwen asked Ruby so many questions it made Ruby dizzy, and whatever answer Ruby gave to Gwen's endless questions,

Gwen wanted to know why. "What makes you say that?" she would ask. Gwen seemed infinitely curious about Ruby. Like Ruby was study material.

But it was Gwen who didn't realize how special she was, with her dark careless hair, delicate features, wide smile, and insatiable curiosity. Being with Gwen felt like playing your favorite game. And Ruby adored games. Like her idea for the un-birthdays.

For the inaugural un-birthday, Ruby bought stamps and sent formal paper invitations in the mail to Gwen and each of the boys, inviting them to an "un-birthday party." Even though Ruby could've handed out the invitations in person, she mailed them instead so they could be received like a surprise.

For the party, Ruby baked a cake. On the day of the un-birthday, the boys ran around the house finding leftover party decorations. They made a special chair for Junior, who was the designated un-birthday person. The chair was covered in ribbons, streamers, balloons, and scraps of wrapping paper cut into fringe—whatever they could find to make it look festive.

Every person attending the un-birthday party was to bring something they already owned, wrapped in fancy paper or newspaper, decorated with ribbons and stickers—a gift for the special person. Cards were made from cereal-box cardboard, glued, colored, and glittered with great concentration. The chocolate cake was peppered with Smarties and all the candles she could find in the drawer. It promised an inferno. There was a stir of excitement in the house as they prepared.

"Go get the un-birthday hat," Ruby encouraged Aaron and

he ran off to the bathroom to retrieve the crocheted toilet paper cover made with sparkly yarn. For one night the cover would be repurposed as the most coveted hat in the house.

Gwen showed up with a bottle of chilled champagne for her and Ruby, and sparkling apple juice for the boys.

"We need to do a toast," Gwen insisted, popping the champagne cork and filling Ruby's wineglass until it overflowed. Ruby popped the apple juice cork, much to the boys' delight.

"Cheers." Gwen hoisted her glass in the air, encouraging the boys and Ruby to do the same. "As my dear old dad used to say, *I'd rather have a bottle in front of me than a frontal lobotomy.*" Ruby laughed and they clinked their glasses together.

Ruby got instantly happy-drunk on the champagne, which was sweet and too easy to drink. She lost track of the pot of curry on the stove and burned it so that it smelled like hair chemicals. And so, instead of the supper Ruby had planned, they did "the civilized thing," as Gwen put it, and ordered pizza. Then they turned off the lights for the spectacle of the candles and sang "Happy Un-birthday to You."

To see Junior made so happy by the cake, the candles, and the repurposed gifts pleased Ruby. Junior beamed in the glow of the attention. The purpose of the un-birthday was to make the un-birthday person feel special for no reason at all.

The party was a roaring success, but later Ruby and Gwen fought, again.

It happened much like Ruby imagined it might. They were both quite drunk, and Gwen got mad at Ruby for saying Gwen liked to have things her own way.

"What do you mean by that?" Gwen challenged, on the defensive. Gwen wasn't always a happy drunk.

"You know. You *seem* like you're really easygoing, but deep down you're a control freak. You say so yourself." Ruby made the comment in a drunk, *I'm teasing you* kind of way, but Gwen was primed for fury.

"*Control freak?*" Gwen's voice rose and Ruby smiled, maybe at what Gwen said or how she said it. Ruby couldn't even remember the reason she smiled just then, but the smile sent Gwen into a fit. "Now you're mocking me?"

Ruby didn't think she was, but unfortunately she kept smiling.

Ruby knew that Gwen, despite the front she put up, was oversensitive to being mocked or laughed at. But Ruby was in no condition to take that seriously at the moment.

Gwen's violent reaction happened so fast that later Ruby couldn't remember the exact sequence of events, but she did recall being pushed up against the wall, her windpipe crushed under Gwen's forearm. Gwen was so close that Ruby could smell her unwashed hair. Ruby's smile faltered a bit but didn't disappear entirely. Gwen's eyes were full of rage as she pressed her forearm harder across Ruby's throat.

"Stop," Gwen hissed, getting closer. "Stop. Fucking. Smiling."

Ruby's breath rasped against her windpipe, but otherwise she didn't protest. It was the level. The *level* of Gwen's anger that surprised her. And still she couldn't buy into it; it all seemed sort of funny to her in the moment. Perversely enjoyable. Later, she would chalk it up to the effect of the champagne. Ruby couldn't take anything seriously after drinking that much sugar and bubbles.

A little thrill shot through Ruby as she saw Gwen prepare to hit her. As Gwen drew her arm back, hand open, ready to strike, Ruby half closed her eyes and turned her face slightly away in anticipation.

"Don't touch my hair," she whispered. She tensed for the blow.

Gwen paused. The waiting went a split second too long and Ruby opened her eyes. Gwen looked at her raised hand and then at Ruby. She took a step away. Ruby coughed. Gwen said nothing but looked at Ruby like she'd just woken up. Gwen's arms fell to her sides as if they were suddenly very heavy and she turned and walked out of the room, shaking her head. She didn't even bother to slam the door.

More than the violence itself, Ruby was troubled by Gwen's failure to follow through with it. She dissected the moment all night. All the next morning she was distracted by the mystery. Slowly she settled on the idea that in the middle of their most intense and intimate moment, Gwen had seen something in Ruby that made her lose interest. Made her lose her commitment to it. Lose her commitment to Ruby.

Was it Ruby's new boyfriend? she wondered. Ruby had just started dating a guy from work called Mark. Gwen thought this was hilarious and made fun of him every chance she got.

"Mark's last name should be Eraser," she said. "Then he could cancel himself out."

"He's okay," Ruby said. "You should get to know him."

Gwen made a noise in the back of her throat like Ruby was telling a joke.

Or perhaps the quality of Ruby's smile had changed as Gwen prepared to strike her. In anticipation of the blow, maybe Ruby had given herself away? Given away that she secretly enjoyed the idea of Gwen hitting her. Because Ruby knew, somewhere deep down, that Gwen hitting her would either bring them closer together or drive them fully apart. Whatever the trigger, Gwen had lost interest in the intimacy, in the urgency of the moment, and ultimately in Ruby herself. As if Gwen suddenly couldn't be bothered even to hit her. It was as if their whole time together boiled down to that one moment. It was only worth it if it went too far.

BUT GWEN'S VIOLENCE WASN'T the reason Ruby mailed Gwen the *never contact me again* letter. She sent it because of what followed. Gwen took a job in Vancouver, decided to move two provinces away and leave Ruby behind with her messed-up life, shitty eating habits, and rambunctious kids.

"YOU JUST SAID YES to the offer?" Ruby asked, trying to process Gwen's news.

"Yup."

"Just like that?"

"Mm-hmm" was Gwen's infuriating reply.

"You didn't even talk about it with anyone before you just said *yes*?" By "anyone," Ruby really meant "Ruby."

"Nope," Gwen said.

Gwen's one-word responses made Ruby murderous. But she wasn't finished making a fool of herself yet.

"Maybe I can come to Vancouver? Moe would take the boys."

Gwen pressed her too-long fingernail into a mosquito bite and remained silent.

"I could spend a few days there? Maybe I'll like it and want to move." Ruby laughed to suggest she wasn't serious.

"Maybe?" Gwen answered as if she, too, doubted the possibility.

"I could try out your cardboard suitcase for you," Ruby joked. "Take it on a road trip."

Gwen tried to laugh, but the tone was off and Ruby couldn't read it.

"So, you're really leaving?" Ruby hated how pathetic she sounded.

"Yup."

Ruby held herself together, grinding her teeth and wishing Gwen to be struck by a falling tree or a guillotine. Ruby got up and pretended to go to the bathroom. As soon as she rounded the corner out of Gwen's sight she stopped and gave Gwen the finger, double-barreled, through the wall. She waved her arms, emphatically jabbing her middle fingers in the air. *Fuck you,* she thought. *Fuck y—*

"What are you doing, Mommy?" Aaron was watching her.

"Jesus, kid," Ruby said, swinging her arms behind her back. "You scared me." Ruby laughed as cover. "There's a fly in here. Did you see it?"

The boy shook his head no.

"Do you want to go get the flyswatter? We can smack it."

"That's okay," he said, turning to run off. "I'm going outside."

Of course he knows there's no fly. Why would he go get the flyswatter for an imaginary fly? She went into the bathroom and splashed water around in the sink. "Fuck you," she said looking in the mirror. And then more kindly, she reminded herself, "I love you."

And just like that, within a week Gwen was packing her shit and moving away. She softened a little and told Ruby, "I'll miss you." She held out the promise to call, the promise to be back. The promise that they would talk, as if maybe they were going to work things out. All Ruby could think was, *No fucking way.* All she could hear in her head were Gwen's smug, unforgivable answers. *Nope. Yup.* Ruby's teeth ached from the grinding. It was all too far gone for Ruby. She could only think *Cut, cut, cut* when it came to Gwen.

Ruby had enough counseling and therapy in her life to realize, of course, that she was covering up her hurt and rejection with anger. She was rejecting Gwen before Gwen could further hurt and exclude her.

Of course, this comes from being adopted, you know, Ruby could hear her counselor Carolyn's voice say in her head. *Wounded at dawn*—the original rejection, Carolyn had said, loosely quoting something from the Spanish poet Lorca—she was really a Fine Arts graduate who couldn't find gainful employment in her field. The line *wounded at dawn* had stuck with Ruby all these years.

After the car-packing, as Gwen was saying goodbye and hugging her, she whispered in Ruby's ear, "I'm sorry we fought."

Ruby almost couldn't stand it. She squeezed Gwen tighter and shouted in her head, *Go! Just go!*

Despite this, Ruby thought she would relent after Gwen left. But Ruby surprised herself when she realized she didn't want Gwen back, after all. And besides, she was slightly afraid of being with Gwen.

Ruby wrote the letter to destroy it all, to push FINAL on the big red nuclear button. She was determined to delete any of Gwen's lingering *I'll miss you*s and *I'll call*s.

After Ruby dropped the letter in the mailbox, she thought she would feel relief. Instead, a great sadness enveloped her. She stopped dressing nice. She wore old sweatpants and T-shirts and ate every bad thing she could get her hands on. Potato chips, chocolate, crackers, and beer. Every day she made cookies or brownies and ate them until she was sick. She convinced herself cookies were food if they had oatmeal in them. The boys loved it.

Ruby thought more than once about making herself barf, but instead she just kept eating. Twice a day she brushed and flossed her teeth. It seemed the least she could do.

A week after she dropped the note to Gwen in the mailbox she received a text message. It was from Gwen.

"Wtf is going on?"

Ruby didn't answer.

Then later, again from Gwen: "If you love me like you say

you do, why would you do this? Why not work this out to-gether?"

Ruby laughed out loud at the suggestion. She momentarily considered sending a "lol" back to Gwen but stopped herself. No contact was the way to handle the situation. It was her MO, had always worked in the past. Ruby was sure it would be effective this time.

But then, three weeks after the mailed letter, Gwen showed up at Ruby's door. Dropped off in a cab. She was in town for something. Meetings? Armed robbery? *Who cares?* thought Ruby.

"Can we go somewhere for a beer?" Gwen asked, spotting the boys running through the backyard threatening each other with sticks. *It's always fun until somebody loses an eye.*

Ruby called next door and asked Herman to watch out for the boys. She grabbed her jean jacket and smokes—she had started smoking again—and they left the house. Ruby didn't even bother to brush her hair, just a baseball cap to cover the rat's nest. Her jean jacket was tight on her shoulders.

"You look good," Gwen said.

Ruby sneered. "I smell bad," she said, refusing to repay the compliment. They walked three blocks to the local bar. It was a Monday evening and quiet. The waitress recognized them and said a warm hello. Ruby tried to smile but she caught the waitress's look of surprise to see Ruby so disheveled and fat. In sweatpants, no less. *Yup, that's me all right,* Ruby thought.

Ruby drank her first pint too fast. She felt it go to her head. Her face got hot. She ordered another pint before Gwen had

even made it through half of her first. Ruby filled every silence
with her eyes glued to the football game on the bar's one big
screen. She decided somewhere into the second pint that she
wanted to feel as little as possible. They made small talk. Ruby
didn't want to ask Gwen anything about Vancouver. Instead
she let Gwen ask about the boys. Ruby ordered a third beer.
She regretted going to the bar.

"I have something for you." Gwen took a parcel out of her
bag and placed it in front of Ruby. It was wrapped in three different kinds of wrinkled wrapping paper, patched together
with Scotch tape. A card stuck to the package said *Miss Ruby* in
Gwen's handwriting.

A vein across Ruby's temple throbbed and she thought a bug
might be crawling on her. "Does anyone handwrite anymore?"
she asked, looking square at Gwen perhaps for the first time.

Gwen laughed. "Well, I do," she said.

"I have to go to the bathroom." Ruby pushed her chair away
from the table and lurched in the direction of the toilets. But
instead of going to the bathroom she stopped at the bar and
ordered two shots of tequila. The bartender gave her salt and
lime and she licked the salt from her hand with an exaggerated
motion, downed both shots, one after the other, and bit into the
lime wedge, sucking its juice.

The bartender laughed. "That bad, hey?"

"You're telling me." Ruby belted out a laugh, rolled her
eyes, and winked at the bartender all in one fluid motion, for
which she was proud of herself.

He nodded. "You're all right." Ruby made her way toward
the toilets at the back of the bar.

In the bathroom she didn't immediately recognize her reflection in the mirror, with her flushed cheeks and boring clothes. Bloated and out of control. Discouraged.

"You're *not* all right," Ruby said to herself in the mirror. "So much has already been lost." She was slightly afraid she might cry.

"Fuck *lost*." Ruby was quite drunk now. "I didn't lose anything," she poked her finger at herself in the mirror for emphasis. "*They* did." Ruby pictured herself as a baby, swaddled in messy blankets, being passed from one set of hands to another. No. *Lost* was what *others* did. She swayed on her feet.

Ruby had a choice. Go back to the table and see what Gwen the Destroyer had in mind. Or don't. Don't play Gwen's game. "Play your own game," Ruby said to her new other self in the mirror. *Fuck you I love you.*

Gwen came into the bathroom. Ruby in the mirror, looking guilty, imagined Gwen knew exactly what conclusion she had just reached.

"There you are." Gwen strode up to Ruby. Gwen, with her bad posture, took Ruby's shoulders in her hands and pushed her against the wall. Ruby could smell Gwen's sweat, like pencil shavings. For a second, she thought Gwen might hurt her. Instead she surprised Ruby. She kissed her. Square and full on the lips, a kiss full of ambition, fire, bitterness, impatience: a wanting and vengeful kiss.

Gwen was shrewd that way. She knew hitting Ruby wasn't the way to hurt her. The kiss. A single kiss. In case of emergencies. That was the way to do it, after all.

Rose

2 0 1 5

...

I N THE HEADACHE CORNER OF THE ER, KOHKUM ROSE cried in her silent way and Uncle Gordy told her she'd be okay.

"No, I don't want it," she pleaded, her small hand gripping his arm.

In the next bed, anonymous behind a thin fabric curtain, a woman's heavy sighs suggested their words burdened her. Brightness, noise, too much activity—everything aggrieved their neighbor. Like Rose, she complained of a headache. Her song hatched from invisible misery, she pleaded for lights to be dimmed. Nurses met her protests with indifference and resentment; they let it be known, via their own sharp sighs and condescending replies, that *this* was a *hospital*. Read into that the job of those who worked there: to problem-solve, diagnose, treat—cut and cure. Not care. Eye rolls conveyed the subtext: *Patients have impossible expectations.*

Given a shot of something, Rose finally received some temporary relief. The long and short of what was on the table: kohkum Rose would be put to sleep, and the doctor would shave away a patch of her still-dark hair, slice her scalp to the bone, peel the skin back, fold and pin it like a kohkum's kerchief, and use a special bone-cutting saw to prune away a piece of her skull. After the calcium dust settled, he'd proceed to repair, dissect, and resect, or somehow iron out the bulging, weakened blood vessel threatening her brain. And when he was done, he'd reverse the order of operations and put her back together again.

"Good as new," Uncle Gordy reassured, patting her slender forearm. Without the operation, the blood vessel would burst inside her intact skull and cause calamity. With the operation, a chance to fix the problem. Gordy, who had not thought hard enough about the difference between Rose uncut and Rose cut, wanted her to have the operation.

"Every surgery has risks," the doctor said. "Yes, this one a bit higher than most, I won't lie to you. She could die." He spoke only to Gordy; kohkum Rose and Ruby were rendered incidental. Ruby didn't know which infuriated her more, the doctor's obvious dismissal of "the women" or his message of doom. "Without the surgery," he added, "she *will* die."

Kohkum didn't want to, but signed the papers anyway. None of them, not Uncle Gordy, not Ruby, not Rose, knew anything about second opinions.

Uncle Gordy went for coffee and to call Ruby's auntie Georgina, his older sister, in Alberta. A nurse entered and injected Rose with "a top-up" for the pain.

"Ruby, my girl," kohkum Rose called out.

"I'm right here," Ruby said. She hadn't moved all afternoon.

"I want to go home," kohkum Rose said. They sat quietly

with that while her words swelled around them. By "home" Ruby supposed Rose meant her small house in the city. Later, she doubted that interpretation and wondered if Rose had in mind the place where she was born. Little Six Lake, with its rolling hills and salty water; the place-out-of-place on the prairies. Where the land shifted from a pressed flatness to suddenly curve and fold over itself, treeless, against a white sky. Where the sound of shaken leaves on dry branches rippled across the acres like soft gossip.

Kohkum took off her ring and handed it to Ruby. "Your daddy gave me that," she said. "It's a birthstone for each of my children." Ruby looked at the ring, its gold band bent from everyday wearing, six stones all different colors: yellow, red, green, white, blue, and purple. "You hold it for me, my girl." Ruby nodded like they'd just made a significant business deal. An understanding passed between them in an instant. Without saying it, they both registered the fact that only three of the six stones in the ring still shone with life. Ruby's father—Rose's son Leon—many years dead from a car accident. More than two decades. Hard to believe. By the time Ruby found her family, met her kohkum, Leon was already sixteen years gone. And two uncles, Rose's sons, also gone. How much could one woman give away? She closed her palm around the gift, warm from Rose's skin. Leon's stone the layered red of ripe raspberries, bedroom slippers, or just-spilt blood.

THE FIRST TIME RUBY met Rose and Gordy, they brought a shoebox full of photographs. She had only ever seen one picture of Leon, mailed to her by Rose months before they met. Ruby would always remember taking that first photo out of the envelope: like Leon was being born.

In the course of their three days together on that first meeting, Ruby examined dozens of pictures, over and over—she never tired of it, and Rose and Gordy indulged her. She managed, that time, to set aside any ambivalence toward Leon, the father who let her go. Right or wrong, she deemed Leon less culpable than her birth mother, if only because of his passive role in giving her up. It wasn't *his* body in which she'd grown. *He* didn't have the chance to object, when she was born.

She scrutinized each photo, inspected Leon's features. "Do you think we have the same nose?" she asked, more than once, holding a photo beside her face for comparison. They had already all agreed that Ruby had Leon's eyes.

A photo of Leon: standing in front of a car, the sun in his eyes, his fists clenched as if an instinctive posture. Black bomber jacket, black boots. And those fists. Ruby had a photo of herself with the same fists. She was only nine or ten years old, standing in the backyard in summer, glaring at the camera; small, tight fists clenched, almost ready to run. And something else, something that came back to her later, after she'd had time to sit with the image.

Studying the concept of adolescent subcultures in a first-year sociology class, Ruby had watched a very old film from the National Film Board on juvenile delinquency. A documentary, shot in a small Canadian city. There was something about one of the young men, his demeanor, his brash and bold behavior, likely made more so by the presence of a film crew. As they filmed the small gang of boys, this one stood out. He was dark-haired and, even though the film was in black and white, she could tell he had a tan complexion. He wore a short black jacket and boots, like toughs of the era would have done. A bit James Dean. He'd remained in her memory because she would have thought at the time, *Is that him?* Reflexively. Because that was what she did, her whole life. She would have seen the film, picked out the cues, the likeness in the hair and complexion, and fantasized that he was the one.

In the film, he jumped on the short wall of a fountain, walking its edge while women, wrapped in their coats and scarves and on their way to go shopping or somewhere else, in the middle of the day, stopped to stare and judge. He strutted under their censorious gaze. He laughed and, in the same moment, swiveled his head toward the camera. His one shining black jewel of an eye penetrated through the lens and through time, and hooked itself into the center of her being. With a barb it caught and she could feel it tugging like a line from her chest to him, his grin and look so genuine Ruby could swear she heard the word "daughter." Then he stumbled, swung his arms, caught himself before jumping off the short wall with a laugh, all swagger and sass. The moment broken, but she'd never forgotten that visceral flash of recognition.

ON THE THIRD DAY, Rose gave Ruby a large brown envelope. She'd enlarged a photo at a shop downtown. A rush job.

"That's your dad," she said, but Ruby already knew.

Blown up to 16" × 20", the picture was of Leon as a baby,

wearing a blue knit sweater and hard white baby shoes. Old enough to sit up but not old enough to walk yet.

When Ruby arrived home from that inaugural weekend, the first thing she did was frame the photo carefully, before taking down one of the "family pictures"—a cute northern baby with a runny nose—and replacing it with Leon's picture. Later, she would hang a picture of herself next to Leon's, Ruby on her second birthday, wearing a dress of a similar blue. A mirror for their baby-selves. Compared the noses, the eyes, the eyebrows. His gold-brown skin a similar tone to hers and her boys'.

"Mommy, why are you crying?" Aaron asked.

"I don't know, Minnow, just am," she said, pulling him close.

"Who's that?" he asked, pointing to the new picture of Leon.

"Your moshom," she said. "When he was a baby." It was the only truth she had ever told about the family pictures. "You look like him," she said.

"I do?"

"Let me see." She crouched down, held his face in her fingers, considered it, turned his head side to side, looked from Aaron's face to Leon's picture, serious. Finally, she declared, "You have his nose too!"

She thought about Gordy saying she had the same stance as Leon. "He was wiry. Tough," Gordy said. "He didn't take any shit." Bodies are math, Ruby thought. An identity is an equation that's always true, no matter what. She and her boys had inherited Leon's geometry. The boys were nothing if not nimble, their calculations echoing to a fuzzy parallel.

"Show me them all," Aaron insisted then, pulling her hand. He was getting too big to be carried but she picked him up anyway, like she did when he was little. "This is your cousin," she said, following the routine, stepping in front of the first of the "family" prints. "He lives far away."

"He looks nice," Aaron said, regarding the print of a boy, making eye contact and with his hand near his mouth. "He would probably like to play with me."

"I bet he would," Ruby said. "Someday we'll visit, okay?" They advanced to the next picture.

"This is your uncle." She pointed to the picture of the man on a trapline. "Kocawîs. He misses you."

"What's his name?" Aaron asked.

"Gordy," Ruby answered. "Uncle Gordy." She'd never had a good answer for that one before. Of course it wasn't really a picture of Gordy, but the truth lay in the naming.

"This is kimamasis, your auntie," Ruby said, pointing to a picture of a serious, beautiful Native woman staring into the camera.

Aaron nodded his head. Ruby proceeded to the next photo. "And who's this?" she asked.

"Me!" Aaron proclaimed.

"This is you as a baby," she said. "When you wore diapers and had stinky pants."

"I did not," he protested. She set him on the couch.

"You're getting heavy," she said, and when he looked disheartened she said, "but not *too* heavy." She kissed his cheek and said, "Go play. Where's your brother?"

Aaron jumped off the couch and Ruby swatted his bum playfully as he ran away to find Junior.

For so long, the boys were her only genetic flesh and blood.

They'd spent their lives together in the ceremony of making themselves whole. In the span of one weekend, she'd more than quadrupled her known blood relatives.

ROSE LAUGHED OUT OF nowhere, a clue the pain medication had kicked in again. Maybe she was confused, because she asked after Ruby's dad as if he was still alive. "Tell Leon I'm here," she said. "He'll wonder where I am. He'll miss taking me to the bingo." Kohkum Rose went to Bingo Madness every Tuesday. Leon used to take her, a long time ago. "He's a good boy, you know," she chuckled. "King of the Bingo," she said and laughed again, her chin down.

Kohkum and Gordy liked to recount the story for Ruby. Leon drove Rose to bingo every week, and every week it was the same routine. They parked, went in, she bought her usual two super-packs of bingo cards, he helped her get settled in her lucky seat and made sure her daubers were in good working order. Then Leon would retreat to the back with the other men to smoke cigarettes and drink coffee by the exit until the Tuesday bingo was over. Both Rose and Leon were used to the routine until one Tuesday when the jackpot rolled over for its fifth time. Rose told it the best. They arrived extra early to find the hall's usual quiet buzz increased to a contagious hum. Leon caught the excitement and got the idea to join Rose in playing bingo. "See what all the stir is about," he said. When Rose ordered her two super-packs, Leon ordered the same. Rose just looked at him sideways. Leon had never played bingo before.

Leon set up his cards beside Rose at the table and chatted up all the nearby ladies until the caller started rolling his cage of balls and calling the numbers. Fast. Leon's cards, spread out before him, slid around on the slippery table. He couldn't keep up. He got confused, he missed numbers. His dauber was slow and his eye not sharp enough. Several times Rose pointed to his cards to show him a missed number. She was keeping track of her numbers and his at the same time. Someone yelled *Bingo* on game one and, for a few minutes while the numbers were checked, Leon caught his breath. He reorganized his slippery cards, readied his dauber. He no longer chatted and smiled at the women. The caller started again and Leon had much the same result in game two as he did in game one. As soon as *Bingo* was called in game two, Leon tossed the dauber onto the cards in front of him and pushed his chair back from the table. He'd worked up a good lather, according to Rose. "Goin' for a smoke," he grumbled. When he didn't return by the time the caller started the third game, Rose dove in, madly playing across both spreads of cards, her skinny arm flying, punctuating the cards: *Dab! Dab! Dab!*

Leon stayed at the back for the rest of the night, smoking his cigarettes and drinking coffee while Rose played out his cards. Leaving the hall at the end of the night, the jackpot rolled over for yet another week, Rose poked Leon in the ribs with her elbow and exclaimed, "*Two* super-packs!" Leon shrugged his plaid-shirted shoulders. "Who do you think you are?" she added. "King of the Bingo?" Rose and all her friends within earshot had a real good laugh. Leon had to laugh too and the name stuck. That was what Ruby imagined kohkum Rose thinking about in the hospital bed, the pain meds kicking in—King of the Bingo.

"How's my girls?" Uncle Gordy poked his head around the curtain on his return from coffee and phone calls. Upon hearing Gordy's voice, the woman in the next bed percolated with displeasure. Gordy made a face, mouthed *oops,* and took up his chair without another word. They sat in silence until kohkum Rose looked sleepy and nodded off for a few minutes. "Well," said Gordy, standing up and looking at Ruby, his toes pointed to the exit.

Kohkum Rose's eyes flew open; she had the radar of a bat. "Wait," she said. "I want to tell you something first." Her dark eyes were large and uneasy, intent on Gordy. He stood by her bedside and leaned in. "I want you to know. In case. I want you to know that I want to be buried at Little Six." Gordy squeezed her forearm softly. "With my mom and dad," she said. In the shadow of the blue hills.

"Shush," Gordy said, pushing her words away. "You're going to be fine." Their neighbor began panting, Lamaze-like, and Uncle Gordy opened his eyes real wide. "That sounds like our cue to go," he whispered to Rose and winked. Surgery was scheduled for the next day at 1 P.M.

In the passenger seat of Gordy's old Ford truck Ruby closed her eyes, kohkum's purse in her lap like a sleeping pup. The nurse had made her take the purse as they were leaving. "Don't leave valuables here. They'll get stolen." Rose's ring rested hot in Ruby's pocket. She thought of what was ahead. "Brain surgery" were two big words when you put them together like that. Right up there with "open heart" and "spinal cord." She tried to imagine kohkum, who topped out at a hundred pounds and was less than five feet tall, skinned, her skull open. Obscene. Naked. Her brain touched by pale air, the surgeon's indecent fingers, his shiny instruments, fat attitude, and the false sharp light of an operating room. An untenable violation.

"Let's make a pit stop, kiddo." Gordy pulled in and parked at the bar. Ruby hid Rose's purse under the seat and they went in and downed three pints each, which took the edge off, but that night her sleep was disturbed by the alcohol, her dreams a restless jumble of family ghosts. When Ruby woke at 3 A.M. she anxiously pondered the inheritance her children had come into. The casualties, the longing; affection and revelation. Each an inspiration. Aaron and Junior as children, dazzling outlaws, reckless and faithful with their sticky hands, too-big second-hand clothes, and naughty smiles. Herman, waving one morning from his front step, telling her he'd heard her being frustrated with the kids the night before. "You yelled so loud *I* went to bed," he joked.

Adored at the end of the day, as they slept, when their finally still faces softened. The day's outbursts and passions quiet now, her impatience fallen away and replaced by tranquility. She was terrified to look at them half the time, her love fierce and unnerving.

EARLY THE NEXT MORNING, Uncle Gordy's phone rang. "What do you mean, *gone?*" he asked from his end of the conversation. The look on his face priceless and shifting.

Kohkum, it turns out, was not "gone" as in "passed." Instead, she had disappeared from the hospital. But where? Uncle Gordy phoned Georgina in Alberta and told her the latest news. "Stay put, in case she comes there," he said.

The cops were called, they asked tired questions, as if their report was a nuisance keeping them from their real work. They gave the impression they'd already decided there was nothing much they could do about Rose. They questioned her state of mind. "My kohkum is as sharp as a toothpick," Ruby replied. Uncle Gordy and the cousins tried to guess where she'd go, wondered if she'd become confused, with all the pain medicine, or had the vessel burst and sent her off on a wild brain-in-a-bloodbath tangent? They checked her house, thought of the bus station in case she wanted to go to Auntie Georgina's. The city suddenly seemed impossibly large. A cousin was dispatched to check the bus station and promised to keep them posted. The cop asked if there was anything else. Ruby said nothing. She watched. Just watched. Silent about Rose's words of wanting: "home."

They learned she'd dressed in her own clothes and taken her glasses. She'd left behind her shoes in the bottom of the cupboard, and her teeth in the blue cup beside the bed. They already knew her purse was at Uncle Gordy's house. Rose's ring warm in Ruby's pocket. They must have all pictured it at the same time, the shifting image of Rose out there in the world, vulnerable, her hair loose and wild, her stocking feet on the city cement, talking or smiling toothless. Or lying on the street somewhere, collapsed. Thankfully they were having a tender fall. Ruby's mind replayed the surgeon's hated words:

without an operation, she would die. Ruby had just barely found her. Their relationship still felt underdeveloped, the chance for so many more possibilities ahead of them. No amount of time could make up for what she'd lost, but she wanted more than this.

Ruby longed to know something impossible, how they'd arrived here, just here, exactly. Ten years at residential school qualified kohkum Rose to speak English, become a waitress, a housekeeper in a motel, and a farmhand's wife. After years of being told not to speak her language, Rose had refused to teach her kids Cree, convinced they would be better off without the accent, better able to function in the white world. Her husband, Johnny, more traditional, had wanted to teach their children Cree, but Rose insisted on raising the kids her own way, wouldn't be told. She nurtured them with what she'd been given at residential school.

What no one articulated: this wasn't the first time Rose had run away. She'd run away many times before, starting at the school. Rose and Ernestine. Ernestine and Rose. The first two times, they made their way to the edge of the girls' group, out for a walk, and both times, tensed to run, they chickened out, and instead ended up sitting along the south side of the main building, backs against the school, legs bent at the knees as if holding up the wall. It was there Ernestine extracted a promise from Rose.

"When we leave here, let's live in two houses, side by side," Ernestine mused.

"I want three dogs. And tame cats that can live in the house. They can all sleep on my bed," Rose said, her eyes closed, head tilted back. "They'll purr all night. Like a bunch of little motors."

"You can marry my brother," said Ernestine. "We can be sisters."

"And I won't have a garden because I never want to pull another weed again," said Rose, as if she hadn't heard Ernestine's proposal. They laughed about the hated endless weeds in the school vegetable garden. "We'll eat all day long," added Rose dreamily. "I want to be fat like my Auntie Aggie." They pictured Aggie with her round brown face and kind hands.

Ernestine, who could dream with the best of them, persisted. "If you marry my brother, we can be sisters."

"Who? Toby?" Rose laughed. "He's a baby."

"No, Johnny," said Ernestine. They both let the idea settle in two parts. *Sisters. Johnny.* The one they called kisciyiniw. Old man.

"He has a girlfriend," Rose said, which was practically the same as saying yes.

"I'll make sure he knows you like him," said Ernestine.

The for-real running away came later. Johnny left the school early. Rose and Ernestine met up with Johnny. Rose and kisciyiniw Johnny were married after all. Then, the periodic disappearances, the grown-up running away, for a few hours or a few days, persisted in Rose's life. It was part of what ultimately ended her marriage to Johnny, Ruby's moshom. Kisciyiniw Johnny died young, just a few years after their divorce.

When Rose and Ruby first met they talked for three days, nonstop. Ruby told Rose she'd been a runaway. "Starting when I was ten," she said. She didn't tell Rose what it was she ran away from, or that, even though she didn't have anything to run from anymore, the instinct to bolt from intimacy remained. Rose told her then about her own running away. They sat with that knowledge, a moment of affinity. Ruby had been told her whole life she was chosen. A thing she forever longed for, but never quite believed in. With Rose it felt nearly true.

By silent agreement they mentioned none of Rose's running away history to the cops, in case they took it as another reason not to treat Rose's current disappearance seriously.

RUBY SMOKED OUTSIDE THE HOSPITAL, her dark hair soaking up the hot September sun. She pictured Rose's dark head and the volcano rending her skull, the one that raged for days, the pain at "ten" before she was convinced to go to the hospital, Gordy's pickup truck splitting the road down the middle to get there.

She palmed the ring in her jeans pocket and wished Rose safe, while her family members talked small and they all kept their real thoughts to themselves. Secretly, she rooted for Rose, hoped she found whatever she needed, imagined her back to her early life, when she was tender, loyal, and full of longing. Each time Ruby stroked the stones of the ring, counted them with her fingertips, all six, and dipped the point of her index finger into its imperfect circle, the little red reminder of her father put Ruby in a pensive mood.

Ruby thought often about Leon's death. She imagined it, hoped he lost consciousness in the car crash. Or at least saw a light, or some other vision, to comfort him. Hoped his mind allowed his body to escape pain.

She had visited his grave where he was buried next to his brothers, Terry and Mike. The three names lined up on the flat gravestone. Each with their dates. Leon was only thirty-five when he died. She'd already outlived him. The gravestone was positioned in such a way that it caught and collected fallen leaves. Later she couldn't remember where it was and eventually the grave and its stone, covered in leaves, would exist only in her memory. Ruby wanted to grieve for Leon but she didn't know how. Bound up in her creation, at the root of her web of being, he was substantial and yet fleeting. She knew no ceremony of letting go, so they both remained silent.

ONCE, WHEN RUBY WAS a teenager, Alice told her a story that she never got over. A co-worker of Alice's had related an anecdote about a young Native guy who'd been adopted. When he went to find his family, he found out his mother had died already, so he never got to meet her.

Ruby thought about him, waiting his whole life, not knowing, thinking his mother was out there somewhere, and then when he looked, she was just gone. A double vanishing act.

But Alice's tale continued. She wasn't finished yet. The young guy then went to try and find his birth father, only to learn that the dad was also dead. The grandparents were all passed on too. He went to the reserve and there was just no one left from his family, no one to tell him who he was. Distraught, the young man ended up committing suicide.

Ruby had cringed when Alice related this story. Why? Why did Alice tell her this account? A cautionary tale? That it would be better not to even try? Ruby might find only heartache? Ruby might think about killing herself? It was a cruel story to tell, full of bitter hopelessness.

"WE KNEW ABOUT YOU," Rose said. "We knew something happened out there, with Leon."

"Did he tell you about me?" Ruby asked.

"Yup, he did." Rose nodded. "He even told me he went to that place, where your mother was. The maternity home. But they turned him away."

Ruby laughed. Every revelation exposed how much she would never know.

Rose contacted social services right after Leon died. "I wanted to do it even sooner," she said. "And then," she added, "I waited for you to come home."

Ruby's childhood lies came back to her, tales she told her friends, that she'd been kidnapped as a baby, then abandoned by the kidnappers when they fled the cops. She was the real daughter of somebody rich and important. A king. A prince. From a place where everyone looked like her. She was being desperately searched for. She was somebody's lost treasure. It was only a matter of time before she was found.

Wishing she had known Leon was a familiar sentiment— longing for the impossible. "But I have *this* now," she said, mindful to be grateful for what was good. She felt connected to kohkum and Gordy, but less so to her cousins, who she'd heard say "apple" as if Ruby didn't know what they meant. One of them speculated once about Ruby being born with a "silver spoon" in her mouth. She had no retort. She didn't think they were right, but how did she know? She fluctuated, believing she didn't belong until Rose convinced her again that she did.

WHEN GEORGINA'S DAUGHTER GOT married, Ruby met her relatives for the first time at the hotel. She was thirty-four years old but felt like a child. Gordy walked into the lobby and Ruby knew him right away, her DNA radar right on point. Auntie Georgina, though, was cool to her. Maybe she resented the intrusion of Ruby on the big day. Ruby overheard Georgina ask Rose, "But what does she *want?*"

In an alone moment, Georgina said to Ruby, "My mom was hard on those boys." Referring to Leon and Terry, the two youngest, as *those poor little boys,* she said, about Rose, "She'd give them such a licking." Georgina, the older sister, the often-babysitter, felt sorry for them. "I tried to help them if I could." Nothing about Rose, or her demeanor, signaled that such rage lived in her slight body. But Ruby had a flash of recognition, of empathy, for the exasperated maternal fury of an overwhelmed mother. Recalled, then, overhearing Junior tell Aaron once, "You're lucky. Mom was meaner before you were born."

"WE WOULD HAVE TAKEN YOU," Gordy repeated. "We would have taken you in, for sure."

Something about their compassion, while welcome, made Ruby feel like she ought to put her childhood hardships on display, validating Rose and Gordy's instincts toward kindness. A way to convey that *they* were always wanted too, even if she hadn't known it until then. But Ruby held back, didn't want her story to look like some kind of sympathy hustle, didn't want to reveal her misfortunes around people who'd had their share. So she said only enough to convey the flavor of a complicated childhood.

And the entire time, Ruby lined her tiny nest of mythology with each fragment she picked up, twigs and leaves and bits of string; she hoarded each scrap and built from them what she could. Scavenged a narrative. Accounted for herself. As faulty as it was, as drafty and full of holes.

RUBY COULD SEE HOW things came to be the way they were for Rose. Married to Johnny at eighteen and, six kids later, Rose never had her chance to figure out what she cared about. To figure out if she cared about anything yet. Ruby's dad was dead over twenty years. It all ended the same way for all of them—flat on your back in a box, more or less. Ruby wanted what Rose wanted, because we should all have that chance.

By suppertime they couldn't stand it any longer, so Gordy and Ruby took the truck and drove around the city, searching. An hour after the sun disappeared, they were just heading onto busy Dumeaux Drive from the freeway. Ruby saw a cop car coming toward them, driving in no hurry on the other side of the road, and she wondered if they were out looking for Rose too. Her eyes followed the cops in the car—there were two of them—to see if they were alert and on the lookout. That was when she spotted Rose. She saw her before Gordy. Rose was

walking shoeless on the opposite side of the street, on the narrow ribbon of sidewalk.

"Pull over! Pull over!" Ruby shouted as they flew past her.
"That's her!" Ruby twisted to catch a last glimpse. Gordy
started blasting the horn repeatedly. The four-lane-wide road
had no shoulder. Even in the evening, the traffic was busy and
fast. Gordy turned left then took a right, a right, and another
right to go around the block and get onto the same side of the
street as they'd seen her. "Hurry," Ruby urged. It took forever
before they got back onto Dumeaux Drive. Ruby was sure
they wouldn't find her again, that she would have disappeared,
but to her relief they spotted her. Gordy turned into an alleyway and before he had the truck in park Ruby leapt out the
passenger-side door and ran to the sidewalk.

"Kohkum?" Kohkum Rose looked past Ruby. Small in her
sock feet, she turned her head away from the headlights of the
cars zipping past. The steady white noise of traffic created a
small vacuum of deafness. "Rose," Ruby said and Rose focused on her. Ruby noted she'd gone slightly blue at the lips.
Ruby didn't know if Rose even recognized her. "Where are
you headed? You don't have any shoes."

Gordy caught up to them and moved to grab Rose's arm.
"Jesus, Mom," he said, but Rose's reflexes were surprisingly
quick. She twisted away from his reach and stepped backward
toward the street. Her head turned this way and that as if she
was looking for something. She stood light but tense on her
toes. Her stance put Ruby in mind of a nervous cat that didn't
want to be touched. She put herself between Rose and the busy
roadway. The sidewalk was narrow enough that a couple short

steps and a disoriented person might tread into the path of traffic.

"I can't find my purse," Rose said. "I don't know where my
purse is and Leon didn't pick me up." She looked around as if
she couldn't recall exactly what she was looking for. "Are *you*
taking me to the bingo?"

Gordy made a frustrated sound like the bellows of an accordion. Ruby jumped in and said, "Yes. That's where we're
going. Leon couldn't come tonight. Should we go there now?
Bingo?"

"My purse," she insisted. "My daubers are in my purse."

"I have your purse," Ruby said. "It's in the truck. Right
over there." She pointed and Rose's eyes followed the direction. She nodded.

Rose allowed Ruby to take her elbow and guide her down
the sidewalk. Gordy ran ahead to get the truck. "Bring the
daubers," she called after him. "You can play the regular pack."

In the truck, on the bench seat between them, Rose said to
Gordy, "You can be the King of the Bingo," and then she
laughed so hard she was left panting. Ruby put her arm around
Rose and when she stopped laughing Ruby whispered "King
of the Bingo" into her ear and they both chuckled some more.

Rose's laughter gasped in her chest. She couldn't help herself. Ruby imagined Rose running and running. She'd nearly
gotten away with it.

Grace

1 9 7 5

. . .

FROM THE BACK SEAT GRACE STARED AS DOUG PARKED
the station wagon. She put her hand on the door latch, all the
time watching the enormous structure. The house was all eyes.

While Grace hesitated, Doug pulled the small suitcase from
the back seat. "Sheila," he said to Ma, like a warning or a
prompt.

"C'mon, Sugarbug," Ma said with false levity, opening the
front passenger door. "Let's go get this over with." She stepped
onto the sidewalk.

Girls like you, Grace thought to herself, *go to places like this.*
How did she become one of "those girls"? she wondered.

And this place. Misleading, really, to refer to it as a home.
BETHANY HOME, the sign said. She took in the brick three-story
with its large, dark windows, the whole facade ugly and over-
bearing. A fat queen on her tufted pouf.

Grace didn't want to move toward the house, up the walk,
and into the shadow of the building. Her mind, always on the
active side, as Ma would say, conjured images of drag marks

running along the cement path. Grooves. She imagined fur-rows, worn into the heavy concrete steps where many sets of feet had been dragged unwillingly across the threshold. She knew she was being overdramatic, but all the same, she couldn't help herself.

Grace climbed reluctantly from the relative safety of the car. She had a momentary urge to resist, even as her feet moved of their own accord up the long path, dotted along the edges with disheveled clumps of last year's flowers lying brown and rot-ting in the dirt. Weeds sprang up in the cement cracks. An aura of carelessness surrounded the house. She followed after Ma and Doug up the cumbersome steps and into the cold of the deep shadows. Echoes of laughter did not linger. Her mind shot to an image of lead paint chips picked out of corners like dust balls and gummed by unwitting dumb babies as the house slowly fell apart around them.

AFTER THE PAPERS WERE signed in the major's office Grace was left, despite her small protests, in the creepy house. A chilly goodbye was exchanged between her and Doug, Ma looking on, lost. When it was Ma's turn, she gave Grace a faux punch in the arm, told her to be good. Then she hugged her, and Grace tried not to cry. When they'd gone, Grace received what seemed to be a standard orientation.

"You must pick a name," the major said.

For a moment, Grace misunderstood, thinking the major was talking about her baby. A name for her baby! A twinge of delight surged from her core to a place just behind her eyes.

But before it could settle and manifest itself as gratitude, thankfulness, or even joy, the major's next words wiped the almost-smile from Grace's face.

"An assumed name."

Only then did it become clear what they were talking about. A fake name. For Grace. A fake first name so none of the other "residents" would know her true identity.

"And I'd advise you not to talk about yourself. The details of your life."

When Grace looked blank the major continued. "It's for your own protection. Once this is all over"—the major made a sweeping gesture with her hand to encompass the general area of Grace's belly and its offending beast—"you will see . . . we want to spare you any troubles, any problems in the future. By keeping this all"—repeat gesture—"as quiet as possible."

Inside the house, the walls breathed and memories lingered. Grace felt the emotions of the house like a tremor: despair, loneliness, fear. At first, Grace sensed more than saw the frightened teenage girls with big bellies—uncomfortably big bellies—lurking in the shadows. Despite their enormity, the girls were little more than shadows themselves. So much physicality the place nearly reeked of it, and yet she could tell these girls would do anything to receive a touch of comfort, a squeeze of the hand—some small affection. Hugs were clearly a scarce commodity. In this *home*.

After being officially checked in and orientated, Grace stood in the gloom and it hit her. She felt it through her whole body like a cold pressure. The knowing. She knew, just then, she *knew* girls *died* here. She absorbed the gut punch of knowing

and sucked in her breath. Girls died here, bodily and otherwise. Grace didn't want to be left behind, but it was too late,
Ma was gone, driven away in the station wagon by stupid
Doug. The air resonated with the misery left by small parts—
parts abandoned. Small parts and big. Whole parts, entire beings, in fact. Entire beings severed from their source. Grace
shuddered; looked over her shoulder, as if for an escape route.

The narrow windows were set horizontally, elevated above
her head. Much too high for anyone to look out of. As if there
was no need for contemplative daydreaming here, no one to
keep watch for.

She thought of Leon then and the thought made her grin.
There wasn't a time Leon wasn't cracking a joke or smiling so
that his eyes squinted up in his head. He was from a big family,
full of brothers, where he said he'd learned to laugh. "Laugh
and fight," was how he described it. "If you weren't laughing,
you were crying."

His hands were the first thing Grace had noticed about him.
She could tell a lot about a person by their hands. His were
brown and work-ready. Tough. Once in a while he cracked his
knuckles in an absentminded way that just made Grace even
hungrier for him. The first time he held her hand, she was a
little bit drunk. She let him hold it for a few minutes and then,
couldn't help it, held up his hand in hers and looked at it.

"Your hand," she said.

"What about it?" he said, laughing at her drunk words.

"I think your hands are beautiful," she said, and blushed.

He laughed again. "How about *rugged* or *strong*?" he asked.

"Beautiful's for girls." And then he brought Grace's hand to his lips and kissed the back of it. "Like you," he said.

If she could have she would've taken a bite of him just then, gobbled him up like a chocolate bunny at Easter. Could have bitten the bunny ears right off in one go, that's how delicious he was. Instead, she kissed the back of his hand too.

He laughed and laughed. "You're *all* aces," he said, before he kissed her proper on the lips.

"WELCOME TO THE ASYLUM"—a voice tugged her out of remembering.

A gum-chewing, potbellied pixie of a girl stood in the hall behind Grace.

"Don't those windows say it all?" the girl asked, pointing with her nose. Before Grace could formulate a response, she carried on. "Loud and clear: *No one's coming to rescue you. No one's coming to get you.*" The girl shook her finger and said the words like an invocation, like an official rule she'd heard over and over.

Grace tried to smile but knew it must look more like a grimace.

"Don't worry. Not only are they *not* coming to get you, no one's even here to give a shit. There's no one, anymore, who can fill that bill." The girl paused to crack her gum a few times in quick succession. "I'm Candy," she said, and stuck out one hand, grasping Grace's and holding it tight, looking into Grace's eyes and winking. "The major doesn't like my choice of name. She picked 'Theresa' for me." Candy made a face in imitation of the major—bulging eyes, jaw jutting forward.

Grace laughed despite herself. Put a hand to her mouth.

"She says I should be called Anne," Grace said, wishing she had the guts, like Candy, to disagree with the name.

"I'll let you in on a secret," Candy said quietly. "Candy *is* my real name." She turned and walked into the shadows of the main floor living space that seemed to disappear in darkness under the stairs. Grace followed.

THE MAJOR, STIFF-BACKED and rigid in her chair, called one of the girls into her office, the one called Mary. Grace snickered at the irony of the name Mary had either chosen for herself or had chosen for her, immaculate conception and all.

"You don't want to be called in to talk to the warden," whispered Candy. "And if you do, tell her *just once*."

"Just once, what?" Grace asked.

Candy made a noise like a laugh. "How many times, dummy. Like, how many times you *did it*."

The home was full of an improbable number of girls with the distinct misfortune of being caught out their first time.

The girls were overflowing with advice. A better answer still for the warden: just once, but now you *know better*. Don't specify. Don't say what exactly you know better.

"Yeah, I know better," Ruth chirped. "I know better'n to get caught!" The girls giggled, some rolled their eyes.

"I'm never doing it again," one of the girls exclaimed.

"Yeah, right."

"I'm serious. Not for, like, five or ten years. And if I do, I'm gonna make him pull out."

"That doesn't work," Candy said authoritatively. "It's no better than counting on luck. And look where that got us."

"If a girl gets pregnant it's her own fault," Joan chimed. She'd taken out nail clippers and was steadily clipping away. Grace cringed.

"Oh gawd." Candy rolled her eyes and leaned in to Grace. "Joan believes she's genuinely here to be saved," Candy scoffed. "And quit doing that in here, you dimwit. It's gross."

Joan ignored them, kept on clipping. "You should never open your legs in the first place," she added.

Grace could see there were many ways to be saved here. Saved from your sin. Saved from your baby. Saved from yourself. Girls like Joan, who bought into salvation, wore their punishment like a cross, dragging their belly full of penitence around until they could be delivered and returned quickly and quietly to their old lives. The trick afterward, of course, was in the forgetting.

Even though the girls called the house "the Asylum" and referred to the major as "the Warden," they participated in the charade too. Stripped of free will, they all joined together in a grand display. Pretended they believed it was all for their own good. That they were doing it for love. That it was a choice. But deep down they all knew it was a choiceless choice—no volition behind it.

Grace had participated, so far, in the charade with her eyes shut and breath held. Her Ma, Doug, the minister of their little church, the social worker, and now the Warden, all told her, would keep on telling her, there was no other way. What options did she have, after all? What resources? She had no means. Their questions with no answers drilled into her. Instead they all relied on a good, clean, Christian, deserving, childless couple to be Grace's salvation.

And yet, it was really this old house that was full of sins.

"WHAT'S THAT?" THE SOCIAL worker said, pretending at first not to hear Grace. "The father's Native? An *Indian?*" She rubbed her eyes as if tired. "Oh, dear." She moved like she would write something, but then decided against it—in the end making no notes in her file. Not yet. Instead she said, "But you're so fair? So blond?"

Grace heard this as a questioning of her judgment. Heard it as the social worker's implied *How could you?*

Just then, Grace thought about her friend back home. Jill. She thought about Jill and her perfect family. Jill wouldn't understand any of this. Not really. This kind of thing would never happen to her. The social worker's tone made Grace think about how Jill's mom didn't like Grace and was always giving her the hairy eyeball. Once, Grace overheard Jill's mom call Grace "cheap."

The social worker sat back in her chair and said, "Let's see." She nodded her head as if telling herself she'd made the right choice. "Let's just wait and see what comes of it, once the baby's born." They'd seen this sort of thing before. Maybe there'd be a way to cover it up.

MARY DISAPPEARED OVERNIGHT. The girls were told to strip the sheets from Mary's bed and remake it with clean ones. No one was surprised except Grace.

"What happened to her?" she asked.

"The same thing that's going to happen to all of us." Candy smirked knowingly. "The medical wing, dummy."

Grace looked blank.

"She *went over* last night. Isn't that a scream. That's what they call it here, when you go to have your baby. *Going over.* Sounds like dying or something."

Wake up in the morning and if one of the girls wasn't there it would likely be said that she *went over* last night. Over to what, each girl would find out soon enough.

ON HER THIRD MORNING at the home, Grace ran away. Impulsively. Enveloped by the sudden urge as she lay awake in her bed under the scratchy brown sheets that had rubbed her skin raw in only three nights. She hadn't had one dream since she arrived. Couldn't bear one more second in this place.

It was early, well before 6 A.M., the sun just preparing to rise, giving a dim, twilight effect. She tucked her coat under her arm, slung her girlish purse over her shoulder, and carried her extra shoes in her hand. She couldn't think how to retrieve her boots from the mudroom and so determined to make do with just shoes, even though it was only the beginning of May and the ground was wet with rain, and even the snow hadn't completely melted yet.

She slipped quietly down the back stairs—not the wide staircase she had first seen when she entered the un-home, but the narrow and rather steep back stairs that led to the kitchen. The ones the girls used regularly. So as not to be seen, she assumed. To remain in the shadows. Bodies rustled and moved all over the house but she couldn't stop to worry about them. Straight through the back door she walked, coat in hand, no gloves, no hat, her coat didn't even do up anymore, over her almost-six-month bulge. She could see her breath in the morning twilight as she bent to put on her shoes, slid her coat over her shoulders, and tucked her hands in the pockets. She walked away.

No idea which way to go, she turned right and walked up the sidewalk. She didn't know the city.

What now? What now? Her mind ran, but, caught up in the immediate thrill of escape, she couldn't formulate an answer.

"Hey!" came a voice from behind her. Grace's neck tensed but she kept walking. Faster. She refused to turn around. Footsteps ran behind her, and Grace waited to feel the cold hand of the Warden snatch her arm.

"Wait up, jeez," Candy complained behind her, out of breath from running while so heavily pregnant.

Grace exhaled. Awkward, pleased, she joked, "I didn't know you could run at, like, nine months pregnant." She punched Candy lightly in the arm.

"Well?" said Candy. "What're we waiting for? Let's get the hell out of here, dum-dum."

THE GIRLS TURNED LEFT then right, walking as if they had a purpose, but really, they had no idea where they were, or where they were going. Grace didn't care. She wanted to be lost. She took no notice of landmarks or street signs, didn't want to find her way back. Uphill seemed to be the wrong way to go about this, but they found themselves trudging up a long hill anyway, traffic lights and the sound of cars at the top. The wind tugged at Grace's open collar and an icy finger ran along her narrow chin. She turned the collar up to protect her face and neck. Her ears blazed and began to numb. Even so, as the sun rose behind them, it brought with it a sense of hopefulness. At the traffic lights, a small gas station with signs of life. Wordlessly they crossed the road and stepped through the door, relieved to be out of the wind.

Small and crowded with knickknacks and gadgets, the store reminded her of the small-town hardware run by the Millers back home. The warm air coupled with the scent of old newspapers, engine oil, coffee, and fresh bread welcomed her as if she'd arrived someplace safe. A small café in the back where a couple of old men, much like her grandpa, sat at the Formica tables, hats on, hands on thighs, chairs askew, booted feet firmly planted on the floor.

"Oh gawd, I gotta pee," Candy exclaimed. "No time this morning, you were in such a hurry," she laughed, rushing away to the café toilets, leaving Grace alone to navigate the store.

The twenty-dollar bill hidden in Grace's purse provided some immediate comfort. Would it get her a bus ticket? A room somewhere? Something she really wanted, whatever that was? She lingered over the newspapers. Looked at plastic-wrapped foods. A man at the counter watched her—his eyes on the back of her neck. Part of her wanted to sit in the café and nurse a hot cup of coffee as long as possible. But first, she gathered the nerve to approach the counter and look at the man, whose eyes were not as unfriendly as she'd expected. Curiosity, instead of unkindness, on his face.

"Can you make change for the pay phone?" she asked.

"Is it a local call?"

She shook her head no.

"Okay. 'Cause if it was a local call I'd just let you use the phone here," he said, tipping his head slightly toward the phone behind the counter.

"No. It's long distance," she said, her hands trembling as she dug the money from her purse, tucking her left hand under the bag to try and hide her ring finger. She watched his face as he counted the quarters into her hand, sure he was looking for the absent wedding ring.

INSTEAD OF PINCHING HERSELF to see if it was all real, if she'd really gone this far, she picked up the handle of the pay phone in the cramped foyer of the gas station store, dialed the number for home, inserted quarter after quarter. Her whole body shook.

"I left," she said, breathless, turning her back away from the door to protect her secret because, she thought, you never knew who you could trust anymore.

"What? Who is this?" Doug shouted down the phone line, suspicious and angry.

"It's me. Is Mommy there?"

Silence. Heavy breathing. She could hear him thinking.

"Doug?" Grace hated the meekness in her voice. Hated the near-tears in her throat. "I left."

"What do you want me to do?" Doug asked.

Grace had no answer. "Can I talk to Mommy?" she asked again.

"Don't expect to stay here." Doug's voice was so cold and flat Grace's teeth hurt.

A black-and-white topographical map was pinned to the wall beside the pay phone. Grace read random words. *Hard surface. Relief feature. Cut-line.*

Grace hung up. She looked closer at the map, read through fat tears: *esker.* Willed herself to memorize that an esker was a relief feature.

IN THE STORE, HER TEARS nearly dry but annoyingly close to the surface, Grace found Candy lingering in the confectionary aisle. Grace watched as Candy dropped a chocolate bar into her coat pocket. She wished she was as careless as Candy. Wanted to be the one stealing chocolate bars for once. Instead she grabbed Candy's arm and whispered, "What are you doing?"

Candy stepped away from Grace and laughed loudly, attracting attention from the clerk, which was the opposite of what Grace wanted.

"Put it back." Something about Candy made Grace feel like a hall monitor. Uptight. Uncool.

The clerk was really giving them the stares now.

"Fuck off," Candy said, but with a smile. Her eyes gleamed, full of energy.

As if it were all a game. Grace considered the idea for a moment. Maybe it was. All a game. She imagined how she might play it. This game. Running away was part of the sport. Maybe the challenge was finding a way to get a job, maybe a job in a little store like this one. Rent an apartment, buy a baby crib. Keep her baby. They all secretly wished it. She knew they did.

The clerk came out from behind the counter.

Candy took another package from the shelf and put it into her other pocket.

Grace moaned "Goddammit," rolling her eyes.

The clerk's attention fixed on them now, he came down the aisle as if he meant business.

Candy didn't look up but instantly clutched her enormous midsection and let out a wail Grace expected could be heard halfway to Alaska. Candy bent over, holding herself as if she might spill. Moaning. Very convincing.

The clerk's face blanched. Grace looked at him, her expression terrified for a different reason than he thought.

"Help me, idiot," Candy whimpered.

"I'm going to *kill* you," Grace whispered back.

Still supporting her stomach with two hands like it was a

pumpkin, Candy limped toward the door of the store. "Take my arm," she hissed at Grace. Grace did, and together they hobbled, bent and strained, past the clerk with the phone receiver in his hand. Candy gave a few huge squalls of anguish as they reached the exit. Together they tumbled out the front door and started walking fast down the street. They took a corner, then another into an alleyway.

Candy doubled over, laughing. "Oh my gawd, did you see his face?" she shrieked.

"You scared the shit out of him," Grace said.

"I know!" Candy pulled two chocolate bars from her pockets, handed one to Grace. "Breakfast," she said. "Eat, dummy. It's gonna be a long day."

AT LEAST THE SUN'S OUT, Grace thought as they walked down Thirty-third Street and headed west, licking chocolate from their lips.

"How did it happen—you know, for you?" Candy asked, pointing at Grace's belly.

"I didn't think about it. Then all of a sudden, my period stopped. I prayed, holy shit, I prayed," Grace laughed.

"You got a boyfriend?" Candy asked.

"Leon," Grace said, relishing the chance to say his name. "My stepdad scared him so bad he left town. I wasn't allowed to know where he went, but he's from Manitoba, I think."

"Is he nice?" Candy's voice was hopeful.

"Yeah. He might come back for me, when he can," Grace said with false assurance. She added, "I think he will."

"Yeah, I bet you're right," Candy said, wanting to believe in happy endings.

"What about you? You got a boyfriend?"

"Nah," Candy said. "He dumped me as soon as he found out. Says it's not his. Ha!" Candy bellowed. "I just want to get this over with and get on with my life."

"You don't think about keeping it?"

"Are you crazy, dum-dum?" Candy shrieked. She pulled a pack of Razzles from her pocket, chewed for a while, then said, "Why? Do you wanna keep yours?"

"I don't know. I mean, where would I get the money?"

"You could get a job," Candy said. "Probably?"

"I just want to see it, you know? I can feel it stirring in there and I want to see the baby, that's all. Then I feel like maybe I'll know what to do."

"Did you know they can't *make you* give it away? They act like they can, but they can't," Candy said.

"Like what—you just refuse to let it go?" Grace asked, trying to picture this.

"There was a girl before us. Elizabeth. She kept the baby in the dorms. She stayed there and wouldn't let it go. Wouldn't sign the consent."

"Where did she go? After?"

"I think she went home. But no one knows for sure. They just remember her doing that. The girls had a baby around. She let them all hold it."

Grace sighed.

A black-and-white police car cruised slowly past. The girls

averted their eyes and tried to look nonchalant. Two pregnant teenagers, improperly dressed for the weather, out for a stroll. Nothing to see here. The cops turned left at the corner and drove out of sight.

"Sheesh," Candy let out her breath.

"I thought we were goners," Grace said.

"Just keep walking. Pretend nothing's wrong," Candy advised. She fished the last two Razzles from the pack and crumpled up the wrapper before tossing it on the sidewalk. From behind them, a siren whooped once before a booming male voice, over a loudspeaker, commanded, "Stop." Grace turned. The cop car rolled slowly behind them, a male cop watching them closely.

"Ah, fuck," Candy sighed.

The cop rolled down the window. "Candy Johnson. Grace Dunning." Their names like a roll call off his tongue.

Grace's face got hot.

"You two think you should be out walking around in your condition?"

"What condition's that?" Candy asked, her eyes wide, an on-purpose-dumb look on her face.

The cop abruptly jammed the vehicle into park and opened his door, a signal he was finished playing games. Grace started to cry. Even Candy was silent. The officer made for them to sit in the back seat of the car and they did so without protest. Sealed off in the cop car and eventually driven back to the home. And so, their running away amounted to nothing.

The night before Candy "went over" was the last time

Grace saw her friend. As she stripped Candy's bed in the morning she thought about Candy's bravado, hoped it helped her through.

Soon enough, though, it was Grace's turn to learn what happened when you went over. Pain and fear. More than even her active imagination had conjured. No one had explained to her what would happen, what to expect. She found "going over" meant, mostly, laboring alone in quiet shame. The suggestion from the nurses, from the Warden, who made a surprising visit to the ward, and from the obscure, all-powerful doctor was that your remorse could be measured by your self-control in the agony of labor, in the rush of delivery. Now was your chance to be a good girl. *Be a good girl and be quiet, why don't you?*

In response to her whimpering, to her guttural noises, the doctor said, "You don't need to do that. I want you to stop it." Declarative. Authoritative. Stuffing a sock in Grace's mouth like a kidnapper. Like a robbery gone bad. "There. That's a good girl." He patted her knee. Grace shrank. *Don't touch me,* she thought, then added, *Dum-dum.* Thinking about Candy just then made her smile, if only for a moment.

GRACE REFUSED TO SIGN the papers. She kept the infant with her for more than a week. Without the signed papers, the Warden had no choice but to allow Grace and the baby to stay in the medical wing. "This is highly unusual," the Warden repeated, over and over until Grace blocked her voice.

Dark-haired "but not too dark," the social worker remarked

PROBABLY RUBY 135

more than once. The Warden nodded as if grateful to finally be able to approve of something. Gradually Grace experienced less pain and fewer tugging stitches, though her bound breasts nervously tingled each time the baby cried. But she wasn't dark, not dark at all. She could be "passed." The Warden and the social worker both agreed.

Like an exam, Grace thought. Finally, she seemed to have done something right. She passed the baby. Like a kidney stone, complete with a little bit of blood and more pain than seemed right. Like a baton, in a relay race. She passed the baby.

Over her time in the medical wing, Grace sensed the Warden and the social worker being quietly patient. As if they knew she would sign the papers, eventually. So they waited. Grace felt them waiting.

And while they waited, unbeknownst to Grace, just to be sure, just to be on the safe side, they selected a couple who couldn't afford to be too choosy. They picked carefully: perhaps less deserving, not quite as young, maybe not quite so crisp and clean; an odor of alcohol on his breath, a shadow on his cheek, a hint of neurosis like perfume in her wake. All concealed from Grace. Perhaps even—to give them the benefit of the doubt—subconscious to those who make such decisions. Still, this couple was better than her, they thought. Better than a teenage girl. Yes, this would do. A couple who maybe couldn't afford to complain too loudly should the baby begin to show its roots.

"Keep the baby out of the AIM program," the Warden advised the social worker. "With one white parent, you might be able to do it," she added. "Besides, we don't need the girl's mother complaining."

"What do I do about the father's identity? For the file?" the social worker asked.

"What's the father's last name?" the Warden mused, glancing over the papers. "*Black?* That's innocuous enough. You can leave his name there, that should be fine."

"What about the ethnicity question?" the social worker persisted. The Warden sighed.

"Use your imagination," she said, handing over the file and turning to leave the room. She paused in the doorway, thinking, looking at the social worker. "French," she finally declared and closed the door behind her.

UNDER THE COVER OF darkness and in secret, Grace took off her pajamas, the ones her mother had packed, the ones with kittens and pink bows. Everything was a secret here, even if it shouldn't be. Everything was shameful, especially desires. Especially the body. She undressed the baby and lay down with her, pressing their flesh together, luxuriating in the soft, alive warmth of the infant, smelling her dark hair, rubbing her back, cupping her tiny bum, stroking her shoulders with her fingertips. She breathed the baby, in and out. Just breathed. Concentrated on the swell, the taking in. Retaining. "I won't forget you," she whispered. "I promise." She kissed the baby's head lightly. "We fit together. You're part me. I hope you remember too."

GRACE TOUCHED THE BANISTER on the staircase she'd come to hate, nail-bitten fingers pulp-red with anxiety. In the Warden's office she signed the papers in a dizzying fit of anger, futility, frustration. Powerless in the face of their words. With the pen between her thumb and index finger, just there, she saw with devastating clarity that there had never been a choice. Rubbed raw and as sharp as a razor, she signed. Her ankles and face still puffed with toxic fluid, breasts still leaking milk.

Before she left, the Warden's face softened unnaturally. "It's for the best," she told Grace. "Now you can forget."

But Grace knew better. Knew it was forever—*felt* its perpetual shadow on her insides. It was a scar, and she was marked. Her time in the Asylum now part of her permanent record.

Grace cried all the way home in the station wagon until Ma got mad at her.

"What good does it do?" Sheila asked, trying to be reasonable. "Best to forget about it and move on," she said, repeating the advice she'd been given.

"YOU SEEM DIFFERENT," JILL SAID when she first saw Grace after she arrived home.

"No shit, dummy." Grace tried to laugh it off. Then she got more serious and added, "My aunt nearly *died*." She hung her head like she was sad. Even though Grace's cover—sick aunt, out east, on her deathbed—even though it was a lie, it did, in fact, feel like someone had died. Only it wasn't any smelly old aunt.

Jill knew it was a lie, but she never asked Grace to say the truth out loud. That was okay. That helped.

———

GRACE TRIED TO FORGET. She did everything to keep busy, to not have to think or feel. She started going to all the parties, where she flirted with boys. She started smoking. And she drank.

"Holy shit," Jill said. "You're ep-i-*demic.*"

The drugs and booze dampened a frantic despair. Grace often felt like she couldn't take a breath, couldn't breathe deeply enough to continue living. She panicked at the thought that now she was alone. The only word that came to mind was "hysterical." *Hysterical. Hysterectomy.* She became convinced the doctor had secretly removed her entire uterus instead of just the baby. Sleight of hand. Nevertheless, her insides, empty and bankrupt, from time to time still invoked a phantom baby, stirring. Spirit baby.

And while Grace was hollowed empty, everyone else around her developed a case of collective amnesia. As if the Asylum weren't real, as if Grace hadn't endured the pain of birth, as if the dark-haired baby never made passage. The baby was disremembered by everyone but Grace. As if it all never happened and yet it was the single biggest thing.

The months passed and as August loomed, along with the baby's first birthday, she began to drink and party with a new urgency. Every Friday and Saturday was filled with binge drinking at bush parties. Blind drunk and riding in cars, who knows where with who knows who. Anywhere, with anyone.

"Grace," Sheila said one day, so serious Grace stopped in her tracks. "Don't get in some kind of trouble again. Just don't.

God help us, Doug'll blow a valve. He's already got a heart murmur. Not that you caused it or anything, he's had it since he was born. But he's *susceptible*."

Grace knew this meant Sheila couldn't afford to support them all by herself, she'd said as much, many times. "We don't need anything that'll make him fall down dead with a heart attack," Sheila continued. It was hard to make ends meet as a single parent.

Much later, Grace would read somewhere that *girls like her* do one of two things. As if an invisible fork in the road forced them to choose without even knowing. *Girls like her* either found a way to quickly marry and have a baby they could keep—a replacement baby; or, *girls like her* never had another baby, as if they understood there was no replacement. As if they recognized a second baby was just that—a second baby. There was still a first, and she was still unaccounted for. Slowly Grace came to understand that she'd participated in infanticide.

WHEN SHE MET RICK, his blue eyes reminded her of her baby girl, the one she was supposed to pretend didn't exist. They were a deep blue, the kind of color that came from a briny ocean. Or newborn-baby eyes.

DOUG BLOCKED HER WAY out of the bathroom one evening as she was getting ready to go out. She tried to push past him but he stepped in front of her.

He looked at her makeup and said, "Everyone's talking about you."

Grace shrugged her shoulders. "I'm not responsible for what other people think." She stuck out her arm, shoved her hand between him and the door frame. He stepped aside and she pushed past him.

GRACE DREAMED AGAIN.

She dreamed a graveyard of babies. Shoeboxes lined up one beside the other, neat and systematic. Each contained one small, pale, dark-haired corpse. Bodies of evidence. Surely a crime had been committed. First baby would never be recovered. No matter what, first baby had been magically conjured away.

More and more, she dreamed about Leon. Daydreamed he would come for her, poetically, on the baby's birthday. She knew he didn't know the birth date, but fantasized all the same that he would save her and together they would save the dark-haired baby.

When Leon didn't show up by the baby's first birthday, Grace got blind drunk and sought Rick out. She wasn't sure if he was a nice guy, but she told him his eyes made her think of the bottom of the ocean. He liked that, and they slept together for the first time that night.

THREE MONTHS LATER, IGNORING the signs, bargaining-praying, and doing jumping jacks in her room. Running up and down the steps at the town hall when Sheila went in to pay a bill. *Think positive,* she told herself. But even though she was still going to parties, still seeing Rick, she wasn't drinking anymore. Kept hoping it was just a fluke, that her system was messed up because of last summer. She decided not to say anything to Rick. It was pointless. He planned to leave soon. Go back east to see his family at the end of harvest. Or maybe he'd go to BC, he said. Spend a mild winter and then plant trees in the spring. Who knew. Besides, nothing was wrong anyway. Right?

GRACE'S CLOTHES WERE GETTING tight. She was careful not to wear anything she wore last summer because she figured Ma would clue in right away. They got a ride from Jill's dad to go shopping and Grace shoplifted a loose poncho. She planned to wear it every day.

AND THEN THE SERIOUS snow was on the ground and harvest was over. "Do you have to go?" she asked, the last time she saw Rick. It was cold enough to see her breath.

"I'll be back," he promised, but instead of looking at her he gazed over her head. Grace wondered what was there, in the distance.

Grace wore her coat all winter. Stayed bundled. Hiding in plain sight. *I'm so fucking fat,* she thought. *I'm such a dum-dum.* She floated numbly through winter like an under-darkness dream.

———

IN EARLY SPRING, in the living room, making decorations
with her cousins for the oldest one's wedding, Grace started
getting menstrual cramps. She psyched herself up that she was
finally getting her period again. She practically danced down
the hall and into the bathroom. She locked the door and found
blood on her panties. Relief broke a cold sweat on her forehead. Finally. She got a pad from the cupboard. The cramps
were serious so she decided to lie down for a while. She fell
asleep and was woken by Ma calling her for supper. The cousins were gone home. As soon as Grace stood up she doubled
over with cramps.

In the bathroom she found blood and mucus on the pad.
She'd seen this before. This wasn't her period. She looked at
her watch and timed between the waves of contractions. About
two and a half, three minutes. While she knew what this was,
she didn't know what to do about it. Her mind went into a
blank denial and she forced herself into autopilot. Back in her
room, Grace put on her poncho and went to supper.

"What's gotten into you?" Ma asked. Grace was fidgeting
on her chair, swinging her legs under the table to distract from
the pain. All so she could keep her face as calm and ordinary as
possible. She kept her eyes on her food, cut it up and ate it,
even though she was far from hungry. Ma had made the highly
unimpressive breakfast-for-supper—Grace's fried eggs peered
at her from the plate like greasy alien eyes. She fought the nau-
sea and glanced away, caught Doug looking at her like she was
fucking weird. She felt a contraction building and pinched her

arm to distract her attention. "I have to go to the bathroom," Grace said, standing abruptly.

"Well then go, for heaven's sake," Ma laughed, like it was ridiculous.

Grace looked at herself in the bathroom mirror and decided she felt a lot worse than she looked. Her face was slightly flushed but didn't betray the agony she felt as her uterus rhythmically tightened. Grace returned to the supper table and chopped up her food. She pushed her plate away.

"You've only eaten the egg whites and a couple bites of your toast," Sheila protested.

"Maybe she's decided to go on a diet," Doug said, like it was any of his business. "You shouldn't let yourself get fat," he said, ducking his head down as he shoveled food into his mouth.

"Yeah, that's a great idea, trying to reduce." Sheila sounded relieved. "You're so young and you've got the rest of your life ahead of you. It's too early to get fat," she blurted. "I can try one of my Weight Watchers recipes tomorrow, if you want."

Grace groaned and rose from the table.

"She's so bloody sensitive," Ma said to Doug as Grace left the room.

He grunted, then replied, "I'm going over to the hotel."

"You mean the beer parlor," Sheila said.

Grace didn't hear if Doug answered.

LOCKED IN THE BATHROOM, Grace sat on the toilet and rocked herself through the contractions, one after another. Finally, she went on her hands and knees on the soft bath mat where she swayed forward and back, eyes closed, just going with the tides of her body. She put her hand in her mouth, bit down, and rocked, rocked, rocked. Silent. Ma hadn't noticed yet how long Grace had been in the bathroom.

Soon her body remembered. Not afraid anymore, she just let it happen. Bearing down, she made a noise she couldn't help, a long, low sigh, and the baby slid out before she was even ready. Grace still on her hands and knees, the baby just shifted onto the bath mat, easy as anything.

Grace curled up beside her, put her hands all around her— her body still warm from being inside Grace's. She looked at the infant's deep blue eyes. For the first time. And again. Like the first time twice. Déjà vu. She pressed her close, covered her with a towel. Grace's legs started to shake as she rubbed the baby's face with her fingertip, wiping away a smear of blood. The infant kept her eyes open and was perfectly calm. She just looked at Grace. And Grace looked at her. They stared and stared. Mesmerized, Grace rubbed her hair softly with the towel.

MA WAS AT THE DOOR.

"Open the door," Sheila said, rattling the knob.

"I don't want to," Grace said. Her voice sounded funny, even to her.

"What do you mean you *don't want to?*"

"You're gonna be mad at me."

"What have you done?" Sheila jangled the knob some more.

"I just. I don't." Grace paused, as if searching for words. "You're going to be mad at me," she finally repeated.

"Okay," Sheila said slowly. "I promise. I won't be mad." She was quiet for a moment. "Grace?" she insisted. "Do you have a baby in there?"

Grace hesitated and then answered yes in a small voice.

"Grace, where did you get a baby from?" Sheila's voice was curiously composed. "Come on, honey. No one's going to be mad at you." Sheila shook the door again. "You haven't done anything that can't be undone."

"I know," Grace said, caressing the baby's head. "It's a girl," she said.

And then, surprisingly, Sheila said, "If you've taken someone's baby, it's okay. We can fix this."

"I need a minute," Grace said, urgently. "Why can't you let me have this one thing?"

A few seconds later the lock clicked in the handle and Sheila was in the doorway with a hairpin. She took it all in like an assessor, the blood, the towels, and Grace curled in a ball on the bath mat with a tiny quiet baby. "Goddammit," she said. "I thought you stole someone else's baby." And then, quickly reevaluating, Sheila shifted gears. She was nothing if not calm in a crisis. "Okay," she said. "We can get this cleaned up before Doug comes home from the bar. *We can fix this.*"

"I'm so dumb," Grace said. "But isn't she beautiful?" Grace held the baby's hand, looking at its tiny translucent fingernails.

"She's beautiful, Sugarbug," Sheila said gently. "But you know what has to happen, right? You know we can't do this."

"Ma, *please.*"

"We can *fix* this," Sheila asserted. "We can still fix this. I can clean this up before anyone knows. Before Doug gets back." She started filling a bucket with hot soapy water.

Sheila put Grace into bed, gave her two Valiums, and promised not to go anywhere without telling her first. She lined an apple box with a clean flannel sheet before hastily wrapping the baby and the placenta, all together, and placing the bundle in the box. She put another blanket over the whole thing.

GRACE WANTED TO STAY in bed, to let the Valium take over, let it cloud her thoughts until they flowed away from her like syrup. She could feel it coming, the sweet relief from the drugs, but down the hall she heard her baby crying, a thin cry that told Grace the infant already knew this was it, this was good-bye. The bawl cut through the haze and Grace choked on a sound that came from the center of her diaphragm. She sat up, swung her legs out of bed.

In the dresser drawer she found a pen and a scrap of paper. She wanted the baby to know something so crucial it built like a bubble inside her chest. She stared at the blank paper, finally wrote, *You are,* and for a moment couldn't think, overwhelmed by how important the note was and how she had to get it right, this one thing, the only thing she could give to her. A name, the note, it was all Grace could offer. The note had to encompass all that she wanted for her, all that the baby needed for Grace to be able to let her go, again. All Grace could think was, *It has to be right.*

Charity, she wrote. And then: *I loved you first.* Grace looked at the note and thought that wasn't quite it. The baby with the big blue eyes deserved something more, something that stood out. Grace wanted her to have comfort, reassurance. She scribbled out *Charity* and wrote, above it, *Cherish.* She folded the note into her palm.

Steadying herself along the wall, she hurried down the hallway to the bathroom. The joints in her legs were tethered by loose rubber bands.

"Grace, go back to bed, for heaven's sake," Ma said, trying to intercept and steer her out of the now-cleaned bathroom.

"No." Grace pushed Ma away, eyes fixed on the box in the middle of the room. "I need to say goodbye." As she knelt beside the box, a gush of blood escaped between her legs. She didn't care. The baby wasn't crying now but alert, alert to Grace's presence. She touched the top of her head, letting her fingertips linger on the pulsing soft spot. Her nerve endings absorbed the baby's warm energy. Ma made an impatient sound and Grace tucked the note deep inside the warmth of the blankets before Ma picked up the box and carried it from the bathroom.

"Go to bed, Grace. I'll check on you when I get back."

SHEILA GRABBED HER KEYS and left out the back door. The box on the passenger seat, she circled the block at the hospital before deciding on the emergency department. She left the box as close to the entrance as she dared. In the middle of the path.

Surely someone would find it. Someone would find it soon, she told herself, as she hurried away, empty-handed. No one would walk past without investigating. The baby would be found.

In the car she whispered, "I'm sorry."

She hurried home before Doug returned.

SHEILA NEVER SPOKE ABOUT the babies again. Grace, on the other hand, spent years quietly fantasizing about rescuing them. When she drank, she wallowed around in remembering, talking to herself. She said the names of the men who'd let her down. *Leon. Rick.* Often interchangeable. Her song a conjuring plea. But mostly she grieved for Leon. Bargaining for him to come and get her. Promising that together the two of them would rescue the dark-haired baby of her dreams. The baby with eyes as deep as the ocean. The missing. She'd tell him, when he came—whoever came—she'd tell him: *The baby has your eyes.*

Angel

1994

...

THEY BOTH LOVED ANGEL, IT WAS TRUE.

It was early summer. Moe and Ruby hadn't even been married a year yet when Angel arrived at their place in her shitty Chevette packed to the roof with everything she owned, which wasn't much. As they helped her unpack the car, Ruby registered the strange assortment of goods that accompanied her. Her guitar, which made sense, and a small black duffel bag stuffed tight with clothes. But the other things: a plastic colander, wooden shoe rack from IKEA, skateboard, snowshoe poles, a hedge trimmer. So random. As if she'd just grabbed anything and stuffed it into the car.

It made Ruby imagine Angel, angry, leaving Wanda.

"Oh yeah? Okay, fine, if that's the way you want it. I'll go, then. But I'm not leaving without *this*," picking up the hedge trimmer and shaking it like a threat. "And *this*," grabbing the colander off the drainboard. Stomping out to her car and flinging the items in, then back to the house to tell Wanda what else she wasn't leaving without. Giving Wanda the chance to maybe say she was wrong. To ask Angel to stay. Something like that. Ruby could just picture it.

The final two items, the shoe rack and the snowshoe poles, snatched angrily from the front entranceway. And Wanda, shutting the door as Angel drove off, tires squealing, the residue of her life stuffed into the Chevette like a badly played Tetris screen. Ruby could picture it pretty good. That was probably how it went down between Angel and Wanda, more or less. It made Ruby want to ask Moe exactly how it ended between them, him and Angel, all those years ago.

THE FIRST WEEKS WITH Angel at the house were filled with the three of them drinking endless beers in the backyard. Every night they heard the phone ringing off the hook in the kitchen, but Angel didn't want them to answer it. They all assumed it was Wanda. Instead, Angel played the guitar and sang. Moe built a firepit from leftover bricks from one of his landscaping jobs. He borrowed a lawnmower and cut the grass. He patched the crumbling patio. Their neglected yard took shape around Angel, who sat in the center of it all, her own weather system, oblivious to the storm she caused.

ONE NIGHT, HERMAN SHOWED up from next door, drawn by the music. He admired the firepit, Angel's long legs, and the freshly cut grass.

"Here, Ruby." He handed her a joint. "Yard-warming gift," he laughed. She lit it and passed it around. As the buzz set in,

Angel plucked out the repeated notes of Clapton's "Cocaine."
She sang the lyrics while the rest of them shouted "Cocaine!"
into the night air and laughed themselves sick. Stoned, a little
drunk, Ruby watched Angel in the light of the fire, admired
her straight white teeth and full lips, the way she closed her
eyes sometimes when she sang, or looked down, as if mesmerized by her own voice. And then mid-song she'd suddenly
look up and catch Ruby's eye and a smile would transform her
face and it was like Ruby had been handed a priceless gift. Moe
watched Angel too, his face wide open, eyes shining, helpless.
Angel's beautiful hands stroked the guitar like a lover. Watching Angel, Ruby couldn't help but imagine her with Wanda,
loving her, strumming a nipple, full lips pressing here, and
here. Moving down her body, pressing, nipping, licking, kissing. Angel naked. Her curvy hips and sleek legs, entwined with
her lover's. Angel was perfect in a way Ruby had never been
and never would be.

RUBY'S MOTHER LIKED TO tell a story, about when she adopted
Ruby. "One side of her head was completely flat," Alice exclaimed. "Can you imagine?" Ruby didn't have to imagine,
there were baby pictures. Not a good look. For nearly the first
nine months of her life she was in a foster home and when she
left she couldn't even sit up. Her "now-mother," which is sometimes how she referred to Alice, tried to tell Ruby it was because
the foster home neglected her. That is: the foster home Ruby was
in before Alice came to rescue her. She also told Ruby all about
the ugly boils that were on her "bottom" because of being left in

dirty diapers all the time. Alice liked to carry on about how much of a screamer Ruby was. Her way of underlining her belief that Ruby had always been dramatic.

Despite what her mother thought, Ruby believed the real reason behind the flat head was because she had a secret twin sister. She imagined they pressed their heads so tightly together, bonding there in the liquid darkness, sharing brainwaves along with their mother's amniotic fluid, that they couldn't help but be marked by the experience. She relished the idea of another person out there just like her—with thoughts like hers, who knew how she felt. Ruby had a secret twin sister and she didn't know what had happened to her, but she felt her twin-ness acutely. She felt her. Right there on the left side of her head, which reshaped itself by the time she entered school. But at night, even now, she pressed that side of her head into the pillow as if some unremembered comfort could be recaptured by doing so.

Ruby couldn't help it, she'd never been able to help it, but all her girlfriends, eventually, became entwined with her sister-longing. At some point, she started to wish they were her sister. *Closer. Closer.* That's what her mind said. Not obsessively. Not in a Stephen King *Misery* way. Just in a longing way. A desirous way. A needy way. She knew it was juvenile, but it was also true.

"LET'S HAVE A MOVIE NIGHT," Moe suggested one evening. Moe and Angel had been at the library all afternoon and had borrowed a documentary on penguins. The three of them made popcorn and turned the lights down. Ruby thought she would lie with her head in Moe's lap, like she always did by the end of a movie night. Instead, Moe and Angel used the penguin documentary as a tool. Ruby learned: Some animals were polygamous. Especially penguins, but it didn't stop with them. There were monkeys and birds and others who displayed traits of poly behaviors. Documented for hundreds of years, two or more female penguins could gather to share a male. Or vice versa. Triptychs. They built a life together, mating, season after season. It happened. It was natural.

But Ruby found it even more interesting that researchers first discovered this tendency in penguins in the late eighteenth century and they kept it a secret. Her question was, Why? Her speculative answer was, They kept the penguins' secret perhaps because it was their own secret. Hidden desires. It hit too close to home.

Penguins couldn't fly because their wings had adapted into flippers for swimming. They spent half their life in the ocean. Everyone adapted. It was natural.

THEY WERE ASKING RUBY to adapt. Moe and Angel.

"How long have you guys been talking about this?" What she really meant was: *You guys left me out?* Instead, she laughed and threw the movie case across the room.

"THE DISCUSSION" STRETCHED OVER days, became part of the fabric of everything they did until Ruby felt strained by its presence. More than once Angel asked, "What are you so afraid of?" She smiled in a way that made Ruby want to do something dramatic like jump up and scream, or pluck her eyelashes out one by one, or kiss her, all at the same time.

A book from the library on "polyfidelity" informed all their arguments. Ruby was supposed to be reading it, but every time she tried, her mind jumped to Moe and Angel kissing in the backyard. *Moe and Angel, Moe and Angel.* More than just kissing, of course, but they didn't really talk about that. Ruby felt like she was swimming through a sea of murky water—she didn't know where she was going and she had no defense. At any moment she might realize she couldn't breathe.

"I'm not afraid," she told them. "Don't tell me how I feel." They really didn't know. She'd spent her entire life responding to danger by constructing *unafraid.* Brave, full of bravado. This was not what *afraid* looked like. But their new reality made Ruby uneasy and anxious. She couldn't quite articulate what was happening.

THE FIRST TIME ANGEL held Ruby's hand a thrill fluttered through her chest, her rational mind went soft. Angel stroked Ruby's fingers in hers and she could think of nothing else she wanted more. Angel kissed Ruby the way Ruby'd seen her kissing Moe, and Ruby pressed her body against Angel's with an urgency that surprised them both.

RUBY DIDN'T KNOW WHAT she wanted, wouldn't make a commitment either way, which drove Moe wild. They argued, sometimes for hours. Ruby would try to disengage but Moe insisted they "communicate."

"We need to resolve this," he said, meaning Ruby needed to get over what he saw as her "jealousy," which had become a bad word in their ongoing discussion.

"I'm exhausted," she cried. "I don't want to be doing this."

"Admit I'm right," he persisted.

"Okay. You're right. How's that?" Rage burned behind her eyes.

"You don't mean it."

Did he realize he sounded like a child?

"Look. I just said you were right." Ruby's voice shook. "Now move out of the way so I can go to bed."

"No," Moe said so calmly that she had the urge to slug him. "Not until I believe that you mean it." Moe stood in front of the door, blocking her exit from the kitchen.

She could hardly believe they were having this confrontation. All because she was having a hard time accepting what he wanted, what he and Angel both wanted—what Ruby sometimes wanted too, but they weren't giving her the space to sort it out. Sharing Moe. Sharing Angel.

"I think you're angry because this is forcing you to experience your own feelings," he said, starting his arguments over again. "Did you even *read* that chapter on jealousy?"

The phone rang. Ruby moved to answer it but Moe said, "No. It might be Wanda." She didn't think Wanda had been calling lately, but she kept this to herself.

An hour later she laid her head on her arms at the kitchen table and told Moe she believed him, he was right, she would try harder to understand his perspective about love and loving. About non-monogamy. Finally, he moved and she escaped to the bedroom.

Despite everything, despite being so angry she sometimes hated Moe, she still wanted to be married to him. It was important to her that Moe was Métis. His was essentially the only Native family she had. That was why it was so impossible for her to leave Moe even though he gave her so many reasons to want to. He was tied to all the things she missed and wished for. He was still her "big Métis hope." Moe was part of her fantasy about his family, about finding out that they were somehow connected—related, maybe, in a distant way. That really, truly, and by blood, she *belonged*.

It was about wanting a second chance to redo everything they'd already done, but with more intentionality. More thought. More magic. Like Moe's blue ribbon-shirt. Métis blue. With white ribbons and decorated with infinity symbols. She admired that shirt and at the same time was jealous of it too. He wore it on special occasions and to cultural events, like Batoche. She imagined them getting remarried and him wearing his ribbon-shirt for their re-wedding. And her second-wedding outfit would echo his Métis ribbon-shirt somehow, adorned with white ribbons, or she'd carry a Métis-blue bouquet. Instead of a plain skirt and worn-out shoes in his parents' living room. And Moe in his black Bowie T-shirt and his dad's blazer.

She recalled how she'd found the ring on sale for ninety-nine dollars in the Consumers Distributing flyer. Possessed by

an idea, Ruby was determined, and Moe was willing. At the
store, she'd filled out the paper at one of the stands, scribbled
the code for the ring with the tiny blue mini-golf pencil before
they stood in line together. As they waited for the clerk to retrieve the ring, she'd slipped Moe fifty bucks. Moe took the
money, but was irritable. Perhaps he'd never imagined getting
married this way. Perhaps he'd pictured it differently. Or
maybe he'd never thought about it at all.

SHE WONDERED WHY SHE couldn't be happy. Did sadness
make happiness more potent? A penguin will steal an egg or a
chick if something happens to its own—moved by a desperate
sadness and the drive to do what their biology tells them they're
meant to do. Moe was driven too. There was a fire behind his
need—he'd researched, found evidence to prove his new be-
liefs.

MOE AND ANGEL KEPT telling Ruby she shouldn't feel jealous.
The book kept telling her she shouldn't feel jealous.
"Jealousy isn't a real emotion. It's a socialized state. It's
hard to step outside that mold."
Moe accused her of being selfish.
Whatever their words were supposed to mean, she spent
countless hours trying to figure it out.
She wanted to believe, to prove she was willing to push her-
self to discover how strong she was, to break the hold she

hadn't even known social convention had on her. To prove she wasn't selfish. To prove them wrong. She genuinely wanted to understand. They set up a rotating schedule for spending different times together, one-on-one. Moe and Angel; Angel and Ruby; Ruby and Moe. The new favorite word in their house was "communicate." Angel kept her own room; Ruby and Moe kept theirs, since they were "the primaries." The new vocabulary and rules gave Ruby the sense of always being one step behind.

They started to write love notes and snippets of poetry, left the finished pieces for one another to find, like sweet surprises. Angel's pieces were always directed to both of them, nothing just for Ruby and nothing just for Moe. And forget the poetic device of no punctuation or few capital letters. Angel wrote in all caps, added exclamation marks, pressed hard, left marks.

ONE DAY, REACHING INTO a bowl of sharp utensils on a top shelf, Ruby impaled her palm on the food processor attachment. When she saw the bloody puncture, she immediately thought of stigmata, even though she'd been raised with little to no religion. She thought about how delicate the human body was, how mortal, how easily wounded. The mark felt good in her hand; she held it in her palm and it sparked something greedy. Her mother Alice had once been a believer, attended church, had Ruby baptized. The only way Ruby knew she'd been baptized was because she found the certificate in a drawer in the dining room hutch. It was blue-green, on thick paper, and heavy for its size. Mostly unremarkable, aside from the line that said *Date of Birth,* which was filled out with *August 24, 1976.* Ruby had always been told she was born in 1975. She was twelve turning thirteen when she found the certificate. Or maybe she was eleven turning twelve. The certificate sparked new insecurity in Ruby. *I'm not who I think I am.* How could she be sure of anything?

At seventeen, Ruby had badgered Alice for her adoption papers, but only after she had conducted a secret systematic search of the entire house. Alice was hurt by Ruby's request. She took it personally. She thought Ruby's desire to know where she came from meant Alice had done a bad job or wasn't a good enough mother for Ruby.

"I'm sorry I don't meet your expectations," Alice had said harshly.

"Jeez," Ruby protested. "Why do you have to make this about you when it's not? It's not *all* about *you,* you know."

"You grew up in a good home," Alice asserted. "You were special. We chose you."

She pictured her mother choosing, probing for spots, bruised peel, flesh wounds to be trimmed away, testing the limbs, tugging the leaves, squeezing the cheeks like nectarines, checking the firmness, running a thumb over smooth skin, fingertips pressing, knuckles knocking. Was she special like dragon fruit, like mandarins at Christmas? Or special like a two-pronged carrot or a potato with a big hole in the middle?

Weeks, maybe months later, Alice handed Ruby an envelope which contained a page and a half of typed words. Non-identifying information that said her birth mother was a fifteen-year-old high school student with blond hair and blue eyes who was intelligent and liked to read. Swedish.

Ruby, with her dark hair and inky eyes, had never once felt Swedish in her life.

She focused on her birth father's description. Dark-haired and French. Over time, the French word *Métis* worked its way into Ruby's consciousness until it all made sense to her.

"What are you?"

"French."

"Métis?"

She nodded.

"That's okay, we like you anyway."

According to the paper, her birth father played sports, liked baseball. Four brothers, one sister. His parents, her biological grandparents, farmed, labored. They were all of average height and weight. Ruby read and reread the thin words and finally understood something about herself.

Moe came home one day with Herman's old Indian motorcycle, which they all found hilarious.

"We should call it 'Métis' motorcycle," Ruby joked. "Now that it's ours."

The bike was Moe's payment for two months of hard labor, landscaping Herman's front yard. The bike was decrepit, loud, and missing the proper lights. Moe had no license to drive it, but that didn't bother him.

Angel and Ruby went to the street at the front of the house to look at it.

"It's beautiful, sweetie," Angel gushed, rubbing his arm.

"Is it missing the muffler?" Ruby asked. She wanted to say, *We could use the money instead.*

He straddled the bike and started it. The engine belched then erupted in a roar, leaving no room for words. He shouted over the motor, "Wanna go for a ride?"

She shook her head no, but Angel climbed on behind Moe, slipping her arms around his waist, hugging him close, pressing in behind him. Ruby said nothing, knowing she wouldn't be heard over the engine anyway. Angel watched Ruby, eyes wide, smile broad. She kissed her pretty fingertips and blew the kiss to Ruby, who caught it and cupped it in her palm. They roared away in a cloud of blue-white exhaust.

"YOU DON'T LIKE THE bike, do you?" Moe said to her hours later, when they finally returned and Angel had gone to bed. Moe and Ruby were lying in their bed in the dark, not touching.

"Angel likes it enough for both of us," she said.

"That's not fair."

"Well, there's only room for two anyway."

"Do you want to go for a ride?" he asked.

"That's not the point. Can't you see how many things are only made for two?"

"We'll get a sidecar," he said. "You can ride in there. You'd probably like that better, you'd feel safer."

"I'd feel like an appendage," she said.

"You're being overly sensitive." Moe reached over, pulled her in for a hug. He stroked her face and said, "I love you.

Look. I'm here, aren't I? I wouldn't be here if I didn't love you. I adore you, you know that."

She breathed deeply to calm down. Instead of sleeping, she was awake all night trying to figure out how she'd gotten it so wrong again.

IT WAS HER NIGHT to spend time with Angel. Moe was working in the shed out back, tinkering with the motorbike, painting the gas tank, soaking filters in gasoline. Angel and Ruby shared a bottle of wine in the kitchen. As Ruby watched Angel pour generously into Ruby's tumbler she vaguely recognized that she was drinking a lot more now than she used to.

"You're stuck," Angel said, "in your social norms. You've been programmed." Her tone was understanding and full of pity for Ruby's unenlightened state. They held hands across the table and Angel caressed her thumb and fingers, one at a time, over and over. She watched their two hands together. It was hypnotic.

"We're all oppressed. We've all been taught that sex and our bodies are shameful." Angel was an unconventional beauty. Dark. Gutsy. Sweet and spicy all at once.

They talked for an hour at the table and Ruby relaxed into the wine.

Moe came into the kitchen smelling of gasoline and engine oil. He looked at them sitting at the table. "Ruby's drunk again," he said and laughed.

"I am not," she said, irritated.

"Sure." He smiled knowingly at Angel, who smiled back. It

was a conspiracy. "Ruby's drunk again" discounted anything she said or did after it was declared.

LATER, MOE AND RUBY lay in bed again in the dark. She was on her back, stiff, not touching Moe.

"Why don't you want to kiss me the way you kiss her?" she asked into the dark.

"What do you mean? I don't. Want to kiss her. That much."

"You do. I've seen you." This was the frustrating thing about Moe. Either he played dumb or he was dumb. Either way it was an untenable position.

"Are you trying to tell me you don't love her?" Moe asked. "I've seen the way you two carry on."

"Isn't that exactly what you want? You want me to fall in love with her because then it gives *you* permission to fall in love with her," Ruby said.

Moe grunted. "Are you afraid there's a limited amount of love?" This was it. The dogma. "We're not going to run out. There's no top limit. Love isn't some nonrenewable resource. Your thinking is so narrow and selfish," he accused.

"*I'm* selfish?" she exclaimed. "That's hilarious."

"If you can't be happy then no one can."

WANDA OR NO WANDA, she started answering the phone again. Her mom called to say her dog Zed had died. Ruby wondered if Alice would be lonely now. "Do you want to get another one?" she asked, trying to be helpful.

164 L I S A   B I R D - W I L S O N

"No," Alice said firmly. "God, no," she repeated, in case Ruby didn't believe her the first time. "I never want to go through this again."

Ruby didn't tell her now-mom about Moe and Angel and their new arrangement. She could just hear her say, "But you've only been married ten months!" like it was a crime or something. She wouldn't know how to explain the situation to her anyway, and she didn't want to give her any more reasons to dislike Moe. Alice had already made it known she thought Ruby could have done better. Ruby thought Alice would most likely scoff at the idea that Ruby thought she was doing something special. But why not? Can't every love be special somehow? Even if it ends up kicking the shit out of you?

Somewhere deep inside, Ruby was still imagining things would go back to normal. She still wanted them to live happily ever after. It occurred to her that the relationship she thought she was building was not the same relationship Moe was imagining.

Ruby started crying on the phone.

"What's the matter, sweetie?"

"I don't know," she said. "I guess I'm sad because Zed died?"

SHE LAY WITH ANGEL and let her hold her in her arms, skin to skin, her head resting near Angel's breast. Angel's skin was soft. Smooth and hairless. Her secret twin, her pressed-head twin, and the deep longing of an undefined absence. Angel was a surrogate for that lost love and sister-comfort. Moe a surrogate for her entire lost Métis family. She allowed herself to wonder, Why not? If it brought her relief, why was it wrong?

But there were nagging questions. If it was all true, what they said, why was she so sad? So tied up in knots? Why did she cry in secret? Why did it feel like she was living in the center of an unsettled question? After they made love, even as they held each other, she felt a deep despair, the onset of sadness in her throat, driving her to press herself against Angel's body, flatten her cheek against Angel's chest, listening for a heartbeat, much like a child. And even as she sighed and pressed and pulled close, smelling her skin, building the sweet-after into a memory, in that immediate moment there hovered a delicate misery, a small kernel of knowing this was unsustainable. *I miss you,* she thought stupidly.

MOE AND ANGEL WENT out on the motorbike. It was their night together. She didn't ask where they were going. She fleetingly, secretly fantasized about them crashing, being smoked at an intersection by a pickup truck running a light, or taking a corner too hard on a fast road. Smeared. Reckless. Careless.

She thought about taking the motorbike key and swallowing it. She thought about ways to make it disappear.

MOE JOINED HER IN their room later and they fought about Angel, as usual. Their bed had become a boxing ring. After they finished fighting, she practically had to beg for a hug, which they negotiated in excruciating blame-detail before he grudgingly put his arm around her. *Don't tell me jealousy isn't real,* she thought. She wanted to punch him with her fists. Lying against his shoulder feeling the rage swell and crash inside her, all she wanted to do was strike him. She envisioned straddling his body and punching him in the face. But the face was too intimate, so she transferred her imaginary punches to his body, punching him in his chest, sides, ribs, her imagined fists seeking out the places where he was soft. So mad at him, lying there in the awkward embrace of their shared infidelity. She gave him the finger in the dark.

ON A FRIDAY NIGHT the three of them got dressed up and went out drinking. At the bar they got drunk, but when it became obvious Moe and Angel weren't getting as drunk as Ruby, Ruby broke away from them, turned into motion: a whirling mass of chaos and flow, rushing, dancing, flirting, laughing loudly, here and there. On her way to a Category Five, she couldn't stop herself. In her wake, anger and loss, wanting and understanding. From her wildness she grew fervent, feeding, feeding, feeding.

She danced with a guy and told him, "See those two over there?" She pointed, made eye contact with Moe and Angel, who watched her. "That's my husband and our girlfriend. We all live together." Ruby threw her head back and laughed, letting him kiss her neck. "Isn't she pretty?" Ruby slurred.

"So are you," he said. Suddenly, Ruby wanted everything to

be more dangerous than it had ever been before. The ground barely swayed, hardly missed a beat.

Eventually, Moe and Angel pried her from the bar. "What's the matter?" She clutched Moe's shirtfront trying to stand up straight. "Isn't this what we do now?" The evening aborted, Ruby raged and howled, made unreasonable demands. She pleaded; she became sweet. In the end, they were all exhausted by it.

That night they left her alone in her bed, the bed she normally shared with Moe. "Are you stupid?" Ruby asked herself, before passing out, aware of Angel and Moe closed off down the hall in Angel's bedroom. The next morning, she was sick of herself. So sick of herself she vomited. She moaned. She did not feel better. Later they had to forgive her before she could forgive herself.

MOE AND ANGEL WENT out on the bike again. Ruby stood on the front step and watched them roar away. Herman was out in his newly landscaped front yard. She waved at him. He came over and she asked, "How's the yard?"

But Herman didn't want to talk about his yard. He said, "Moe's a good guy. You two are cute together."

"Did you ever know you loved someone more than they'd ever love you?" she asked him.

"Moe loves you," Herman said. But Ruby wasn't just talking about Moe. She was also talking about Angel. Seeing the two of them together, it didn't take much to recognize it was more about the two of them than it was about her.

Ruby started to cry. She put her hand protectively over her stomach. "What the fuck's wrong with me?" she asked Herman, to which he had no reply.

A COUPLE OF HOURS LATER, from the bedroom window, Ruby saw Wanda's car pull up. Moe and Angel had just returned on the motorbike.

Angel and Wanda greeted each other. Wanda's body language was open and warm. Angel was, as always, a frayed wire.

Moe left them, headed to the backyard, his dark head bobbing in time with his steps, a little Métis jig in his pulse.

Ruby continued to watch Wanda and Angel talk. Finally, Wanda reached out, took Angel's hand. Angel pulled away, but only slightly; their hands stayed together. Ruby could tell she halfway wanted to be drawn in by Wanda. They talked more, they laughed at something, and Angel let Wanda pull her in for a hug. They held on and on to each other. Ruby wondered if one or both of them were crying, familiarity and relief in their postures.

Moe would be mad. She knew this.

If Angel left with Wanda, Moe would be mad.

Even more, if he found out it was Ruby who'd called Wanda, well. He'd be mad.

It was like crashing the bike, only better.

It was like swallowing the key, only easier.

She rubbed her belly some more, felt a bit guilty. Like the penguin who stole someone else's egg.

"Kisâkihitin," she whispered to her belly. "I love you."

Blondie

1991

...

HER FIRST DAY IN THE CITY SHE CAME UP WITH AN invisibility plan. She got a cup from the 24-hour Burger King and that was the first place she tried it. She pretended she was deaf. She looked at the cashier with her eyes wide and held her mouth straight. She made like she was watching the cashier's lips carefully and then she signed to her. Ruby could do this because she took American Sign Language on Saturday mornings for three years. Back when she wanted nothing more than to learn a secret language.

If she had a superpower it would be invisibility. Pretending to be deaf was the next best thing.

This place felt a little bit like death. She'd found a way to keep the vultures away, at least for a while. They thought she couldn't hear them calling her "jerkoff." It was okay, she had her own names for them too. Some of them anyway.

It had only been four days and she'd finally figured out where she could sit without getting in shit with someone. She pulled her sleeves down to cover the scars on her arms and kept her hood up to cover her shaved dark hair, hoping people would think she was a boy and leave her alone. Being a girl came with its own distinct set of problems.

So far, she'd gotten away with it. With joining the streets when she knew nothing about its subculture of power-tripping hate and false love. By pretending she was deaf. She gave anyone who tried to talk to her the look—eyes big, mouth straight. Watching carefully.

SHE'D ARRIVED ON THE longest bus ride ever, had no idea why she picked Toronto—because it was far away, she guessed. She should have picked somewhere smaller, for chrissakes. She was just trying to put a lot of distance between herself and her so-called family. She didn't need any family, thank you very much. That's what got her into this mess in the first place.

It was absolutely a wonder that anyone at all still went in for "love." Or whatever they called it. In fact, she learned quickly this was a thing with street kids—they mistook street culture as some sort of "family" and acted like they were all in it together, some big love fest. Until one of them fell out of favor and then the rest turned on that one with a viciousness usually reserved for high school cliques.

SHE LIKED THE SKINNY older guy who sat across from her, though. She thought his name was Win. He sometimes smiled at her and nodded a little bit, but mostly he kept to himself. He liked to talk to himself and organized his stuff around him like a little fortress.

The first day, when she decided she needed to try and melt into the background, she got the cup from the 24-hour Burger King and sat outside the liquor store and waited. No one gave her anything and no one even really looked at her. She didn't mind, for now. Her first concern was to stay away from the guys interested in "new meat." And to get a little something to make being on the streets bearable. At the moment she felt largely on top of it all because of what she didn't want any of the other deadbeats to know—that she had a bit of money. Not much, but anything is something.

Outside the liquor store again, a guy in a black concert T-shirt, probably in his twenties, slowed down to take a look at her. She grabbed the chance and held up her cup with one hand and with the other thrust a note at him. He took the note, probably thinking it was asking for money. He raised his eyebrows as he read it. She thought he'd say no to her request, but he just walked off with the note, into the liquor store. She monitored the door where he'd gone in and waited, keeping an eye on the exit. Lots of people came out, one after the other, but he didn't appear. She started to think he might have found another exit, so as to avoid her, but then she spotted his AC/DC T-shirt as he moved through the automatic door. She stood up, taking her empty cup with her. He tipped his head toward the parking lot and she followed him, looking around to make sure no one was watching. Literally no one could give two shits.

He stopped beside a beat-up green Nova. "It's seven," he

said. She stared at his lips, fully in her role. She put her tongue between her teeth, like she was concentrating really hard. Like it was difficult to understand him. He looked at her and seemed to recall "the issue," which she literally spelled out in her note: *I'm deaf,* she wrote at the end of the ask. "Se-vun," he mouthed with exaggerated slowness.

She fished some crumpled ones out of her front pocket. She knew it was really six-fifty but some guys liked to get their little bit too, even if it meant ripping off a runaway.

She handed him the bills and counted out four quarters into his palm, then held out her hand for the bottle.

He removed it from the paper bag in the crook of his arm, held it out to her. As she grabbed it, he held the top of the Smirnoff bottle and prevented her from taking it. She raised her eyes to look at his face.

"What's your name?" he asked. She stared at him blankly and he pointed to himself and said, "Steve." Then he pointed at her and raised his eyebrows.

"Roo," she said stupidly, stopping herself before saying her whole name.

"Roo?" he asked, laughing. "Well then, *Roo,*" he said, "you wanna make some extra money?"

She pulled at the bottle but he held tight. He tucked his head down and forward to be sure he was in her sightline. Raised his eyebrows.

She shook her head no and took a small step back, but kept her hand on the bottle.

"Fair enough," he said, letting go. She turned away and

took off through the parking lot, away from his car, tucking the bottle into her jacket pocket.

She was walking up Dundas near Sherbourne, enjoying a few furtive shots, when some guy started shouting at her. At least she thought it was at her. But she didn't look because she remembered she was supposed to be deaf. She tucked her head down and kept walking. Suddenly he was in front of her. She looked up, startled.

"Do you speak English?" he shouted in her face.

She gave him the blank look. Eyes big, mouth a straight line. She concentrated on his lips. They were angry and fat. She felt nervous. She made the sign for *I'm deaf* at him. And then a couple of other nonsense signs, just so he'd get the picture.

"What the fuck," he spat. "Don't you know who I am?" he yelled, waving his arms and puffing out his chest.

Charles Manson? she thought but stopped herself. He wore a fanny pack and she stared at it. She couldn't tell if he was seriously dangerous or just a regular lunatic. His face was all red.

She made a couple of other signs that she hoped would convey her hopelessness as a conversationalist. He glared at her.

"Go fuck yourself, you deaf little cunt," he said and stormed off.

She bent her head low again and walked on, sweating and a little angry. *What the fuck,* she kept saying to herself. *What the fuck did I do?*

When she calmed down, she started to get worried. Charles Manson called her the c-word, she realized, which meant even crazy nonsensical people must recognize her as a girl, despite her best efforts at disguise. Maybe she was fooling no one.

SHE TOOK HER CUP to the main drag, where tourists went by. It was the height of the day and they were all out. And it was getting hot. She couldn't keep her hood up the whole time or she was going to die of heatstroke.

She spied Win, a friendly face, and sat down on the sidewalk across from him. Not too close, plenty of room between him and her, between her and anyone else. Didn't want anyone freaking out on her. She noticed that Win was turning as brown as a nut in the relentless sun. His short dark hair had been cut recently and he had bald patches all over his head. He looked like he might be molting.

She thought about her mother's efforts to keep her out of the sun as a child, always insisting on a wide-brimmed hat because of the way Ruby instantly browned up in the sun. Alice sometimes rubbing cut lemons on Ruby's skin when she'd had too much sun, while Ruby protested and pulled away.

A blond woman in high heels and a skirt, accompanied by a guy who had the air of a boyfriend, came striding up the sidewalk. Their purpose appeared to be Win.

"Hi Win!" she exclaimed. "How are you doing today?" She talked too loudly. Her voice, important and self-controlled, carried up and down the street. "Do you remember me, love?" As she talked to Win she crouched down, her skirt riding up good and high on her thighs, likely giving Win an eyeful. Win's skinny arms went up around his head, bent at the elbows, kind of like the way a baby in distress would put its arms up. Ruby thought he was protecting his ears.

"Okay. I'm okay," he grunted. "Yup. Okay." He looked like he was trying to smile politely. Blondie's boyfriend remained standing, as if he was her Secret Service bodyguard. Even Ruby could tell the woman was too close to Win, was in his space. She'd stepped across his barrier. Win started to rock back and forth as Blondie talked in her loud voice.

"Did you get something to eat today, Win? Have you been drinking water? It's hot out here. You have to keep hydrated."

Watching her bend down there on the hot sidewalk, Ruby thought, *I bet* she's *never been called the c-word.*

When the woman stood to leave, she glanced at Ruby and caught her eye. Ruby looked away quickly but it was too late. She'd aroused her attention. Ruby carefully avoided eye contact but felt the woman staring at her. She moved closer.

"You're new, aren't you?" she asked in her too-loud voice.

Ruby ignored her. After all, she was deaf.

"Hey, kid," she said, "I haven't seen you here before." Her voice starting to take on an edge of annoyance. She wasn't used to being ignored.

Ruby still refused to look up.

The woman said to her boyfriend, "I know the kid can hear me. What the fuck?"

"Leave 'im alone," Win said.

"Okay, well. We'll see," she said. "Come on," she commanded her bodyguard, followed by the sound of her heels clicking away.

Ruby looked up. Win was rebuilding his fortress. She

watched him until he looked at her and she smiled at him. He smiled back then resumed his rearrangement of items around him in a semicircle. His protection.

NIGHTTIME WAS THE HARDEST. She was never too sure where to go. Nowhere seemed safe and yet she needed to stay warm and try and sleep a bit. The first three nights were spent in the 24-hour Burger King. There were lots of people sleeping in there. No one said a thing and no one bothered her. It felt safer than some other not-great options.

On the fourth night she couldn't stand to be in the fluorescent lights any longer so grabbed her backpack and went for a walk. She stayed on what seemed like a wide, busy road, but soon the lights ran out and it became deserted. There were no businesses on the street and no human activity that she could see.

It took a while before she noticed a man walking behind her in the dark. She listened to his footsteps and glanced over her shoulder several times. She walked a bit faster and he kept pace with her. She sped up to a near run and he shouted at her, "Hey!" He quickened his steps too.

"Hey," he yelled. "Stop," he commanded. His voice angry.

She stepped onto the wide road, four lanes of nonexistent traffic at this time of night. He started to run then and so did she. Bolted diagonally across the road toward the other side of the street. That's when she saw it. A business of some sort. A glass door with light on the other side. She ran toward the door, his footsteps hard behind her.

She reached the door. CITY CABS was printed on the glass.

She pushed the heavy glass door, half expecting it to be locked. It gave and she stumbled into a tiny waiting area covered in brown paneling with beige carpeting on the floor. Behind a glass cage sat the cab company's dispatcher, an older, heavyset woman.

"Can I help you?" She was clearly surprised to see Ruby.

Ruby didn't even consider playing the deaf trick with her.

"Okay, um, yeah." She had to think fast. She looked out the door to see if the man was going to dare to follow her inside.

"What do you need?" the woman asked again, reaching under her desk.

"Um." CITY CABS was also printed across the glass above her head. "Can you call me a cab?" Ruby asked.

"You want me to call you a cab?" she asked, as if she didn't believe her.

"Please?" Ruby said. "There's some douchebag following me. And yelling at me. I don't want to go out there." She checked the door again.

"Someone's following you?"

She nodded.

The woman pulled a baseball bat from under her counter, appearing ready to break someone's face. She was very convincing.

"Well, okay," she said, staring at the door. "Let the fucker try something." She picked up her mic and said to Ruby, "It might take a few minutes. But I'll call someone. Just wait. You wait right there."

Two wooden chairs with worn-out upholstery occupied the space. One faced the door and the other was right beside it.

Too anxious to sit in either one, Ruby stood in the corner, as far away from the entrance as possible. Unable to see out because it was bright inside and dark outside, Ruby watched her own reflection in the glass: a scrappy kid, hood up, with a too-big backpack. She hoped he wasn't out there watching, but sensed he was. *My second Charles Manson in one day,* she thought. Then she ducked away from the door, realizing that there was nothing stopping him, really, from coming in and dragging her away.

After fifteen silent minutes the woman, like a fortune-teller, said, "Your cab is here," and ten seconds later a car pulled up in front of the door. Ruby thanked the woman and ran out, scanning the immediate area for danger. Jumping in the front seat of the cab, she let out her breath in relief.

"Where to?" the driver asked.

"I don't know. Is the bus station open all night?"

"Are you catching a bus somewhere?"

"No. I just need somewhere to go. Some guy was following me so I don't want to stay around here."

The cabdriver cocked his head and looked at her doubtfully. "Some guy's following you?" he asked.

She nodded yes.

"And you don't have nowhere to go?"

She shook her head no. "I don't live here," she said. "I'm not from here."

"Where do you live?" he asked.

She didn't want to tell him, so said, "Another city?" She paused, then added, "I just came here to try and find my dad."

Okay, it was true, her so-called dad was missing from her life, but he was not missing in the way her words implied. And she highly doubted she would find him in this city if he were.

"Well, okay," the cabbie said, satisfied somehow. He put the car in gear and pulled away. After driving for a few minutes, he said, "If I can help you find a place to stay, do you want me to take you there?"

"What kind of place?"

"Like a shelter. For just women. They can maybe help you."

Ruby agreed. *Anyplace safe,* she thought.

When he parked, he told her to wait in the car. He went to the door and pressed the intercom buzzer.

Ruby thought about her story, being here to look for her dad. She could have said she was looking for any number of missing parental units. She thought about her notebooks at home, in which she'd written letters to her unknown mother. *Dear Mother, I bet if I was with you you'd only tell me lies to make me feel better. Dear Mother, I committed you to memory before I was born. Someday it will all make sense.*

Soon the front door opened and the driver talked to a woman. She looked over to the cab, sizing up Ruby. Back to the cabdriver. Looked at Ruby again. She seemed unfriendly, but finally nodded her head. The cabdriver came back to the car, opened the door.

"Come on," he said. "They'll take you in."

Ruby hesitated and he said, "It's a safe place to spend the night. Then you can do whatever you want."

She got out of the cab and went in.

———

THE NEXT MORNING, she washed up in the bathroom with several other women. No one said anything to her until some-one called out "Ruby" from the hallway. She'd gotten so used to being isolated even amid people, it was surprising to hear her name. "They want you in the office," the woman said, hitching her thumb over her shoulder.

Two women sat behind a desk. One of them, to Ruby's sur-prise, was Blondie with the short skirt who'd talked to Win on the street. Ruby sat down and tucked her hands inside her sleeves. They asked her so many questions she wished she had pretended to be deaf when she arrived. She started to tell them the sad story about coming to Toronto to look for her long-lost dad. Somewhere early in the story, though, she got tripped up. It didn't make sense. "What's your dad's name?"

"I'd rather not say."

"Look. You're a minor. You can be sent right now to juve-nile hall. It's like detention. I'm sure you don't want to go there."

They were clearly not going to take any shit from the likes of her. She picked up her backpack, ready to leave.

"Wait." Blondie moved to stand in front of the door. "I'm sorry," she said. "I didn't mean to threaten you."

"We only want to help you," said the other woman. "Let us call your mom. Or someone." Ruby realized then that Sandra, her social worker back home, was right. Ruby didn't belong on the streets. She didn't belong on the mean streets anywhere.

They called Ruby's mom. "Her name's Alice," Ruby told them. She smiled sweetly. Ruby knew this wouldn't go well.

Blondie got frustrated on the phone. Ruby could tell Alice was really giving them the gears, telling them she didn't have enough money to pay for the bus ticket back home. It made Ruby smile, even though it wasn't funny. She could tell Blondie had thought this was going to be a breeze. Ruby's mom had news for her.

"But she's not safe here," Blondie said into the phone, her voice rising. "She's vulnerable."

Ruby didn't hear what her mother said in response to that. She tuned them out. She tuned out all the noises until they figured it out with Alice.

Finally, they hung up the phone. They both looked at Ruby in silence.

"Next time," Blondie said dryly, "run away someplace closer to home."

Ruby burst out laughing, big and strong. It was the first good laugh she'd had in a long time.

Dana

2 0 0 6

. . .

Step One: POWERLESS

ON A MONDAY NIGHT, AT HER FIRST MEETING IN THE church basement, with their chairs arranged in a circle, Ruby noticed him right away. Noticed his too-long dark hair and beard. His rather unclean clothes. When the circle came around to him, he echoed the others.

"Hi, I'm Dana and I'm an alcoholic."

"Hi, Dana," the group intoned.

Like lots, he was here because of court. Ruby scrutinized him from across the circle, decided immediately he was iffy. Rough, but with an attentive voice. His posture like that of a feral animal. When he spoke, he lowered his chin and looked up through his eyelashes, smiled with the side of his mouth. Was this calculated? He turned his head, moved his eyes, locked them onto Ruby's. And he knew. Knew he was giving off a gravitational pull. A planet looking for its moon.

When it was Ruby's turn, she couldn't do it. Instead she said, "Hi, I'm Ruby. This is my first time here."

"Hi, Ruby," they chorused in return.

Ruby reddened and stared at her shoes—a pair of bright yellow Gazelles pitching the prospect of happiness.

At the break she stood at the refreshment table considering her options, acutely aware of Dana stirring and fussing with his coffee longer than necessary. She imagined he would speak to her, and she was right.

"Good one," he said, and when she looked at him his dark eyes watched her playfully. Was he making fun of her? She wasn't sure how to take him.

She gave him a puzzled look. "Good one?" she parroted.

"Yeah. You dodged the whole *alcoholic* thing," he laughed. "Good one," he repeated.

Ruby laughed her laugh, just to show him what she was made of, then blushed so hard she could feel it in her hair follicles.

"Can I ask you a question?" he said, his eyes mining her features.

Well that was quick, Ruby thought. But he didn't ask her out, as she expected. Instead, his question made her hair prickle.

"Are you related to any of the Blacks?"

"I don't know," Ruby said after a pause. "I'm adopted. I don't know my family."

"I bet you're related," he said keenly. "You look like them. I thought you were one right away." He briefly waved at her face. "Blacks from Little Six."

The new information, the names, *Blacks, Little Six,* tumbled into Ruby's psyche, eddied around her neurons, rolled into her bloodstream, and mixed with her DNA. She shivered with the possibility. Slowly, from that moment, those words, names, connections began to work their way into her narrative. Just like that.

"Nice family," he said, continuing his elaborate coffee preparation. She watched his hand set down the mini milk carton, stir the beige contents of his cup with the plastic stick. "You should find out. I bet you're related, you look just like them." He nodded his head at her.

Ruby had prepared for a recognition like this, for a long time, maybe even her whole life. But she didn't expect it to be so physical, his words. *You look just like them.* She felt the promise of what he said in a rush of endorphins. It was better than any drug she'd ever done.

"Have a cookie," he laughed, pointing with his chin at the package of dry cookies on the table. "You look too serious." He paused, then confessed, "They're terrible. Dollar store. It was my turn. I suck. I got no other excuse." His knuckles were scabbed from fighting or at least from punching something. Paint under his fingernails.

"I don't even like cookies," she said, cringing as the words came out of her mouth. What the fuck was wrong with her? "I mean, yeah, I . . ." She trailed off, no idea what she meant. People started taking their seats in the circle again so she turned abruptly and walked away from him. Electrified.

Step Two: BELIEF

FOR THE NEXT MEETING, RUBY MADE COOKIES, DROPPED the boys and half the cookies off at Moe's, taking the rest with her. She handed them to Dana and said, "Amends," which made Dana laugh, hard.

"Step nine," he said. "You're a quick study," and he winked at her. He actually fucking winked. Who does that? She practiced winking all the way to her seat. Unlike Dana, Ruby's winking seemed to involve her whole face. She resolved to get better at it.

In the circle, Ruby couldn't look straight at Dana without feeling her face grow hot. She watched him from the corners of her eyes. Flecks of white paint on his jeans looked like bits of ripped-up paper. Accidental brushstrokes and distracted thumb wipes. She watched him watching her.

At the break they shared a smoke and he said, "Let's get out of this place."

Step Three: GOD

AT THE BAR THEY ORDERED BEER.

"Yup, you look a lot like them Blacks," Dana said.

"Which part?" Ruby asked, wired, on a towering high ever since their first meeting, since he'd first mentioned Blacks from Little Six. "*Which part* what?" he asked.

"Which part of me makes you think that? Makes you think I'm a Black?" Ruby tested the words on her tongue, *I'm a Black*. Dana couldn't appreciate how important the knowing was to Ruby. It was everything. She'd woken up that morning dreaming about family, then tried to get back to the last dazzling image she'd had.

"They're a good-looking family," Dana teased. "Good-looking women in that family, yup."

On some level, Ruby could identify the emotional exaggeration of it all, but still she couldn't help it. When Dana talked about her potential family, said those words, *your cousins, your relatives,* it fueled her, fed her habit.

As a teenager, Ruby had searched her mother's small house, top to bottom, each room, every possible spot, hunting for her papers, letters, documents, anything that would yield a clue about herself.

She'd started in the master bedroom, with the smell of her mother's lingering perfume a reminder of Ruby's transgression, her trespass. Ruby's skin tingled as she listened in the silent house for the sounds of anyone coming home. Methodically, she advanced, her arms moving, hands opening the drawers, all ten of them. Carefully removing and returning the contents of each. Then to the closet. Dragging a chair from the kitchen, she started with the top shelf. Every shoebox, every corner. She turned up nothing. Where do mothers hide such things? A cardboard accordion folder in the bottom of the closet, behind the rack of shoes, looked promising. Full of papers. This could be it. Had to be it. But they were boring old bills. Dated 1979, 1980. The mortgage for the house in 1966. Nine years before she was even born. Things must have been more hopeful then. Dreams of having their own baby. The accordion folder yielded only disappointment. Ruby inspected it twice, unable to accept that it held nothing of what she was after.

From her mother's bedroom, she had moved on to the other parts of the house. The top shelf of the front hall closet. Unlikely, but a good hiding spot was all about the unexpected. The kitchen, with its silverware box, junk drawer, the hard-to-reach cupboard above the fridge. Ruby turned up nothing.

On the living room shelves she scanned the books, searching for one that stuck out. Something obvious. The Bible? Not likely, she smirked. Not likely to be read. She opened it anyway, nothing there.

In the basement, a promising old brown trunk. Locked. She went back to her mother's bedroom, retrieved what had looked like random keys tossed in a drawer, one of which finally fit the trunk. But the chest held nothing more than some old magazines, papers, and old school textbooks of her so-called father's.

She had turned the house upside down. Removed and replaced hundreds of items in their spots. Left few traces of her explorations except for the disturbance of dust and some micro movements that, if Alice had detected them in, say, a drawer or a corner of her closet—clothes pushed aside and moved back into place incorrectly—if she'd noticed anything out of place, she'd said nothing. A person knows how they leave their stuff, on a day-to-day basis. Small shifts would have been noticeable, Ruby convinced herself, looking back. But Alice had said nothing. She made Ruby come out and ask for what she needed. Alice never made anything easy.

———

BETWEEN BEERS DANA DRANK shots of tequila. He licked the salt and bit the lime like he was making sexy luuv. Ruby licked her lips and wondered what that would be like because she knew it was only a matter of time. His lips wet with lime juice, Dana kissed Ruby. A salty, warm, wet, boozy kiss. Her favorite kind. His beard tickled her face. She reached up and put her hand around the back of his neck, using her whole palm and fingers, moving her hand up the base of his skull, where neck meets cranium, and thought how beautiful, this graceful curve and rounding of anatomy. Ruby lingered in the luxurious softness of his hair, wanting nothing more than this very moment.

"I could do this." She sighed. "Just this. I don't need anything more." But of course, that wasn't true. They kissed again and she concentrated on tasting his limy lips. "What do you want?" she whispered.

"I want the works," he breathed into her mouth. "The full Ruby," he said, and she laughed.

At Dana's place, Ruby stifled the uneasy sensation that they didn't realize how lucky they were. That it would never be exactly like this again.

Step Four: FEARLESS MORAL INVENTORY

THE TWO OF THEM IN DANA'S SMALL STUDIO APARTMENT, drunk but not drunk enough, lay under the sheets as they had become accustomed to doing. Out of beer and out of smokes, they debated where to get money.

"You could ask your mom," he coaxed, but Ruby had told him before that this was out of the question—she'd not only burned that bridge but incinerated it and buried the ashes deep.

"*You* could ask *your* mom," Ruby said, throwing the ball back to Dana. But Ruby already knew where this was headed; still she diverted. "Or you could finish a painting," she countered. A painting would solve it. He'd only sold one so far, fussy about saying when it was finished. Even when it looked good to Ruby, he couldn't be persuaded.

"Van Gogh only sold one painting in his whole lifetime," Ruby offered, remembering her grade ten art class.

"Nothing's ready," he sighed sadly. "I could work on something later but I have to be motivated and right now I just need a drink." He rolled halfway onto Ruby and nuzzled her neck. "You juicy broad," he said, trying to make up. "I love your dimples." Coaxing her to where he wanted the decision to go.

Too easily, she gave in. "I could pawn my wedding rings again," Ruby offered. This was the effect Dana had on her. "But we have to get them out when you sell a painting."

"We will," he promised. He jumped up and searched the floor for his jeans.

Step Five: ADMIT THE EXACT NATURE OF OUR WRONGS

THEY SHOWED UP AT A MEETING ROUGH AND HUNGOVER, and somewhere in the middle of the first half, Ruby seized on a brief moment of clarity. A realization. She left the circle to go to the bathroom, locked herself into a stall, and was sick. When finished, she sat on the toilet and cupped her breasts in her hands, testing their weight, squeezing to verify a certain tenderness she already knew was there. She thought about her boys, spending the week with Moe, her hangover forcing regret to the surface. She missed them.

Step Six: DEFECTS OF CHARACTER

DANA FINALLY SOLD A PAINTING. HE CAME BACK WITH forty-eight beers and a couple bottles of wine, handing Ruby forty bucks for her rings.

Ruby hadn't mentioned anything yet. Instead they drank, and when Ruby got restless, hemmed in by the walls of his cheap room, they went out. They walked to a bar that neither of them was familiar with, full of gray-haired people slouching at their tables or curling around the curved edge of the bar, in the middle of the afternoon. Ruby's mission was to stay drunk enough.

When she'd had as many drinks as she could without getting sloppy, she told Dana. Told Dana the news. It was quick, didn't take long. Like ripping off a Band-Aid.

"Are you sure?" he asked. He refused to look at her. He licked the salt, downed his tequila, and bit the lime. He looked at the door. It was literally that fast.

"I'm going to get smokes," he said, standing up.

"I'll go with you," Ruby said.

He pointed to her full beer. "You stay, finish that. There's a store just across the street. I'll be right back." He kissed her on the cheek like a grandpa and strode out.

Ruby waited over an hour, finished her beer and drank two more before admitting to herself he wasn't coming back.

Step Seven: HUMILITY

HER DOCTOR DIDN'T FLINCH, INSISTED ON A PHYSICAL EXAM, dispensed a humiliating lecture on contraception, agreed to make the referral, and asked, "How are the boys?" bringing Junior and Aaron into it, reminding Ruby of the pressing sense that it was as much for them that she acted. To afford them the chances they deserved. Not one more living thing should be dependent on her. Dressed again, Ruby shriveled as she hurried from the doctor's office like a bandit making off with the goods, contracting her pelvic muscles and trying to forget everything.

Step Eight: LIST OF
PERSONS HARMED

THE NURSES BEHAVED DECENTLY, FOR THE MOST PART. RUBY changed her clothes and waited alone in a little room, contemplating the notion that she didn't have to go through with this. She thought about dramatic moments in movies where a woman might walk or run out of the room. But then the nurse called her name and she followed numbly down a long hallway.

The operating room made her light-headed. She noted the stirrups and averted her eyes, as if they told an obscene story she was trying to forget. Her fingers quivered, partly from nerves and partly from twenty-four hours without a drink. The room was cold. The anesthesiologist administered a quick and efficient sedative. Ruby woke up in a recovery bed tucked into clean white sheets. Every call and text to Dana went unanswered.

Step Nine: AMENDS

AFTER A COUPLE WEEKS OF RECOVERY, AND AGAINST HER better judgment, Ruby went to the Monday night meeting. Dana wasn't there and Ruby sat through the first half of the meeting anxious for a drink, some air, a cigarette. At the break she went out the back door and was about to light a smoke when Dana stepped out of the shadows.

Ruby's insides lurched. She turned away and shouldered the wall as if holding the building up, lit her smoke, and ignored him.

Dana approached Curtis, a regular at the meetings, a leader in the group, also out for a smoke. Ruby listened as Dana confessed to Curtis about his court papers, which he took from his back pocket, unfolded four times, and smoothed with his scarred fingers. He needed someone to initial for all the meetings he said he went to, most of which were untrue. Panic gripped Ruby's guts. Maybe Dana wouldn't even talk to her? How unbearable. She wanted to punish him, to ignore him, but what was the use if he didn't even notice? What Ruby really desired was for Dana to care. She wanted him to have come back for her, not for the court papers or any other reason. Curtis told Dana to come in for the rest of the meeting and talk to him after it was over. Ruby stamped out her cigarette and veered to go inside.

"Ruby." Dana said her name like a shot. Curtis disappeared. Dana tipped his chin to look at her from under his eyelashes. He looked like he was at the tail end of a bender. He held out the paper. "Would *you* initial for me?" he asked.

Ruby let out her breath from between her teeth. She paused, just looking at Dana, at his messy hair, his dirty clothes, his liquid eyes. She studied him so long that he finally looked away, broke eye contact. He stepped closer. She was still. Thinking.

"I met a guy called Eric," he said. "Eric Black. I'm thinking he might be your cousin." She knew what he was doing, keeping his tone natural, setting a shiny lure. He knew to say it as if it happened all the time that someone mentioned *her cousin* in conversation. As if she had bona fide cousins. Like she belonged somewhere, to some people who she resembled and who, in turn, looked like her.

He knew how to play it.

That was all it took.

Step Ten: PERSONAL INVENTORY

AT THE BAR, DANA DECIDED TO TEACH HER TO PLAY DARTS. She enjoyed him standing behind her to turn her hips, line up her body, hold her elbow or wrist, show her the right position. He stood too close, pressed his chest now and then against her, and she leaned back into him. Reacquainting themselves with each other's touch, breath, bodies. Ruby ordered another beer and when the waitress commented on her dart-playing Ruby belted out her tremendous laugh.

"Do you want to have a go?" she asked, purposely flirting with the waitress. The waitress exchanged a long glance with both her and Dana.

RUBY WOKE UP AGAIN at Dana's, only this time it was different. The waitress. The waitress had spent the night; they all must have fallen asleep together. She'd woken Ruby by closing the door, but Dana remained fast asleep. It was exactly like him not to notice. People came and people went and Dana stayed the same. The midmorning sun crept in the window, past the gauzy curtains, to stain the floor. Dana slept, the sheet twisted around his waist. Ruby considered how it was the same but not the same. She knew it was only a matter of time.

Step Eleven: PRAYER AND MEDITATION

FUCK DANA.
  Repeat.
  Like a mantra.

Step Twelve: PRACTICE, PRACTICE, PRACTICE

RUBY VISITED HER DOCTOR TO FOLLOW UP AFTER THE surgery, after everything. She asked Ruby how was she doing.

She meant mentally, emotionally. The doctor was much better at writing prescriptions and explaining medical procedures. Ruby found her concern peculiar.

"I'm going to AA," Ruby admitted. She had no idea why she said this, but the doctor brightened.

"Do you have a sponsor?" she asked. Ruby's focus sharpened. Was her doctor in AA? Ruby wondered. This was news.

"Yes," she said without thinking. "Dana." She stopped talking then, aware that Dana's name made it sound like her sponsor was female—same-sex sponsors were an unofficial AA rule.

The doctor nodded. "What about counseling?" she asked. "Do you have someone to talk to?"

Ruby shook her head no. "It's been a while," she said. A while since she tried counseling.

"If you need someone I have a couple of referrals," she offered. Ruby nodded her head, thinking probably not. She possessed no desire to examine her life. No fearless moral inventory here. The doctor scribbled on a piece of paper, handed it to Ruby. Two names, locations.

Ruby folded the paper three times, put it in the pocket of her good wool coat, along with the fallen-off button and a green restaurant mint.

Before she hit the exit, she'd forgotten all about it.

Johnny

1950

...

I T WAS AT THE BOARDING SCHOOL THAT THE HEADACHES
first visited Johnny. The pain started in the base of his skull and
progressed to the front of his head like a too-tight hatband.
Still he didn't recognize the pain until it was fully upon him,
blinding him and making his eyes water. It never let up and
over the course of that first morning it steadily intensified, in-
creasing to such a level that he could barely function, clouded
in a stupor of pain. Despite his agony, Johnny wasn't allowed
to remain in bed or go to the infirmary. The young priest dismissed him with an excruciating rap to the head. "Be more
obedient and your troubles will clear up." The priest turned his
back and walked away.

A VIOLENT STORM CONTINUED to rage in his head and Johnny
resisted the angry vortex that urged him to strike back. Yet
anyone who knew Johnny knew he didn't have any violence in
him. He'd been at the boarding school since he was only six,

taken away from the teachings of his grandfather, from his special bond with his mother. At the school, Johnny was notable for the abuse he took from the priests. Eight years had passed since he'd come to the school and still he didn't forget the way his backbone had ached for months after he arrived, as though he'd been scooped out from the inside and left hollow. He couldn't forget the way sadness pressed on him from all sides, how he wore it like a heavy buffalo robe over his back.

Many of the other children thought Johnny was brave for the abuse he took; they secretly admired his strength and the way he held himself. They could see that he was a watcher. Patient. Others, though, thought he was stupid. The priests sometimes hit him until they were too exhausted to continue, their arms numb and rubbery from exertion. Some were inclined to kick at him then as they stood panting with the effort. They made him eat the brown soap, locked him away in hungry, dark places, but still Johnny never once let on that they were hurting him, never once responded in anger or tried to retaliate. Even a beaten dog will eventually turn on its attacker, try to protect itself, they said. Some found it unnatural.

Johnny spoke his language, out loud, when he felt like speaking at all. What looked like defiance to some, others saw as fortitude, stoicism, or perhaps outright heroism, at least that's how they would describe it later, looking back. The priests, for their part, thought he was hopeless, an idiot—that he couldn't be taught. They did all those things to him but they never stopped to look at him. What those other children, some of them, had known was that if the priests had only stopped to see what was there, behind his eyes, they would have understood the nickname he'd earned. Some of the boys called him "kisciyiniw," in Cree. "Old man" in English. *Kisciyiniw Johnny,* they said in the dark in the dorms. They whispered it like a passed-on secret. "Kisciyiniw" because, even though he was just a child, he had clearly always been an old man. He had the grace and understanding of one of the old people. If you took the time, you'd see it too.

Kisciyiniw Johnny didn't voice his pain after that first morning of the headache. Instead, he learned to anticipate and ride the waves of agony. His body moved automatically through the duties of his regular day, with classes in the morning and, in the afternoon, the physical work of hacking with a hoe at the hard clay dirt in the potato garden. Finally, he was free to find a quiet place to retreat, inside himself, and within the pain.

The aching in his head lasted three nights, and it was on the third night that Johnny traveled not only within and through the pain but also beyond it. He could see the old barn where his body was curled in a rigid ball on the dirt floor, his eyes squeezed tight as he concentrated on riding the waves of pain. As he slowly became detached from the scene, he saw himself lying there in the dirt. He wondered for a moment, without panic or astonishment, if he was dead and his spirit was rising to dance in the sky in the place of the ancestors, but something told him this was not the case, that he should not be afraid.

What kisciyiniw remembered of that night was leaving his body behind and rising in the air as though effortlessly flying, floating above the world he normally inhabited to be given an aerial view. He remembered seeing the grounds of the school through the twilight and traveling to the place where the dorms were. Kisciyiniw Johnny had no control over his direction or destination. At that time of evening, the children were allowed to stop working. Most sat in small groups and talked quietly; some were allowed to be in the schoolyard playing a game of baseball with a ratty ball and decrepit bat. Many sat alone, reading or simply looking off into space, while some of the newer ones secretly cried so as not to be heard by the priests or other boys.

Johnny longed to go to those boys, the ones who cried, and show them that he felt their pain, to provide some solace or strength for them if he could. Instead he traveled, as if in languid flight, past the boys' dorm and to the private chambers the priests kept. There, he was not surprised by the tiny world of comfort that each priest had constructed for himself. Still with his aerial view, Johnny observed Father William in his chamber, drinking his tea and reading a book that was not the Bible, but a book on flowers and gardening that he had brought with him from England.

Kisciyiniw Johnny was also able to glimpse into the hearts of some of the priests. Father William desperately missed his country and its customs, and was dismayed to have found himself serving God in this desolate and cold place where the seeds he ordered from his native country could barely be convinced to sprout from the hard dirt before the short growing season was over and the ice and snow returned.

One of the chambers was unoccupied, but kisciyiniw Johnny could tell by the orderliness of the chamber it must belong to the young priest who had slapped him on the first day of the aching head. The narrow bed was neatly made and a pair of plaid slippers peeked out from beneath the bed. His books, all of them religious, included a prized seven-volume set, leather-bound with gold writing on the spines, on the history of the Old Testament, as well as a less impressive-looking set of dull blue books. He read: *Mystical City of God as told by the venerable Mary of Agreda.* All the books were lined up like soldiers at attention on the shelf above his small desk. The desk surface was clear except for the blotter and a pen in its holder. The chair was pushed in precisely parallel to the desk.

This young priest, he saw, was desperately in turmoil within his own spirit, using order and rigidity as an antidote to what he viewed as his own indecency. At nights, when he found himself dreaming of the budding young girls he had known as a boy, he would shudder from his fantasy, hand wet with shame, and immediately berate himself for his weakness. He would then remain awake for the rest of the night saying fervent prayers for forgiveness and guidance while kneeling on the hard surface of the floor and reveling in the deserved pain it brought to his knees. The next day the boys paid penance for the young father's guilty heart in various forms of abuse.

Finally, kisciyiniw found himself at the chamber of the fat priest who was rumored by the boys to be very bad. This priest lay on his narrow bed snoring lightly while a shiny line of drool escaped from the corner of his mouth, his paunch irregularly rising and falling. From time to time, his breath appeared to stop altogether, only to jump-start with a huff after an impossibly long duration.

The boys did everything to stay out of this priest's sights, but kisciyiniw had seen the way the dirty priest had his favorites. He knew which boys those were, not only because they were often stared at by the priest, watched in such a naked manner that kisciyiniw could not believe he was the only one who noticed, but also because of the way the favored boys themselves began to grow fat. Well, not *fat* exactly, but rather, less lean. Most of the children in the school were in a constant state of hunger—there never being quite enough food provided to compensate for the hoeing and digging in the garden, the mucking in the stables, or the hard work of repairing and maintaining the school. Certain boys, though, seemed to resist acquiring that lean and sinewed look that the other boys had in common. These boys were healthier than the rest, at least in appearance. This was because the pudgy priest went to great lengths to provide extra meals for some. And in addition to the meals, the priest had a stock of candies in his chamber that he used to entice "his" boys to visit him.

Kisciyiniw could see that this priest's heart held no remorse for the things he did to the boys in the little chamber. One boy was the same as the next in a long line of disposable children. Kisciyiniw saw the blackness and felt the agony of the child who had most recently been in the priest's chambers, tasting, as if he were that child, the sweetness of the candy turning bitter as the salt of the child's tears and the bile of shock met on his lips.

The child's despair rose in kisciyiniw's throat and beat within his aching head like a bird trapped in a house. At once he understood what the fat priest had done to those boys; what he had taken from them. The agony of knowing rose like a wail, piercing his own ears, threatening to burst his heart from its cage of ribs.

It was the last thing kisciyiniw remembered about the night. The next thing he knew he was waking up, lying in the dirt of the barn, the earliest light of dawn seeping through the many cracks and holes. The headache, mercifully, was gone. As he roused himself, he noticed the blood staining his hands, his shirt, his pants. Still he was not alarmed; he knew he wasn't hurt.

He made his way to the small creek behind the school. He removed his stained clothing and plunged it into the icy water, scrubbing the stains with fine beads of sand until the cold was too painful to bear, until it felt like ice had penetrated his bones. He then scrubbed his hands with sand, working the dirt from beneath his fingernails and the red from every crack in his skin. He worked until his hands were raw. Finally, he walked into the small stream and knelt to wash his body. As he dressed in his damp clothing he considered that he had no way back into the school. Every night the young priest went to each of the doors, jangling his keys, and one by one made a show of locking them so as to prevent any more runaways. Kisciyiniw Johnny realized that he may have been missed already, chalked up as a runaway who would have to be reported to the police as soon as morning broke. He decided he wasn't going to stick around to see if they came looking for him. He put on his socks and hard boarding-school shoes. He was prepared to walk the soles off them to return to his family.

Later, rumors reached kisciyiniw Johnny's community and

eventually found their way to his grandfather's cabin; rumors that the fat priest had been found in his bed on the night Johnny disappeared. The priest's chamber was covered in blood, his wrists slashed so deeply that officials estimated he'd bled out in a matter of minutes. Rumors of a razor blade surfaced but were quelled when none was officially reported. After the body had been removed, some of the boys at the school were forced to clean the chamber. One of the boys entered the chamber but after a few moments went out and refused to go in again, despite the beatings. He later reported to the other children that an uneasy, terrified spirit lingered there.

It seemed an obvious suicide to the police and the coroner, and the coroner's initial ruling had been so; however, the pressure applied by the priests and the church was tremendous until the final ruling on the fat priest's death became "accidental" so that he could be buried in consecrated ground with full rites.

The boys attended his mass and burial and were obligated to pray for his soul, but the only real mourning that occurred was for the loss of the extra meals. Soon those plumped-up boys returned to their previous states of semi-starvation, but relished a sinful satisfaction for the suffering the priest must have endured in his death. In all of the commotion, kisciyiniw Johnny was somehow overlooked, perhaps on purpose and perhaps not. In any event, his disappearance from the school went unremarked.

Kisciyiniw walked over a hundred miles to return to his family. He didn't die. He went back home and learned about the old ways from his grandfather. The way a boy should.

Cary

...

CRANKY WITH A HANGOVER, RUBY BROKE UP WITH Molly over the phone from her hotel room in Calgary. By evening she was already changing her mind. Or at least she was experiencing deep regret. To feel better, Ruby took herself out for supper.

She put on a simple, lightweight shirtdress, leaving the top buttons undone. The effect was sensible with the possibility of flirty. She admired herself in the mirror, thinking she was genetically lucky to have inherited a good structure—slim legs and a slight frame. Lucky, also, to be in control again. At least in control of her eating.

In the bathroom she painted eyeliner above her lashes with a tiny precision brush. Her hand trembled slightly and she thought about how lovely the first glass of red would be at the restaurant, that first soft sip warming her throat and chest. She stroked mascara on her upper lashes and dabbed it on the bottom ones. She painted her lips a deep burgundy-bronze color, perfect for smiling. She rubbed her lips together and poked with a fingertip to smooth the edges. In the mirror she practiced smiling at herself, using all her teeth, working herself up to a friendly demeanor, a good mood.

AT THE RESTAURANT SHE sat facing the room. *Back to the wall,* she thought, and smiled. An old trick—see people before they can see you. She knew it was a bit paranoid, implied: *trust no one.* But oh, how she longed to be able to. Trust someone. Or so she thought, in moments like this. Hangovers were always full of regret and longing.

"How are you this evening?" The waitress was adorable, with a deep red shade of hair and lipstick to match. Ruby smiled at her.

"Do you have a wine menu?" Ruby asked.

The waitress fumbled with the menus and Ruby raised her hand to make her stop. "Never mind"—she shook her head and laughed like they were sharing a good-humored joke. "You must have a half-liter of red? Just bring me that."

"A half-liter?" the girl said.

"Yes. Red wine. You pick. Bring me something nice." What the waitress didn't know was that Ruby had been here before. Knew there were only two reds on the menu that came in a half-liter. To Ruby, either was acceptable.

The waitress stared at Ruby, so she added, "You pick. I'll let you decide what you think—dry or sweet—how's that?" Ruby relaxed into her seat, opened her body language, playful. "And you know what?" she asked.

The young waitress leaned in expectantly.

"I love your hair," said Ruby. "It's working perfectly with your lipstick."

The waitress laughed and Ruby smiled to see her enjoy the unexpected compliment.

The winter her mother died, Ruby lost forty pounds, took up drinking with the resolve of a professional, and started a secret love affair with Molly. She entered a state that asserted, quite simply, that nothing really mattered in the end. What are we living for if only to die? All her day-to-day efforts were ultimately meaningless. She would die, her kids would die, and it would mean nothing in the end. Absolutely nothing. That's exactly what she thought, repeatedly, like a chant, in those days and months after. *Absolutely. Nothing. Matters.* At first, she said it to herself in a way that was unbelieving. Like, *Hey, look at this thing I've just discovered. It's all a hoax. This life. It's all* bullshit. *After all is said and done, absolutely nothing matters. Holy shit.* And she would dream vividly, dream after dream about purple blood, whale slaughter, low tide, and, once, about dying in a head-on car crash with a cherry-red Mustang. In the dream, after the shocking crash, she knew she was going to die and her main emotion was relief.

ONE MONTH BEFORE RUBY'S mother died, Alice experienced one of her rare lucid moments. "Am I going to die?" she'd asked Ruby.

"What?" Ruby replied, not because she hadn't heard her but because she was buying time.

"Am I going to die?" Her mother was so small in that moment, looking up at her, afraid and alone.

And what did I do? Ruby thought. *What was my response? Asshole that I am?* Ruby shook her head, remembering. *I laughed.* Regrettably, she had.

"Ha ha. No!" *Silly,* her tone implied. "Of course not. We're going to the hospital and they're going to give you a shot of vitamin K and you're going to be just fine." *Just fine.* She'd convinced herself of it, even though her mother had not been "just fine" in a long while.

RUBY JOINED A BEREAVEMENT group for people who'd had someone die. Someone died, yes, but why should grief be reserved for the dead? There were so many griefs. At the group meetings each week they painted and listened to music, once in a while heard one another's stories. For some reason Ruby thought more about Bart in that group than she did Alice. She thought about his funeral and couldn't remember his casket. The other participants in the group were white women. There were ones with dead husbands, and a mother with a dead baby, but no other woman with a dead mother. No other Indigenous woman. The ones who had lost a spouse bonded with one another. The young mother, who regularly visited her baby's cremains, was on her own. Ruby went through the motions, liked her paintings well enough, finished the group without resolving anything. It had taken meeting Molly.

The first time she spoke to Molly, Ruby twirled a glass of

wine in her fingertips, smiled her cutest smile, and stated grandly that *poetry* had *saved her*. Molly, a well-known poet, threw her head back and laughed. Ruby watched Molly's throat and realized their conversation, and Molly, were the first things, other than wine, that she'd been interested in since her mother died.

"It's true!" Ruby protested.

Molly settled down and looked at Ruby, as if for the first time. "Tell me," she said. "I want to know."

"Spiritual things, religion, *pfft*"—Ruby dismissed those notions by waving her hand in the air. "I envy people who have that. I want to be able to believe in the endless festival. But I don't," she frowned. "But poetry," she continued, "poetry has a way of rising to the occasion." Then she stated extravagantly, *"The poets can be my clergy,"* making fun of herself so she could see Molly laugh again.

On the sidewalk in front of the house, after they'd left the party but couldn't seem to part from each other's company, Ruby said, "I wish you could kiss me," and just like that her wish came true.

A secret, reckless, ridiculous, and impossible love affair. She couldn't tell anyone about Molly, couldn't say Molly's name because people would recognize it right away. Molly, however unconventional she might want to appear, was extremely concerned with her "public and professional reputation."

"And also with your *heterosexual* reputation," Ruby said, accusingly. "You would hardly know it's 2018 and the great majority of the world is just *over* that."

"And you're not? Concerned?" Molly asked.

"It's complicated. I'm married to money now. Literally married to my job."

Molly had laughed so beautifully when Ruby told her about her husband. "His name is Richard-also-known-as-Dick. Tricky Dick. And," Ruby added, "I've slept alone for the entire two years we've been married. I don't trust him to have my best interests at heart."

After working her way, part-time, through two university degrees, one in the arts and the other in business admin, Ruby struggled to find a decent-paying job. She'd found work teaching life skills to adults, where she regularly learned more than they did, and at the same time picked up shifts serving at a bar. She attended her college's networking events to try and find a break into the corporate world. Dick, a business owner—several businesses, in fact—courted her. Not as an employee, but romantically. Ruby was flattered, assumed they both saw each other as a novelty—something out of the ordinary for each of them. Now she thought of Dick's motives differently.

"He's trapped me," she told Molly after one too many drinks. "He made me a *shareholder*"—she put up her hands to make air quotes. "Now I'm *implicated*." Air quotes again. "But he doesn't hit me," she told Molly. "And I'm not poor anymore. I just didn't see it coming." She explained to Molly, drunkenly, about being manipulated by Tricky Dick into signing suspicious documents. "It was like a puzzle, when I figured it out." She said this as if she knew what all the entanglements were, but, really, wondered all the time if she'd even seen the full picture yet. But she'd seen enough.

"Well," Molly said of the whole heterosexual business, "it's not like I'm a *lesbian*. It's not like I'm going to run away with you and get *married*. And I'm not into labels. I don't want to give others the chance to label me. You of all people should understand that."

"You're a *poet*," Ruby said. "Everything you write is taken as autobiography. Your readers are labeling you with every poem you publish. You know that, right?" But Ruby had to concede that Molly was right on some level: those nouns were hard to squirm away from, and people, for some reason, were fixated on applying a definition, however inadequate, before they could finally relax.

The next day, after their fight, Molly sent flowers to Ruby's office. She signed them *From your GF*. Ruby chose to read it as *Girl Friend*. She took it as a concession.

FOR TWO DAYS BEFORE the cremation, Ruby's mother's body lay at the funeral home in a simple pine casket that was missing one of its fasteners. A closed casket, fitting for such a private woman, covered in a plain white woolen blanket. It was just Ruby at the funeral home with the body. There was no one else. She worked and worried those fasteners, through the blanket, with her fingertips as she stood by the casket's side and throbbed from a spot in her chest. She stroked the woolen cover near the place she thought her mother's hand might be. In some ways a closed casket was both a blessing and a torment.

Alice appreciated pretty things, nice shoes, insisted on quality, but at the same time enjoyed instant coffee in the mornings and white-bread toast. Bought carnations and grew marigolds with their bitter-secret scent. She liked a lot of things that didn't cost too much. Life had taught Alice how to make do.

Would she have forgotten about me if I'd let her? Ruby wondered. In the end Ruby was there for Alice because it wouldn't occur to her not to be there; she was Alice's witness. Ruby ran away as a teenager but she always came back. Sometimes we choose our family and sometimes we are chosen. We're lucky and we're unlucky. Alice was the only mother she had. Ruby learned for herself the things she wasn't taught to know. Being an Indigenous girl.

"I SHOULD HAVE TOLD YOU," Ruby whispered, leaning over the casket, touching the fastener through the blanket. "I should have told you I don't hold anything against you." Ruby knew Alice had lived, as most mothers do once their children are gone, with a culpable feeling of letting Ruby down, of having done her a disservice in some way. Ruby said, "Guilt is for suckers. I know you did your best."

From the funeral home Ruby went to the nursing home to pack her mother's few belongings into a box. She took the Nivea cream from the nightstand, unscrewed the cap and held the jar to her nose, the smell enough to make her tear up again.

She recalled the sensation in the back of her throat—Nivea cream, when she was a child—when she snuck into her mother's room and ate it by the mouthful, one tube-squeeze at a time. It slid down her throat and she was filled with the smell-taste. Now, instead of a tube, she bought it in a jar. In her bedroom at her own house Ruby found the smell was not quite the same. She had no belief that she would see her mother again, or that her spirit was present, somehow—there was no comfort in that. Some comfort in the Nivea cream and the smooth red pearl-like bath beads from the 1980s. When she held them up to her nose they smelled like her mother used to, before she got sick. They reminded her of a time long ago, of innocence. Or *perceived* innocence, anyway.

Ruby remembered her mother's question that night—"Am I going to die?"—sounding like it came from the bottom of a tall thin glass. Ruby asked herself over and over why she was so mean, so dismissive, so impatient, *so not the daughter my mother wanted or needed*.

Later, she asked Molly, "Why do we resist our mothers so hard?"

Molly had no answer other than "Sometimes we love each other in fierce and confusing ways."

Molly published a series of poems called *Grief, Found* that went on to win the largest poetry prize in the country. When Ruby could bring herself to read them she saw her experience with her mother's death all over the poems.

What Ruby didn't talk to Molly, Dick, or anyone else about was the way she felt the dormant black seeds of her first miserable death—her teenage boyfriend, Bart—bloom uncomfortably in the wake of her mother's death. The same feelings of confusion and despair, of utter emptiness. She found herself one second squeezing tomatoes in the produce section and the next needing to drop everything and leave the store, overwhelmed by an urgent sense of sorrow. Was she surprised that this new death gave rise to one so old? Probably, since she thought she had buried Bart for good, cut off the grief, bold and quick. She couldn't stand the lingering, not then and not now. When people left, they left—and she moved on. She'd fooled herself for a long time, thinking she had that power.

THE RED-HAIRED WAITRESS BROUGHT Ruby a small crystal glass of amber liquid, set it down in front of her.

"Oh, this isn't mine," Ruby started to say, thinking for a moment that there was a mistake, and then, before the waitress could say it, Ruby looked up to see who had sent the drink. A man at a table across the room—she turned her head to see him better—looked at her intently, met her eye, and nodded, smiling slightly. Sheepish. A big man, a bit heavy, with curly hair that needed to be cut. And good lord, thought Ruby, a full, unruly, brown-gold beard. The beard sent her thoughts veering toward Dana but she stopped herself, welcoming instead the fleeting image of kissing the stranger and having his pot-scrubber of a beard rub her chin, scratch at her top lip, tickle the divot under her nose. He was alone at his table. She couldn't tell if he had finished his meal or was just beginning.

"From the gentleman," the waitress said, a bit off-cue. "Port. Very nice selection."

"Well." Ruby laughed just a little, deep in her throat, delighted. "Tell him thank you. I'll save the port for after my meal, then," and she pushed it forward with her fingertips. She looked again at the man, not usually her type at all. For one thing, younger than she would normally go for. Maybe even in his thirties. Unless he'd aged well—it could happen. After all, the beard was like a disguise, but there was no gray in it. He smiled at her again and she nodded her head to him, looking amused. He rose and walked across the expanse of the carpeted restaurant, his drink in his hand, to join her at her table.

"I'm Cary," he introduced himself and reached to shake her hand.

"Angel," Ruby said without missing a beat, giving his hand a firm squeeze.

He laughed. "Yes, you are," he said, and Ruby joined him in his laughter.

IN HIS BED, HER CELL phone buzzed. They'd just finished a sweaty and notably vigorous session, and he'd surprised her by letting her tie his wrists to the bedposts with a couple of his dramatic red ties. She grabbed the cell from the side table, checked the screen, and recognized the number of her doctor's office. She hit DECLINE and tossed the phone into her purse. It was bad enough they called her during the daytime—now it was extending into the evening. She'd ignored the calls for well over a week already.

"Anyone important?" he asked. She liked that he was curious but assumed no right to know anything about her. She was especially gun-shy of men, or women for that matter, who acted entitled or possessive when there was no history to back it up. This fellow, Cary, he seemed as agreeable as a goldfish.

———

RUBY THOUGHT OF HERSELF as the "work hard, play hard" type, putting in her time so she could be a bit reckless when the work was done. For years she'd held it all together under that banner. The earnest drinking had started the very night her mother died. Dick took her home, sat her at the table, and put a bottle of good Scotch in front of them with two glasses. They sat at the table and drank. One of the few things they'd done together in almost a year.

But that wasn't all. More recently, she'd been slipping. She didn't know another way to describe it. From time to time she forgot things—alarming things that she knew, and yet they vanished from her mind like she had no control over what was happening inside her head. The order of operations got turned around. Confused.

One morning she had found herself sitting with the phone in her hand, staring at the number pad. She knew she was calling the supervisor in Calgary. She knew she had called him a hundred times before. She knew the numbers she was supposed to dial. But for some reason she couldn't figure out which number came first. She had no idea where to start. It was a horrible sensation and she got up and walked out of her office, down the hall, and into the ladies' room where she locked herself in a stall, sat on the toilet seat, and quietly freaked out.

The second time, she had perched on the bench at the foot of her bed with her shoes on and her socks in her hand and could not solve the problem of what had gone wrong. She had no recourse except to take all her clothes off, put them in a pile on the bed, and start over with getting dressed for the day. By the time she got to the socks and shoes it came back to her how it worked—*socks first, then shoes.*

These episodes frightened her and she finally made an appointment with her doctor.

"WHAT WOULD YOU LIKE?" Ruby asked Molly, early on. "What would you really like?"

"The perfect verse," Molly said.

"I only have love. And a little bit of leftover wine. And these"—she opened her palm and displayed two wine corks on which she'd written the dates and occasion of consumption. And both their names. As if she needed a special reason for drinking.

CARY, SHE FOUND, DIDN'T need to pretend. About the drinking. On her second evening in Calgary, they lay in bed listening to k. d. lang sing "Hallelujah." The song sent tears running down Ruby's cheeks, into her ears and her hair.

"This is stupid," she said while Cary brushed her damp hair back from her face. His glass jar of ice and amber whiskey rested on the bed, propped against his chest.

"What's stupid?"

"I don't even *like* this kind of music," she pleaded. "Now I'm all snot and sadness."

Cary had created some impressive playlists. Thousands of songs. They were rarely without music. "Let's Dance" was next in the shuffle and Ruby reached for her wine bottle, which was balanced on the carpet and leaning against the nightstand so it wouldn't spill. She sat up just enough to pour the rest of the bottle into her stained glass. Cary steadied his jar.

"Who sings this—" she started to ask, and then exclaimed, "Is this Bowie?"

Cary nodded.

"I went to his concert," Ruby said, setting her glass on the nightstand and flinging herself back on the bed. "I love him."

She danced in the bed, lying on her back, using her arms. "Come on," she laughed, nudging Cary. He grumbled, flipped onto his back, tried to join her in her drunken dance, both of them facing the ceiling, twirling their arms in the air, singing the chorus, his amber glass spinning, shimmying their shoulders, cold liquid splashing.

On the soft inside of her forearms were a series of marks. Horizontal scars running nearly the length of elbow-crease to wrist. If Cary saw them he didn't comment, didn't ask what they might mean. It was probably obvious they stood for pain. But more than that, they *were* pain. But even more yet—a release from despair. It's mostly women who cut. Or so the so-called experts said. In a world of experts, not one of them could be trusted.

The scars were old, started in her angsty teen years. But just because she didn't do it anymore didn't mean much. There were days when the alcohol wasn't enough and she could easily revert to cutting. But she'd always maintained just enough self-control or self-awareness, whatever you want to call it, to understand how the cutting would affect her life, her job, everything she'd built her life around, all that she'd worked so hard for. So much worse was the cutting secret than the alcohol that she didn't dare do it anymore. Had never directly disclosed it to anyone, despite the evidence on her body. And yet, the cutting—well. If the two coping mechanisms were placed side by side to evaluate the effect each had on a person's life, surely the one that society accepted more—the drinking, alcoholism, whatever you wanted to call it—the booze was by far the greater destructive force on a human life than a little cutting, bleeding, and bandages. But the alcohol was the one acceptable coping strategy, if you were careful. Didn't get too sloppy about it.

Ruby thought of her boys, just then. Junior grown, Aaron nearly so. They'd all drunk beer together recently, full of lively stories, at first. Ruby's guard was down, and then alcohol brought out the words. As it will. He laughed while he said it.

"I was so scared of you." Junior. He said it twice.

He laughed.

Sometimes laughter is tears' imposter. Ruby felt too sober. Not drunk enough. Someone once said tears are proof of powerlessness. Well, so is laughter.

She felt wild with wanting them to know all the things overshadowed by that one thing. The imperative of a mother is to be a "good" mother. The bad loomed so large and ugly while the good always receded, shyly, into its own room. Never taking up the same space, never equal. Never a one-for-one trade; more like a thousand good for one bad.

Ruby thought of all the things not accounted for: carefully keeping the soap out of their eyes, building forts from couch cushions, storytelling, clean clothes and hair and faces, saying no to cookies, saying yes to cookies, medicine, listening to their dreams, laughing instead of crying, make-believe, pawning stuff to go bowling, balloons on every birthday, talking when one more word threatened to break her, sitting on their beds until they slept, waking up each morning, believing they were all headed for something better, returning home each time she left, suppressing a bubbling fury, remembering what it felt like to be a child and helpless, thinking she was honestly aspiring to spare them the same feelings, living the contradiction of excess and discipline.

And on the other side, frightened little boys and she didn't know enough not to talk when she should listen. The muttered responses, the excuses—*I tried, I loved you, took care of you, I made a family for you*—weren't for them, they were for her. Her wishes, not theirs. She considered too late that the same thing wrong with her wasn't wrong with them.

It wasn't so much the question of what they inherited, but what they would do with it. Fury and love as big as the prairie sky, edgeless, boundless. What was ever inherited without grief? His fear made her so ashamed she didn't hear Junior say, "I could be afraid of you and love you too." Children aren't the only helpless ones.

"FUCK EVERYTHING," RUBY TOASTED, grabbing her glass and clinking it with Cary's, spilling her drink over the rim. Wine rained down on them and Ruby unleashed her massive laugh. She drank in quiet protest to it all.

"Hahaha," Cary chuckled deep in his throat.

He doesn't get me, thought Ruby. *But he wants to. Points for that.*

MOLLY TEXTED RUBY SEVERAL long, semi-accusatory messages that included lines beginning with things like *The scent of your hair on my pillow* and *I remember everything.* All the words a provocation, and Ruby wasn't up to anything more challenging than mechanically pouring the next glass of wine and periodically tying up Cary with the red ties and fucking him in his rumpled bed.

FRIDAY MORNING RUBY WENT for a run to try and quell the hangover before the meetings she was officially in Calgary to attend. In the bushes at the side of the trail she heaved dryly, the contents of her stomach long ago purged completely on another section of the trail, black bitterness falling like cement into the dirt. But still her body wouldn't quit trying to expel something no longer there.

When she was a teenager discovering the delusion of booze, Ruby's legs and arms were covered in bruises from her repeated fallings down, dark new ones overlapping those yellowing from age. She was frequently sick. Her science teacher, guessing correctly, told her throwing up alcohol was the body's response to being poisoned. Binge drinking, he said, was poisoning yourself. "How stupid can someone be to intentionally poison themselves?" he had asked. The notion stuck with her.

Later, as an adult, she thought about it and wondered, What if the poison was already in your body, and it trumped the poison of the alcohol? And what if you had no way to expel the toxins that were already there? The alcohol was a sort of clearing mechanism, to try and expel the preexisting and fast-holding poison. In that way alcohol, in her mind, became something of a remedy. Medicinal. That was the context in which she came to see her morning runs, too—an attempt to clear the toxins, whatever they were, self-inflicted or organic. She wanted to go back and tell her grade ten science teacher: *We're all poisoned to varying degrees, from the minute we're born.*

She retched once more in the bushes and wiped her mouth with her sleeve. Back on the trail she resumed her run, focused on her feet pounding, her heart in rhythm with her breathing, her body sweating out the venom that always refilled itself almost as fast as she expelled it.

AFTER HER MEETINGS SHE agreed to meet Cary at a restaurant close to his place. She was still hungover from the night before. He'd texted her five times in the course of the day, causing her some mild alarm.

As usual, she chased her hangover with a suppertime glass of red, sipped gently, with food, to give her guts a break. By the time she poured the second glass the effects were as desired and she told him, "I'm supposed to go home tomorrow." He already knew this. More than once since their first night together she'd told him she would be leaving Saturday.

———

JUST AS SHE NOTICED the doctor's office had stopped calling, Dick texted her. "Your doctor's office called me. Call them back, please."

She replied, "I'll try. Busy."

"Stop being a child. I don't have time for this" was the Dickster's only response.

Ruby didn't call her doctor's office back. She didn't want to know what they had to tell her. She considered extending her trip as a way to avoid her real life, back home.

SHE FELT GUILTY FOR being relieved when her mother died. Her mother, who had become not her mother at all. Her mother who thought she had protected Ruby from her explosive and angry father for all those years. Her mother, ladylike. A fine dresser. A bit neurotic. Hard on Ruby. In those last months, her mother completely broke down. *Très petit monstre* was what came out in Molly's book.

"She became a monster." Ruby had tried the line out on Molly, but, even then, found it didn't do justice to the situation. To the picture she wanted to draw. "She stopped being herself," Ruby explained. "She chewed her fingernails and looked up at me from under her eyelids as if she was a bad child." She refused to take a bath or wash her hair. Cried if she was forced. She hid her supper in her room until the whole place smelled like rotten food and unwashed hair. "I hated going there,"

Ruby admitted. "I have no idea where my mother went." Finally she confessed, "I should have been kinder. I could have been."

MANAGING A HANGOVER WAS a tactical and time-consuming business. A puzzle or problem to solve. A thing that kept her busy and well occupied.

But Saturday morning she rolled gently out of Cary's bed expecting stabbing pain, the liquid-leveling sensation inside her skull. Naked, she trundled easily to the bathroom. Normally she would slouch carefully over her knees as she peed, getting a bead on the kind of devastation that was in store for her. Instead she stood easily, leaned in to flush, oddly nausea-free. She caught her reflection in the mirror and thought about her usual hangover-morning routine—find the Advil, Gravol, saltines, and coffee to wash it all down. How strange not to need to go on autopilot for the ingrained order of operations. She took a moment to adjust.

Her cell phone pinged. A text. It was Dick. "Your doctor says it's a B-vitamin deficiency." A second message displayed. "You can stop worrying." Maybe Dick was more sensitive than he let on. She always felt a bit more forgiving when they were apart.

BACK IN CARY'S BED, they fucked too quickly and Ruby was left feeling restless and aggressive. Cary lay on his stomach on the bed. Ruby watched him for a few minutes.

"You're not going to fall asleep, are you?" She slapped his ass cheek once, not too hard. She waited and he didn't respond. She pictured him starting to cry into the pillow and thought how intolerable that would be. "Does Cary need a spanking?" she asked playfully.

He still didn't answer but wiggled his ass slightly.

She slapped him again. Reached for her drink. "You might like that," she said. "A little spanking." She slapped his ass again, enjoying how it jiggled a little. The skin starting to flush where her slaps landed.

Cary moaned softly into the pillow.

"Is Cary a bad boy?" she teased, slapping his buttocks again. She slapped him four, five, six times on the same cheek, raising the color. Still he lay still. She reached around, found him erect, and laughed spectacularly. She slapped his cheek again.

"Say yes," she said. "You have to say yes."

"Yes," he moaned into the pillow.

Ruby laughed again and spanked him as hard as she dared, then pressed her fingers to the red skin to quell the blow. "Jesus Christ," she said. "I love spanking you!"

Cary rolled onto his back, pulled her close for maximum skin contact. She straddled his body, twisted his nipples. "You like that?" she asked.

"Maybe." He put his hands easily around her rib cage. "Or maybe," he flipped her over onto the bed, leaned over her, kissing her with his old-whiskey breath, pushing her arms out wide, "maybe I'll tie *you* up for a change." He took one wrist and put it into the tie still looped over the bedpost. It hung loose around her wrist.

"And do what?" she asked, laughing, letting him move her other wrist and pull the tie around it. This one he yanked tighter.

"Oooh," she said, wriggling on the sheets. "Someone's frisky now."

As he retightened the first red tie he said, "I could tie you up and keep you." He tried to laugh, not looking at her. He checked the restraint at the bedpost. "Not let you go back," he added.

Something shifted. Her senses sharpened. She tugged at the ties on her wrists. "You don't have to do *that*." She kept her voice light even though his comments alarmed her. "I'll come back to visit you. Probably a lot."

"Or maybe you'll just forget about me," he said morosely. "Some sucker to have a fling with in Calgary and then you go back to your real life." He sat beside her on the bed now, running his fingers lightly up and down her midriff, raising goose bumps on her skin, his eyes distant.

"You don't even have to tell me your real name, *Angel*," he said.

"Yeah?" she said, working hard to keep the easy teasing tone in her voice.

"I know you just fine without it," he said.

"Oh, you do, do you?" Ruby's mind raced.

"Your story is written all over your body," he said. He touched Ruby's sharp hipbones, one and then the other. Across her abdomen he skimmed the scars of bearing children before running his fingers up her ribs, one at a time, as if counting them. He looked wistful, sitting there, naked. *So boyish,* she thought. She wiggled away from his fingers as her nipples hardened.

And then he did the unforgivable. He lifted his hand and stroked her inner forearm, tied above her head. With his whole large palm, he stroked her scars, just once, but fully, his hand covering them, warm and matter-of-fact, he stroked with a downward motion of his arm.

Ruby's guts tightened. She seethed with a surprising and instant anger. She hated him right then, more than she had hated anyone in recent memory. Ruby wanted to pull away from his touch, but she forced herself to keep a poker face, look at him, calmly.

"The only things I have going for me right now are you and a 750-piece puzzle I've nearly finished," he joked.

"I won't forget about spanking you," she said. "I'll definitely come back for that." She laughed falsely.

He snapped out of his daze. "You liked that, didn't you," he said, the teasing tone back in his voice now.

"Yum," she replied. "Hey. I have to pee again." She shook her wrists, which she already felt loosening up. He untied one then the other and she rolled away from his touch, relieved.

AT THE AIRPORT CARY parked properly, despite her protests, and hauled her bag to the counter for her. Outside security, he lingered.

"Stay," he said. "You can spank me every night."

She handed Cary a wine cork with the date and their first

names on it. *Angel + Cary.* She wasn't angry anymore, just tired. She kissed him on the cheek.

"Be good?" he said.

"I already am!" She laughed her too-loud laugh and people turned their heads. She went through security. Didn't look back.

Mel

1 9 7 6 , 1 9 8 9

...

THE DAY THE SOCIAL WORKER PICKED UP THE DARK-HAIRED infant from the foster home on one of the alphabet-lettered streets and drove it across town to its new home on the east side—no larger than the one it had just come from but supposedly more proper—she looked away. First, from the foster home conditions. She pretended not to notice the smell from the baby's crib. The fact that the baby, almost nine months old already, couldn't sit up. She tried not to feel the soggy bottom end or hear the baby squeal with fear or pain—who knew which? No one had bothered to get to know the child's sounds yet.

Then, on drop-off, the baby shrieking, the social worker looked quickly away from the adoptive father's too-bright eyes. She focused instead on the new mother, Alice, and the care she took to keep a clean house. All was in order as the social worker dropped the cranky baby off and checked the appropriate boxes on her papers.

———

SIX MONTHS LATER, WHEN the social worker did her home visit, she was in a hurry. She could see the dark-haired baby was in good shape, had gained weight, was crawling around on the spotless floor, and, most significantly, was no longer bawling a blue streak. *Check, check, check,* went the social worker's pen.

"She had boils on her bum," Alice was saying.

The social worker nodded, jotted down *boils* in the file.

"When she arrived here. She had the boils. Already . . ." Alice trailed off.

The social worker nodded but didn't write anything down.

"I took her to the doctor, got salve. They're all cleared up now."

"Do you need reimbursement for the salve?" the social worker asked, pen poised. "I might be able to put in a requisition."

"No. I mean, that's not what I meant." Alice's face turned red. "I just wanted you to know. When she came from the foster home she had these boils. They were terrible." Her voice sounded like she was pleading.

The social worker stifled a yawn.

"But they're better now. They're all healed," she said proudly.

"That's great news," the social worker jotted *healed* but no mention of the foster home. *Keep it simple,* she thought.

The husband—the social worker checked her notes for the

name—Melvyn, Mel, yes, she would note that Mel made an appearance in the kitchen. Although he was unshaven, smelled slightly of night-before alcohol, and was apparently between jobs, the worker declined to note any of these facts in the file. The man did, after all, have a lovely English accent that somewhat redeemed his poor showing on the home front.

Mel poured himself a cup of coffee, turned to face her, leaning one hand against the counter behind him. He refused to sit. Instead he towered over them in the small kitchen. His voice was too loud. But most men tended to be that way when they thought they were being challenged. The social worker had no intention of confronting anyone if she could help it. Besides, she had nowhere else to place the baby anyway. *This looks like a fine enough home to me,* she thought, *better than a single mother with no prospects, that's for sure,* and she packed up her papers, already preoccupied with her next appointment. The social worker officially closed the file at one year.

ON HER FOURTEENTH BIRTHDAY, the girl, now named Ruby, looked in the phone book and picked up the phone in the afternoon when no one else was home. She used the extension in the basement, feeling like she needed to hide. Like she was betraying someone. Breaking all the rules, spoken and unspoken. She dialed the number for social services.

"Can I talk to someone about being, um, *un-adopted?*" she asked the receptionist. In the background she could hear babies crying and busy waiting room sounds. She was put on hold before the phone rang through to someone else.

"Sandra speaking. How can I help you?" The woman had the voice of a heavy smoker, rough and on the raw side.

"Um, okay. Well. I was adopted?" Ruby tried to explain. "In, like, 1975?" Sandra on the other end was silent, so she continued. "My family, well," she hesitated. "It isn't good here. I'm, it's . . . It's kind of hard to explain."

"Well, first of all, let me tell you something, missy," Sandra croaked. "It doesn't matter that you were adopted, okay? So just get that idea out of your head right now."

Ruby didn't like the way Sandra talked to her. But Ruby had, over the last couple of months, developed an attitude. Trying to be a tough case. She added a hard edge to her voice and persisted with Sandra. "So I can't, like, *undo* it, or something?" She asked the question as if Sandra was lying to her.

"No. You can't just *send yourself back*." Sandra laughed hard, which turned into a cough. Ruby's face burned with humiliation as she waited for Sandra to be able to continue. "Those are your parents, legally," Sandra said, still amused. "You can't *undo* an adoption."

Disappointed and embarrassed, and a little bit angry, Ruby said, accusingly, "Well, you guys put me here. Social services put me here. And it's not right. What can I do, then, to get out of this?"

"First you'll have to give me your name. We can start a file, send it for investigation. Are you in danger right now?"

Ruby thought about the empty house. "No?"

"Okay then, tell me your name and what the problem is, exactly."

"Um," Ruby said reluctantly. Big pause, and then she carefully took the receiver from her ear with both hands and quietly set it back on the phone cradle.

SIX MONTHS EARLIER, Alice and Mel had split up for the umpteenth time.

"This time it's for good," Mel vowed.

On one of their awkward but obligatory father-daughter visits, Mel picked up Ruby in his car and took her to see his new place—a run-down rooming house where, as it turned out, he lived with more than a dozen international university students. Mel's room was at the back of the house and was the only one with a parking stall and its own private entrance.

Dingy pink, yellow, and off-white linoleum squares covered the floor of Mel's new apartment. Ruby looked around. An old table and two chairs in the kitchen area and a small bathroom right next to it. An old brown couch pushed against the back wall of the apartment. Mildew and other people's cooking smells. A few of her father's clothes hanging from a closet rod built into a corner.

A chair blocking a small locked door caught Ruby's interest. Mel showed her how the door led to the rest of the house. She peered down a long empty hallway with a common kitchen to the left. The students, the house's regular residents, all used the front door of the enormous house, where their mail collected on a tiny table; their doors were either on the main floor or upstairs.

"I don't use this door. Ever," Mel told Ruby, closing the door. Obviously not a student and too old to be living in a university residence, Mel wasn't allowed in the students' space.

After the door there wasn't much else to see. Ruby was quiet and so was Mel. They ended their visit early.

They were about to get into the car for Ruby to go home.

"Hello, Mr. Valentine," one of the students greeted Mel, saying his name carefully, as if trying it out for the first time.

"Cheers," Mel said brightly, more enthusiastic than he'd been all afternoon with Ruby. Mel shook the student's hand. "And call me Mel," he said, before he introduced Ruby. The student, Sam, was friendly, smiling. They chatted about the weather, and Mel asked Sam about his studies. Ruby wondered why, when her dad talked to strangers, his accent seemed to get more intense. Watching Mel talk with Sam, Ruby realized Mel was lonely. She wondered, for the first time, what he did in all the time when she didn't see him.

RUBY'S MOTHER WAS ALREADY seeing an unemployed musician named Jay. Exactly what Jay was unemployed from was unclear to Ruby. Jay sat all day at the kitchen table, taking up all the space and playing his guitar in an unserious way. Sometimes he sang at an annoyingly high pitch that only he thought sounded good. Her mother called him "babe" and touched him a lot. Ruby always made a point of rolling her eyes and leaving the room as dramatically as possible.

ONE DAY, RUBY TRIED to visit Mel unannounced, at the rooming house, but his parking spot at the back of the house was empty and he didn't answer his door. For almost an hour, she waited on the back steps. The door was locked but she got up to try it several times anyway. She slouched back on the steps and waited again for another half an hour. Getting cold, she finally thought to check under the mat for a key. Nothing. She stood on her tiptoes and ran her fingers along the ledge of the trim at the top of the door. Dirt and then something, a light metal object, fell to her feet on the mat.

She let herself into the small apartment. Ruby looked around at the sad-sack excuse for a home. She had maybe been hoping it would've improved from her memory of it, but it hadn't. She moved the chair blocking the small locked door, peering again into the empty hallway. The door was incidental, but intriguing. Ruby thought of the portal in the back of the closet in *The Lion, the Witch and the Wardrobe,* leading to a whole new world. She stared for a few seconds longer before closing the door and locking it back up.

In the cupboards above the sink, a can of beans, a saltshaker, and a bottle of vodka, more than half full. In the fridge some ketchup packets, a near-empty jar of marmalade, and a half carton of eggs. Something spilt and crusty on the bottom shelf.

Ruby took a small tumbler off the drainboard, filled it half full with vodka, put the bottle back. Little sips from the tumbler resulted in warm tendrils flowing down her throat and into her chest, then filling her belly with fire. She continued to sip, sitting at the kitchen table.

When Mel arrived home, she was drunk on his vodka. And Mel wasn't alone. His woman-friend watched as he called Ruby's mother and yelled into the phone, then sent Ruby home in a cab. "Sometimes I hate kids," she heard Mel declare to the woman, who laughed stupidly. Her perfume was overpowering, and before Ruby left she threw up in front of Mel's parking spot.

JAY SAT AT THE kitchen table in his underwear and sang songs about loving and losing a girlfriend. He sang earnestly and longingly, his face contorting and his voice high.

In her mother's bedroom, pretending to use the mirror, Ruby said, "You're his rebound, you know." Her mother's face went long and Ruby immediately felt bad.

RUBY WENT OUT WITH her new boyfriend, Derek, and two of his friends. They shared a twenty-sixer of Five Star whiskey. It was her favorite brand because of the plastic star that you could peel off the bottle. She wanted to wear it like a sheriff's badge but instead put it in her pocket to take home. When she was a little girl her dad gave her all the plastic stars from his bottles to play with. She had a box full of them under her bed.

Derek's friend Rich started singing the Foreigner song, "he's a dirty white boy, dirty white boy," shoving Derek and punching him in the arm. Derek laughed along. Derek liked to imply he was Italian, but Ruby knew better. He was just like her, adopted and Native. He laughed along with the song. Ruby, drunk, joined in, and soon she was singing the song's chorus at the top of her lungs. "Dirty white boy, dirty white boy."

———

JAY SAT IN THE kitchen and watched Ruby make Kraft Din-
ner. "You're not going to eat all that, are you?" he said. Then,
to her mom, "She better be careful, she'll get fat."

Ruby's mom made a small sound of disapproval, moved to
the kitchen sink, and started rinsing dishes.

Jay needs to fuck right off, Ruby thought, but kept it to herself.

"Isn't that right, *big bum?*" Jay laughed.

Ruby, with her back to Jay, rolled her eyes pointedly at her
mom, tossed dishes loudly into the sink, and left the room.

Ruby knew something about Jay that nobody else did. Ruby
was once kind-of-friends with the daughter of the last woman
Jay lived with. The girl told Ruby a thing or two about Jay.
Confided, or almost confided, about Jay maybe touching her.
Something like that. It wasn't very clear to Ruby, who, to be
honest, was only half listening anyway. The last time she saw
the girl, the kind-of-friend had put on weight, suddenly gained
like thirty pounds for no apparent reason. Ruby began to see
how Jay's constant criticism could undermine a person's self-
worth. How Jay probably did the same thing to the friend that
he was doing to Ruby. How the friend might have simply given
in and become whatever demeaning names Jay insisted on calling her.

RUBY, DEREK, AND DEREK'S two friends walked all over the
city, drunk and aimless.

"Let's walk to my dad's place," Ruby suggested. "My *adoptive* dad," she corrected herself.

"Is he there?" Derek asked.

"I think he's out of town." Ruby had no idea if this was true.

When they arrived, the car wasn't in the parking space. Ruby found the hidden key and they spilled into the tiny apartment.

"Your dad lives *here*?"

"Yeah, what about it?" Ruby challenged.

"Let's smoke some hash on the stove." Derek looked in the drawers but there was only one knife. "We can't hot-knife with only one knife," Derek said to Ruby in a whiny voice, as if it was her fault.

"We can flatten out a spoon," someone suggested. "I've done it that way before." The guys started banging on a spoon at the kitchen table while Ruby wandered around the small space.

In the bathroom, she looked at her dad's small green first-aid kit, which had once sat on the back of the toilet in her house. She opened it and found tiny tubes of ointment, alcohol swabs, paper-wrapped rolls of gauze, and flat bandages in a variety of sizes. There were instructions with diagrams printed on the lid. Instructions to make a tourniquet. Or how to fashion a splint. Treat burns, fractures, fainting. Had anyone ever needed such dramatic aid from this first-aid kit? she wondered.

Just then Mel came home. The boys, cornered and guilty, ran through the small door into the international students' hallway. Mel chased them and for a second caught Derek by the shirt, but Derek snapped out of Mel's grasp and ran after his friends and out the front door of the old house. Mel stopped at the door before coming back to the apartment.

"Sit down." He pointed to the kitchen chair. His hand was shaking. He reached for the phone, his eyes still on her. "Are you stupid?" he demanded.

Ruby shook her head no. She wondered if he might hit her.

When Mel turned his attention to the phone and started yelling at her mother, Ruby bolted through the regular door, leaving it to slam behind her. She caught up to Derek in the alley, his friends having taken off in a different direction. Ruby grabbed Derek's arm and together they cut across two streets before daring to walk.

"Your dad's scary," Derek said, out of breath.

"*Adoptive* dad," she said, then added, "Tell me about it. He puts the *fun* in *dysfunctional*," Ruby laughed loudly, to prove she wasn't scared of her so-called dad.

IN THE PARK ACROSS from his house, Derek kissed Ruby and backed her into a corner near the tetherball poles. After a while, he pushed her hand down so she would touch his dick through his pants, but she pulled away. Ruby let him kiss her while she listened to the chains gently singing as the wind shifted them against the tetherball poles. She was getting bored with Derek grinding his dick against her for such a long time. She began to feel mechanical about it, like a vehicle. Derek undid his zipper and grabbed her hand again, pushing it down. *Why are guys so proud of their ugly hard-ons?* she thought.

"I have to go home," she whispered.

"You can't," he said. "Remember? You're in trouble." He kissed her more firmly.

She had forgotten for a minute. She was a fugitive. She stayed with Derek. She mostly did what he wanted but drew the line at putting her mouth on it.

WHEN SHE EVENTUALLY RETURNED home, they were waiting. "Where have you been?" her mother asked.

"Yeah," said Jay, standing beside her mother, holding her elbow. "Where were you?"

"What's going on?" Ruby glared at Jay, then at her mom.

"You're grounded," Jay said.

"What?" Ruby's voice rose. "You can't tell me what to do." And then she pleaded to Alice, "Mom! He can't tell me what to do!"

"I'm fed up." Ruby's mother turned away and walked into the kitchen. Ruby thought of a cow, fed all the way to the top, so it couldn't take in one more thing.

"Forget it," she yelled at her mother's retreating back. "I'm *not* grounded." Refusing to look at Jay, Ruby stomped to her room, slamming the door.

THE SOCIAL WORKER'S NUMBER started with a three. Ruby put her finger in the hole of the rotary dial. Practiced the short arc from the three to the silver stopper. There were three of them living in the house now. But the third person was the wrong one. Jay was the third. Three was a shit number anyway.

She dialed from the basement extension. After the hesitant, almost languid rotation of the dial, Sandra answered abruptly and Ruby nearly lost her nerve.

Instead she said, "Hi, um, I called and talked to you before?"

"Okay, what's your name, sweetheart?" Sandra asked, sounding a bit nicer.

"Well, I didn't give you my name last time," Ruby started to say.

"Oh, yes. I know who this is," Sandra interrupted her. "You're the girl who wants to be un-adopted, right?"

"Yeah," Ruby said with an outward exhale, as if to indicate she knew the idea was too dumb for words.

"Well, I was worried about you. After we got 'cut off,'" Sandra offered generously.

"Oh. Yeah. Sorry about that," Ruby said, remembering she hung up on Sandra. "I just got, kinda, nervous or something."

"That's okay. You don't have to tell me nothing you're not ready to say. How's that?"

"Okay?" Ruby answered.

"Okay, so, do you want to tell me what's going on, then?"

"Well, partly it's like this . . ." Ruby began to tell Sandra about her dad leaving and about her mom getting a new boyfriend when she heard a click on the upstairs extension. She knew Jay was in the house but she'd thought he was sleeping.

"Hello? I'm on the phone," she said. No answer, but the line stayed open. She heard him breathing.

"Sandra, I gotta go. Someone's listening on the other line."
She hung up and hoped Sandra would too.

WHEN SHE WENT UPSTAIRS Jay called her name. In her mother's bedroom, lying on the bed under the sheets with a smirk on his face, he asked her to bring him a glass of water. He even said please. When she returned and set the glass on the table beside the bed, she saw that he had an erection under the sheet. He grinned like he was too smart for his own good. Ruby ran out of the room to the back door, put on her sneakers, and left the house wearing only shorts and a T-shirt despite the cool fall weather.

She ran. Down the back alley, across the street with the grass boulevard. Northwest toward the river. At the football fields near the university she ran around the perimeter of the field, once, twice, three times, she kept running. Finally, she stopped, winded, and walked west toward Mel's house, a few blocks away.

MEL WASN'T HOME. She let herself in. She used the toilet. Thought about stealing the first-aid kit. Drank from the vodka bottle.

TWO THINGS RUBY REMEMBERED: The smell of a canvas tent. The awareness of her body being observed. In the remembering, a third memory, that it had made her eyes bleed. It made her panic, the knowledge of being watched like that. She held her breath so long all the blood vessels in her eyes broke. That might have been the same time or a different time, when she put the belt around her neck. Her bleeding eyes were proof. She was only a child.

SHE PICKED UP THE PHONE.

She told Sandra she was thinking of running away. She didn't tell Sandra about Jay's erections. Or any of the humiliating stuff about Jay.

"You don't have to do that," Sandra said, about running away.

"I don't even know *how* to run away," Ruby admitted, a little bit drunk, sitting at Mel's kitchen table with the vodka bottle and the phone. "I have nowhere to go."

Sandra gave her an address where she could request emergency shelter. "If you need it," Sandra added. "You know, I gotta tell you, missy. It ain't no bed of roses in that place either."

"What do you mean?" What would that be like, to pack a bag and leave home? Freedom? Maybe.

"There's some tough characters on the street." Sandra paused. "I don't think you're ready for that kind of life."

Ruby's eyes welled up. *I'm trapped* was all she could think. "What should I do?" she finally asked.

"Well, I can't help you if you won't tell me your name."

Ruby was tempted to tell Sandra the truth. But instead she

said, "What I'm afraid of is, that you can't help me even if I *do* tell you my name."

Sandra laughed. "You're a smart one, aren't you?"

"They're always telling me to be good," Ruby complained. "Like they think I have a choice."

Discouraged, Ruby thought about the bridge, mere steps from Mel's new place. *I could drink the rest of this vodka and just jump off the bridge,* she thought. *I could. That would solve it.*

"Tell me how I can help you," Sandra said.

"I'm not sure that you can."

Ruby drank from the nearly empty vodka bottle. She knew she wouldn't tell Sandra about the bridge. She didn't actually want to go to the bridge.

Instead, she cradled the bottle and fell asleep on Mel's smelly old couch.

Moe

2 0 0 9

...

I T WAS JUST AFTER 7 A.M. RUBY DIDN'T HAVE TIME FOR A morning phone call. Not if she was going to get the boys out the door to the early sitter with their lunches and all their school stuff, as well as get herself dressed and ready to arrive at work at least reasonably on time. She really had to keep moving, hadn't built in time for a phone call, especially not one like this.

"I'll wait for you," Dana claimed on the other end of the line.

The open lunch boxes sat on the counter, waiting to be packed with little puddings and juice boxes, white buns, processed meat, and convenience foods that came in small packages—all to be nestled among the bruised fruit and mini carrots that were included for form's sake, so she didn't appear too obviously to be the "bad parent" sending a junk-food smorgasbord to school for lunch. She knew how teachers talked. And judged. She suspected the fruit and vegetables just ended up in the garbage anyway. What kid didn't eat the cookies first, when given the chance?

"I don't know who he is," Dana said next, "but he's probably no good. I'll wait for you. Until he's gone."

"Have you been drinking all night?"

"I will," he insisted, ignoring her. She considered putting him on speaker so she could keep working on the lunches, but she didn't want the boys to hear if he said anything bad. She imagined just setting the phone down and packing the lunches—when she came back he might not have even noticed. "I'm gonna wait for you. 'S long's it takes."

She realized with some alarm that he might start crying. This was new.

"When he's gone, I'll be here. Waiting."

Ruby had no idea where all this patience came from, on Dana's part—this willingness to wait. Most guys didn't talk like that. Instead, they tried to muscle their way in, driven jealous by the thought of another guy in the vicinity. Most didn't talk so much about waiting—they wanted their time *now*. Dana was no different. He'd never waited for anything in his life.

This morning, his assertions were more of a curse than a promise. She knew what sort of a partner Dana would be, if she were to take him seriously. He professed to adore her, but she knew how short-lived that could be. As soon as a guy felt like he'd accessed the inner circle, the loving words stopped and some harder reality took over. Dana was no different. She didn't know if there was something about her that caused guys to act like this, or if it was something in the type of men she attracted. She'd had her share of alcoholics, starting with her dad, which she knew was the biggest cliché, but you couldn't help what was right in front of you. And Moe, also a drunk, different from her dad, but in the end similarly patterned. Like checks, plaid, and houndstooth. Distinct from one another, but ultimately they made you feel the same after you wore them for a while.

As an artist, Dana had done very few days of traditionally paid work in his life. Moe didn't particularly like to work either. Ruby remembered the time just after their first boy was born and Moe had lost his landscaping job after staying out all night partying. He was still drunk in the morning and couldn't go to work. Resentful of the repeated routine, she refused to phone his boss and lie for him again.

Later in the morning, Moe's boss had phoned Ruby to tell *her* that Moe was fired. The boss didn't even ask for Moe—instead Ruby had to take the brunt of the boss's indignant words through the phone line. She was so angry, first at Moe, but also at his stupid boss, whose tone implied she had no control over her life. So she went out that day, furious, still waddling and fat and leaky from having a baby, and got herself hired at a rowdy bar to throw drinks around and chuck frozen breaded bar snacks into an ever-hot deep fryer for drunk men who in turn threw the cheap bar food at the bands they didn't like and later drank with the band members when they stopped playing. All of them, drunk customers and band members alike, somehow feeling at liberty to make lewd remarks to Ruby, or about her, whenever she came within earshot. Things like "Would you do that?" Answered by something like "Well at least she's got all the right parts." All the while, her breasts lumpy with milk glands aching to feed a hungry baby who was

at home with his probably drunk father. Between orders she
would go into the ladies' room and express milk, leaning over
the toilet, just to get relief from the pressure. Cursing Moe the
whole time. The wet spots on her shirt were constant—she
dribbled extra water here and there as a measly means of cam-
ouflage.

And yet, despite the similarities to the other drunks in her
life, the obvious drawbacks—damn. Dana. He was a true artist, and she sometimes reminded herself to look for the grace
and mystery inside him that had to be there for him to make art
like that. She knew the good parts of being with Dana, the
hand-holding and tenderness. How he knew everyone and everyone knew him. How high he made her without ever touching a single drug. She also knew the tough parts. Dana was a
great adventure and great pain both. There had to be more to a
life than self-indulgence and regret.

"Mom"—Aaron stood in front of her to get her attention.
She ignored him. "Mom," he said again. "Mom. Mom! Mom,"
he tried different tones. Then finally he droned, "Mom-mom-
mom-mom-mom."

With Moe, many times she'd thought, *Why am I doing this?
I could be miserable alone.* In fact, she *was* as good as alone, or
so she thought. But there was a stigma applied to single mothers. She felt it keenly at her kids' school. As if there was a code
she had previously been oblivious to, one dictating that if you
could say, *My husband this* or *My husband that,* it would save
you from being put into a compartment—one that attracted
disrespect and abuse. *Single mother.* Being in that compartment

made you powerless. For that reason alone, she referred frequently and firmly to "my husband" at any school events she attended. Parent-teacher interviews. Early in any school year it was almost a given that she'd be called to the office over Aaron's behavior, and she made sure to say, "My husband just called me. He had to go to a meeting and won't be able to make it. I'm sure we can talk without him for now." She'd even gone so far as to manufacture contact information for the second parent on the kids' school forms; though she used Moe's name on the forms as if they were still married, god forbid the school actually tried to contact him. He'd probably hang up on them, too.

So even though there were two parents, somehow she'd been left holding the bag. The guilt was all hers. She was accountable for it all.

"Mom, mom, mom-*momomomommmmm*."

"What, Aaron!"

Aaron looked at her as if he'd been snapped out of a trance. "Umm." He scratched his nose. "I forget." He deflated a bit.

Ruby softened. She set the receiver on the counter and took his hand, led him to the couch. "Come here, Minnow." Aaron plopped down beside her and she pulled him into her lap.

He pushed away tamely—a signal that he didn't really mean the protest. Finally, he settled in her lap, the pout still on his lips.

She smoothed out his T-shirt and asked, "Who's this?"

He looked down. "SpongeBob," he answered, grudgingly.

She lifted the edge of his shirt and asked, "And what's this?" before she tickled his belly button.

He knew the game and squirmed in her lap, didn't try to escape. They both laughed.

"And what do you have in here?" she asked, lifting his arm and lightly touching his armpit, which generated more giggles and body contortions. She did the other arm the same way, as was the custom. When he stopped laughing, Ruby asked, "Hey, do you know what?" But Aaron wasn't finished with the game.

"Do my neck," he insisted.

"Okay," she said. "And what's under here?" She tickled under his chin as he bent his head down and tried to squirm away from her fingers. When he settled she asked again, "Do you know what?"

"Chicken butt," he giggled.

"You're funny," she said. "You're so funny, you were laughing before you were even born. Did you know that?"

His eyes got big.

"That's right, Minnow," she said. "When you were in my tummy I felt you laughing."

"You did?"

"Some babies kick, and you did that too, but I also felt you laughing."

"What was I laughing at?" he asked.

"I don't know, Minnow, but you laughed so hard you gave us both the hiccups." Wanting her boys to have what she didn't have, what she missed, she made a point of telling them how they grew in her body, that she knew them before they were even born. How they came into being. At least they wouldn't have to imagine being imagined.

Aaron wiggled on her lap, delighted. "Maybe that's why you have such a loud laugh now?" he suggested.

Ruby belted out her laugh and said, "It was you? It was you!" in her tickle-voice, and tickled him until he threatened to pee.

"Okay, go brush your teeth," she said. Aaron ran off.

"DANA, I'VE GOTTA GO. I'm late for work," she said, picking up the phone receiver again.

"Is he there? Right now? I'll come over," Dana said. "I'll come fight for you, Ruby, if that's what you want."

"Jesus Christ, Dana," she said, then glanced over toward where Aaron had disappeared. Aaron, whose latest development was to say "Jesus Christ" with exactly the same inflection in his voice as Ruby's. Usually to a teacher he was frustrated with. "Not today, okay?" she said to Dana. "I'm tired. I'm working three jobs trying to get to my cousin's wedding. You know that. I can't afford to be fired."

"I'll wait for you," he said again. "You know I will."

"I'll call you later," she promised. "Get some sleep." She hung up and unplugged the phone.

RUBY STILL PICKED UP shifts at the bar. There were only two other workers: Gus, the owner-manager, who was always there, and a tall, mid-forties waitress named Jan, who towered over Gus in a way that made it easy for him to grope her ass, which was one of the very first things Ruby noticed about the two of them. She steered clear of being alone with Gus or too close to him, vaguely worried he might try to put his hands on her like that. Jan didn't seem to mind, though. Gus was married, a wife and children at home. He worked long, late hours at the bar—basically there every minute it was open. Jan worked more regular shifts but was always there when Ruby went in, her shifts only on the busy nights. The nights with a band.

Like she'd told Dana, she was trying to make extra money so she'd be able to afford to go to the wedding at the end of August. It would be the first time she'd meet her real family. Her "birth" family. After thirty-four years. Her grandmother, Rose, over the phone, said, "You can meet everyone, all at once," as if that was a good thing. As if she wouldn't be overwhelmed. She was too embarrassed to tell Rose she didn't have the money to travel and get a hotel. Desperate her whole life to meet all these strangers who ought not to be strangers at all, Ruby was taking every extra shift on offer.

For today's job, she put on her uniform of gray dress pants, black belt, and crisp button-up shirt with its stiff METRO GUARD crests on either shoulder. Clipped the name badge to the left pocket as originally instructed in the orientation video. There was no hat, which was okay with her. She did get to wear a kick-ass navy blue bomber jacket made of nylon, lined, and with a good weight to it. There was only one crest on it, which she appreciated. *Let's not overdo it, right?* Her shoes a pair of black Doc Martens she'd found at Value Village. Of course, she didn't get a gun, or even a stick—not that she'd want one, a gun. She was allowed to carry an intense, big-ass Maglite flashlight, if she owned one. She didn't. The implication of the flashlight was that she could use it for self-defense if needed. She guessed.

The job was overrun with guys who really wanted to be cops but were doing this until they could make their dreams come true. Some of them would be terrifying with a gun and power. She felt bad for hoping they never got their most ardent desire. Bradley, for instance, was one of these. They'd started at the same time, watched the orientation videos together, in the same tiny room. Bradley was very intense and serious. She'd never seen him smile, not even once. Whenever she was with Bradley she laughed extra hard, for both of them.

She wasn't at all cut out for the job, but she pretended she was. Today's was a double shift. During the day, an office tower. Not much was expected of her. Be visually present. Unlock the elevator from time to time. Answer a few random questions. That sort of thing.

Ruby needed the overtime, especially since Moe's check bounced at the bank last week. *Jesus. Deadbeat.* She just hoped he'd pick up the kids after school and feed them supper.

She was stationed outdoors in a 7-Eleven parking lot, unsure what she was guarding against. Kids in cars who cruised Eighth Street looking for other kids in cars to hook up with? More or less. She gathered the point of her being here was to stop the hooking-up from occurring, at least in this particular parking lot.

A carload of boys with gigantic speakers pulled into the lot. She watched them to see if they'd get out of their car and go into the store. If they were customers, it was okay. Instead they parked and played the loud music so that it poured out of their open windows and filled up the parking lot. Nice. *Don't make me do this,* she pleaded in her head. They sat there for a full five minutes. She walked closer to the car. Looked at it pointedly. Still nothing. The boys in the car laughed and joked, ignoring her uniformed presence.

She walked up to the driver's-side window, the music deafening. She made eye contact with the driver, opened her eyes wider, waiting for him to turn down the music. Finally, after a good thirty seconds or so, he lowered the volume and she leaned toward the window.

"What's up?" she asked. She found it easier to put the ball in their court. Make them explain their presence rather than her explaining hers.

AFTER THE BOYS DROVE away trailing music out of their windows like ribbons, she thought about her trip and her grandmother, Rose. Rose telling her, over the phone, what Ruby'd always wanted to hear.

"Yes, Cree," she said, in response to Ruby's questions. "But also, French-Métis. Half-blood. So not *all* Cree."

Half-blood, Métis—like she always thought she was. And Cree. The trip to the wedding would be like a salmon swimming upstream. In her blood to go there. An irresistible pull.

Only she didn't swim away in the first place. That's why it was so hard to know the way back. She was a little salmon scooped up in a big net.

When she went looking, got in contact with social services to ask questions, she found out how it worked. She could send them her questions, but if the other person never sent theirs you wouldn't be connected. Turned out, Rose had sent something, a long time before, immediately after she'd lost her son Leon. Ruby's dad. In the thick of her grief, she'd reached out to find whatever pieces of him she could salvage. When Ruby eventually went looking, sent in her questions, Rose was there, waiting. Now, on the cusp of something momentous, both excitement and panic gripped Ruby. She was afraid she'd be a disappointment to them; pushed aside parallel fears of herself being let down.

She had a momentary flashback to when she was pregnant with Junior. She'd only been nineteen. Ruby got into the habit of visiting the library every week, where she browsed the shelves, pulling books from fiction to history to self-help to arts and crafts, checking out the maximum ten books each time. Some she read, and others she merely dabbled in. If a book failed to live up to its promise within the first few pages, it was returned unread.

After one such trip, she allowed herself to be drawn into a historical novel set in the 1800s, about a white woman protagonist abducted by a group of Apache in the southern United States. Though she would before long forget the name of the book and its author, she would forever be marred by the mem-

ory of the depiction of the marauding Apache, and one dis-
turbing scene and its bloody details of a man torturing a baby
to death. Repulsed, Ruby had thrown the book away from her,
refused to read any more of it. But she spent considerable time
feeling guilty, first for having read the account at all, as if she'd
transgressed a boundary, read someone's indecent secret. And
also, deep down, the book had inspired in Ruby a sickening
feeling of shame. Shame that somehow as a Native person she
would be associated with the obscene words printed in that
book and who knows how many more books with similarly
horrifying scenes.

When she could bring herself to even touch the book again,
she examined the cover for clues. Read and reread its description as historical fiction. Did "historical fiction" mean it was
true, on some level? How true? Those words certainly lent the
book an air of credibility. In light of the unsettling scene, Ruby
questioned her identity. Would she meet her unknown family
and find something awful? Did she have that sort of violence in
her veins? Where, and from what, was she descended? Confused and upset, she tried talking to Moe about it, but found it
difficult to describe exactly the impression the book had made
on her, how it had her hating herself by association for being
Native too.

"Don't pay attention to that shit," Moe said, irritated. "It's
some white guy's racist thoughts about Indians." Of course, of
course she knew this. But the book continued to fuck with her
head until she convinced herself it was a one-off. She had read
hundreds of books and never come across something like that

before. Moe was right, that particular book was the product of the sick mind of its author. Ruby processed the experience over many weeks, reminding herself that no Native person she knew or had known in her life was anything like that. Slowly the impact faded, and she became less distressed, but the trauma remained—she could never unsee the images the book had painted or undo the feelings they'd engendered.

ON THE OTHER SIDE, no inquiries were lodged from her birth mother or her family. A disappointing letter: *We regret to inform you no one has responded to your search.* Ruby wondered, Would her mother ever reach out? She wondered why she hadn't. She actively resisted feeling rejected all over again.

Ruby requested documents from social services, and her Registration of Live Birth arrived in the mail. The name of her birth mother was struck through with dark black ink, but Ruby's original name was intact. Unexpectedly so. The first time she'd ever seen it. There it was. First name, Eva; middle name, Lilly. Last name, redacted.

Eve, in paradise. And a little flower. She didn't know anyone with the name Eva.

Somewhere in the world, a woman who was her mother had the wrong idea about Ruby. Was thinking of her as an Eva. Ruby knew she would never be an Eva. Eva was an identity crisis.

Dear Mother, I bet your favorite color was green and the word "moss" made you think of the smell after rain and the whispering sounds a forest makes. Dear Mother, when I was born I think you gave me a name that your mother said was ridiculous. She tore up the form and the nurse brought you another where you were forced to write a not-ridiculous name and my very first name was lost to both of us. Dear Mother, nothing smelled like rain or moss anymore after they took me away from you.

Under the father's information, Leon's name had been blacked out by the agency, as expected, but there was something else. The form's pre-printed words *father unknown,* to be circled in the event that a father was not named, were firmly struck through with a pen. X'd out. Rejected. Ruby pondered the document for a long time, reading into the crossed-out words a small rebellion, her birth mother's signal, echoing from 1975, letting Ruby know this wasn't the case, that her mother knew full well who was the father of her child.

EVENTUALLY, BRADLEY SHOWED UP in the car. The only car the security company owned. He was on supervisor duty. That was new. *When did he get a promotion?* she wondered.

"They're shorthanded. I'm just filling in. TPHD," he added. She didn't think it possible, but an even more authoritative tone had crept into his voice.

"What the fuck's *TPHD?*" she asked.

"Temporary Performance of Higher Duties," Bradley explained.

"Does that mean a raise?" she asked. She was positive it involved a ten percent bump.

He ignored her question. "Everything going okay?" His tone had taken on a certain superiority that wasn't present before. As if they hadn't started at the same time, accumulated the same kinds of experiences and hours. Watched the same damn training videos.

"Just peachy," she said.

"Okay, well, I'll check in with you later."

"Okey dokey," she said, which was something her dad would totally say.

Bradley looked at her weird and drove off.

THE NEXT TIME BRADLEY was due to show up, she was having an incident with a drunk from a bar across the street. He kept talking to her like she was his friend. Ruby suspected he was crossing his impulse to try and pick her up with his disdain for authority, which was apparently the dual and confusing effect the uniform was having on him.

"I can't find my car," the drunk whined. This was the big mystery of the night. Where did his car disappear to? "Someone must have stolen it," he said. He told her he was drinking at Brewster's, which she knew was across the street and down a bit. He couldn't seem to remember the location of Brewster's, though, which was just as well. She wasn't about to tell him.

"Maybe you should just call a cab," she repeated for the fifth time. He didn't like her idea.

He went away and she hoped he was gone for good. She scanned the lot for any more hormone-driven teenagers, walked around the building. In back, she found the Brewster's drunk stuffing a 7-Eleven hotdog into his mouth, all in one go.

She watched as he struggled to chew the enormous mouthful, hoped he didn't start to choke to death because that would require action on her part in which she'd rather not engage.

She decided to backtrack and walk counterclockwise around to the front of the 7-Eleven. She'd check on the drunk on her way back around. She tried to take her time. Hoping he'd go away. When she rounded the third corner he was there, a bit closer now. Bent over at the waist and throwing up the hot-dog, and whatever else, all over the back of the parking lot. This was not in her job description. She left him to his business.

Bradley never showed up. *So much for having my back, "supervisor,"* she thought. The drunk stayed at the back of the building for a long time. They seemed to have entered a truce, the two of them. When her shift ended at 2 A.M. she walked away. Didn't say goodbye to the cashier, didn't do one last circuit, just slipped into her car and drove. She didn't need to deal with any more drunks.

THREE DAYS BEFORE THE WEDDING, Ruby almost had enough money to be able to go. Oil change for the beast, gas, hotel for three nights, food, and a small wedding gift. Hoped the car didn't break down on the highway. Maybe she should get a CAA membership? But that was money she didn't have. She called the security company and asked if she could be paid for her last shifts in advance. Was told she'd have to talk to her supervisor to have it approved.

When she finally got Bradley on the phone, she tried the charm offensive, telling him what a great job he was doing. "It's like you were made for this stuff," she said, playing on his desire to be a cop. "It'll be great on your résumé," she gushed. Bradley turned cranky, unappreciative of his underling commenting on his career aspirations.

"I can't do that," he said about the pay advance. "Against policy. No exceptions," he added, as if he anticipated her next question.

Fine. She'd go without CAA. Fingers crossed.

The boys were to stay with Moe.

RUBY'S BAG WAS IN the trunk. Her dress for the wedding was on a hanger on the hook over the back seat, where it would air out in the wind from the open window on the highway. They waited for Moe at the front of the house. The boys played with a soccer ball on the lawn. Their overnight bag sat on the step. Moe was late. She'd tried calling, knowing full well that he never answered his phone. And even if he did answer, he had a sneaky way of hanging up on her by saying, "I'll call you right back," urgent, as if he was about to get pounced on by a lion or run over by a truck. Like she had no choice but to say "Okay" in the same breathless way. Then she'd wait for the return call that never came.

And now something else. A carload of people pulled into the driveway and Dana rolled out from the back seat. Beautiful, dangerous Dana.

"Ruby!" he cried. "Where is he? I came to fight for you."

"I'm just leaving," she told Dana, walking across the lawn to meet him.

"Where to, beautiful?" Dana took her hand and put his other arm around her waist and danced her along the grass. "I'll come with you." Dana didn't need her to tell him where. Anywhere. He wanted to go anywhere with her. She was never a disappointment to him.

She laughed, pushed him away. Told him no, it wouldn't work that way. He didn't listen to her. Anything that sounded like a no and Dana just kept talking. "I love you," he said. "I'll wait for you. I'll fight for you. Just give me a chance."

She laughed even louder and Dana looked hurt.

"It's not funny," he said. "I will."

"I'm going to meet my family," she said, worrying now about the time. Where the fuck was Moe?

"I think I know them!" Dana got excited. "Blacks, right? I'll come with you. They'll know who I am. They're going to love me."

Ruby laughed again. Maybe he was right. Maybe they would love him. But no. She couldn't get caught up in Dana's drama. His ride shouted at him to hurry up or they were leaving. He started to look slightly worried.

"Come on," he pleaded. "Let me come with you."

She saw Moe's truck approaching up the road. He pulled in front of the driveway, blocking Dana's ride. The boys ran to Moe's vehicle and Moe walked over to Ruby and Dana.

"I can only keep them one night," Moe said to Ruby, ignoring Dana. "I've got something on Saturday."

She asked Moe for so little, practically zero. When they'd

split up she had asked him for nothing. He'd walked away and left them all behind as if they were leftover scraps. She'd let him off. She'd been doing it for years.

"I've got a wedding," she said. "A *family* wedding. Out of town. I told you that." Moe, of all people. He'd seen her make up and practice stories for the kids about a kohkum and moshom they never knew, about cousins they never met. Put up pictures. Fabricate a family. Blow air onto the embers of their imaginations. Just so the kids would have family from her side. As an act of rebellion, she put some dust in her moshom's hair from the land where he was made. Blew sun into her kohkum's eyes. That's how she made miskâsowin, belonging, out of words and her only memories—her blood memories.

"Then why aren't you taking the boys?" Moe was thick. "If it's family?"

"Because that's overwhelming," she said. "It's too far in the car for them. And I don't even know my family members yet. The boys will come on the next trip. When I can afford it better."

Ruby remembered the two-day culture conference, last year, in Treaty 4 territory, held beside a lake. She took the boys to the camp. Before they left home she'd taught them how to smudge. Held the sweetgrass braid in the tin pan from the baking cupboard, lit and fanned the braid until it was smoking. She'd taken off her watch and showed them how to cup the smoke in their palms, how to spread it over their bodies. She told them why they did this. Then she made them sit still and think about all the good things in their lives. The boys could barely last a minute being quiet. They tore off as soon as she said "Okay, you can go." But she was proud of them at the opening event when they remembered and participated in the smudging as an Elder went around the room with the sweetgrass braid lightly smoking on a shell.

At the feast, though, the boys had been restless and refused food. A woman beside Junior told him to sit still. Another woman said they were little monias boys, and laughed unkindly. Ruby's face burned. What right did that woman have to look at them that way? Ruby felt a familiar reinforcement of her illegitimacy, but now she also felt it being forced onto her boys, too.

And yet, for some reason, Ruby had stayed. Stayed because she wanted it so much she didn't know how to weed the bad from the good. Instead she blamed the boys for misbehaving. For not knowing what they couldn't know. Sometimes, when she wanted to hurt people, she hurt herself; and sometimes she hurt the wrong people. She squeezed Junior's arm too tightly. She was unreasonable.

She longed for their identity to be medicine, something sacred, something more than tears and loss. Instead she exhausted herself with the constant recovery effort, two steps forward and one step back, a long journey when taken that way. Always inadequate.

Ruby didn't even know how to teach them all the things, or anything, they needed to know to be Indigenous boys, men, humans. Starting when Junior was ten, she told him repeatedly to be wary of the police. "They're supposed to help you, but if you're Native, then they think about you in terms of stereotypes."

"What's that?" Junior had asked.

"If they don't know you, they think things about you that aren't true. They might think you're dangerous or not a good person," Ruby said, struggling.

Ruby could see she was confusing him. "I don't care," Junior said, full of bravado.

"Well, you better care," Ruby said, exasperated. "They might hurt you. Because they think these things."

Junior said nothing.

"It's like when you met Kyle for the first time." Junior's attention sharpened at the name of his best friend. "You didn't know if Kyle was nice or not. But then, when you got to know him, he turned out to be a good friend."

"And he likes wrestling, like me," Junior said.

"That's right," Ruby said, inspired. "It's like that with the police. Like, if they only help people who like wrestling, but they already think all Native people *don't* like wrestling. Before they get to know you. So they don't help you because of what they think they know about you, without knowing anything."

"That's stupid," said Junior.

"If the police stop you, or want to talk to you, what do you say?" Ruby quizzed.

"Call my parents," Junior intoned.

"Yes," Ruby said, triumphantly. "Always ask for your *parents*. Not your mom, not your dad, but your parents. Two of them."

"Can I go now?" Junior had asked, suddenly bored.

After the feast, Ruby had sat with the boys on the end of a dock, looking at the water in the moonlight. The moon was known to draw out tears, and Ruby's were close. It was large and low, rising slowly from the water, pulling itself up. Junior said, "Look, I caught the moon." He showed them how he had the orb between his index finger and thumb, as if he was holding it. They all tried it then, taking turns showing one another the moon in their fingers.

"You could put it into your medicine bundle," Ruby suggested to Junior, trying to make up. She took the moon in her fingers and mimed putting it into a small bag and pulling the strings closed.

"It has to stay in the sky, for everyone," Junior said seriously.

"I know, honey," she said. "Maybe you can put the idea of it in there?"

He shrugged and she thought about how perfect he was. Sensitive in a way she didn't always give him credit for.

That night Ruby refused the moon's tears. She laughed with her boys instead, as they held the moon in their hands, the sound ringing across the water.

"MAYBE YOUR BOYFRIEND HERE can stay with the boys?" Moe looked scornfully at Dana for the first time.

"Hey," Dana said.

"He's not my—"

"I'm going with her," Dana cut in.

Just then she saw Moe's truck start to move. "Did you leave the truck running?" she asked. The boys were in it, Aaron in the center of the front seat, his big brother in the passenger seat. Aaron looked at her with a near-comical expression of surprise. Ruby pointed and Moe and Dana turned to look at the truck, rolling straight ahead toward the neighbor's car—Herman's partially restored Thunderbird—parked on the street.

Ruby pushed past Moe and Dana, ran across the lawn past the carload of people in the driveway, and flung the passenger door open. She jumped onto the edge of the truck floor as the vehicle picked up steam.

"Sorry, Mommy," Aaron said.

The truck was in gear. Aaron had put the truck in gear. They were on a collision course for Herman's prized Thunderbird. She reached across both boys and yanked on the gearshift. The truck slammed into reverse just as they were about to hit the rear end of Herman's car. The gears made a terrible sound and from the grass she heard Moe shout, "Not the fucking transmission!"

Instead of smashing into Herman's car, the truck started to roll backward. There was no room in the crowded cab to climb over the boys, strapped in by their seat belts, to reach the brake pedal. She eased the shifter into neutral and the vehicle continued to roll; only now it was rolling backward and on a decline, no less. She steered, looking out the back window. They barely missed several parked cars. She maneuvered more into the center of the road. At least there was no traffic on the street. What would happen if she put the car into park? Would the transmission fall out on the road? Would Moe blame her and make her pay for it? She had no money. Her irrational thoughts kept her frozen, unable to take any action beyond steering.

"Minnow, sweetie, can you reach your foot over and push the brake pedal?" Aaron started to cry. Ruby was standing on the edge, the open door swinging behind her, steering backward down the street as they picked up speed. What would happen once they reached the cross street? She thought again about slamming the gearshift into park. It might cost her. It might cost her this trip.

Just then a figure ran across the road in front of the truck and flung the driver's-side door open. Dana jumped in and stomped on the brake. They were all flung backward by the sudden stop, and the heavy passenger door of the truck slammed onto Ruby's right ankle, the one dangling from the door the whole time. She cried out and Dana put the truck in park in the middle of the road.

The boys were okay. Aaron looked scared but he'd stopped crying. Junior called him an idiot. Ruby hugged both boys and sat on the road and took off her shoe. Her ankle swelled to the size of a melon in seconds. Not a watermelon, but a cantaloupe, anyway. Ruby refused to admit defeat. She hopped into the passenger seat and Dana drove the truck slowly back to the house.

Dana's ride, fearing more trouble than they were prepared for, backed out of the driveway and called out to Dana.

"Go without me." He waved his hand, waving them away.

"You must like this," she said to Dana. "Coming to my rescue."

"You can't go *now*," Moe said after checking out the boys, making them sit on the step. "And don't move," he told them. To Ruby he said, "You need an X-ray."

"It's fine," she insisted. "I just need ice." Both Moe and Dana laughed. "I'm going," she said. Moe shook his head, but went to the house to get some ice anyway.

Once Ruby made it clear to them she wouldn't back down, no matter what they said, the next question was how, since she couldn't drive.

"Me," Dana said. "I can drive." He barely kept his enthusiasm down. "And *you* can ice," he said, like it all made perfect sense. He had all the terrific ideas. That was how Dana would get his way and meet her family. "It's the only choice," he added.

"I'll ask my mom to look after the boys Saturday, then," Moe offered, softened for the moment by their shared dilemma. He loaded the kids in the truck, grabbed their bag, and went.

"Fine," Ruby said to Dana. "Let's go, then." Upriver. Back to where she came from. Where she'd soon find out how her concoctions through all those years, her family pictures, the partial stories she'd fleshed into narratives, had turned out. Truth being only one measure.

On the other side of the road a magpie hopped in the gutter, looking for something. Pebbles? Seeds? Spare change? Who knew.

"Let's go," she repeated to Dana. "You can be my witness."

Acknowledgments

THANK YOU FIRST AND FOREMOST TO MY BIG TERRIFIC family. To Declan for reading, supporting, and championing. To Oliver for being my window to youth, and Max for your grace and beautiful art. To Robben for being rock solid, and Kaya for blood memory. Sean for your writer's sensibility, Deirdre for being a terrific beta reader, Matt for your generous spirit, and Onóra for your great enthusiasm. To Sinead for so many things—reading, laughing, encouraging, understanding. Mykah, mighty Métis. To Tanner for *really* listening with your artist's heart, and of course for the one-of-a-kind Ruby artwork. Many thanks to my first editor, Warren Cariou, for reading, commenting, discussing, suggesting, persuading, and believing. Big hearts and hugs to Martha Kanya-Forstner at Doubleday for really recognizing Ruby and for giving me a hard push. David Ebershoff at Hogarth for loving Ruby almost as much as I do! To Denise Bukowski for your enthusiasm, backing, and firm support. Melanie for the incredible edits— what an ear! Darryl for your love of literature and great support for Ruby. To the Canada Council for the Arts for supporting my work on this book with a grant. To my writing group, Viz Ink—Rita, Murray, dee, Andréa, Gayle, Regine—for all the writerly love. To my Granada, Spain, writing crew, Fiona, Jacqueline, and Gerry, where much of this book came together. Jebbie and Dodie, you know who you are. To the Saskatchewan Writers' Guild for retreat time to finish a full submission. And to Coteau Books for the support and consideration over the years, I am grateful to have been part of the family.

The following excerpts have been previously published or recognized:

"Kal" appeared as "Counselling" in *The Malahat Review: Indigenous Perspectives* issue in 2016 and the *2018 Short Story Advent Calendar*. It won the 2017 Jack Hodgins Founders' Award for Fiction.

"Alice" appeared as "Fenced" in *CV2* and *Prairie Fire: ndn-country* issue in 2018.

"Rose" appeared in *Impact: Colonialism in Canada* (2017) and subsequently appeared in Missinipi Broadcasting Corporation's *MBC Magazine* in 2018.

I acknowledge the support of the Canada Council for the Arts.

Conseil des arts du Canada   Canada Council for the Arts

ABOUT THE AUTHOR

LISA BIRD-WILSON is a Saskatchewan Métis and Cree writer whose work appears in literary magazines and anthologies across Canada. Her fiction book *Just Pretending* (Coteau Books, 2013) was a finalist for the national Danuta Gleed Literary Award; won four Saskatchewan Book Awards, including 2014 Book of the Year; and was the 2019 One Book, One Province selection. Bird-Wilson's debut poetry collection, *The Red Files* (Nightwood Editions, 2016), is inspired by family and archival sources, and reflects on the legacy of the residential school system and the fragmentation of families and histories. She lives in Saskatoon.

lisabirdwilson.com

This book was set in Fournier, a typeface named for Pierre-Simon Fournier (1712–68), the youngest son of a French printing family. He started out engraving woodblocks and large capitals, then moved on to fonts of type. In 1736 he began his own foundry and made several important contributions in the field of type design; he is said to have cut 147 alphabets of his own creation. Fournier is probably best remembered as the designer of St. Augustine Ordinaire, a face that served as the model for the Monotype Corporation's Fournier, which was released in 1925.